Harrison is fascinated by Salomon, the demon who helped save Ilyhas and Esi's lives. He isn't sure why, but it doesn't matter since he's never going to see him again — until he does.

Sal is still trying to identify the demon who cast the spell that almost killed Jadon's boyfriends, and he needs Harrison's help. Sal hates not doing things by himself, but he can't go into a human building to find the demon, not when he's obviously not human. He's not sure Harrison will find something, but he does, and much more than Sal expected. Sal's ex is the demon involved, and she's still angry with him for leaving Hell. When she locks his powers, he knows he has to follow her back to Hell, no matter how little he wants to.

He hadn't counted on Harrison coming with him, though.

Harrison knows he should stay home, but there's no way he's letting Sal face this without him, even though he's not going alone. Hell can be deadly for humans, but he's more focused on getting Sal's powers back — and on falling in love with him.

But not only is Hell deadly, so is Shaila, Sal's ex, and she's still holding a grudge that's going get all of them killed.

A Demon's Choice
Copyright © 2019 Catherine Lievens
ISBN: 978-1-4874-2618-7
Cover art by Erin Dameron-Hill

Published by eXtasy Books Inc or
Devine Destinies, an imprint of eXtasy Books Inc

Look for us online at:
www.eXtasybooks.com or www.devinedestinies.com

A Demon's Choice
Demons Hearts Book 6

By

Catherine Lievens

CHAPTER ONE

Sal *loved* the human realm. He wasn't sure why — some parts of it were as bad as Hell had been, and he'd spent all his time in his house on the lake until recently — but there was an energy to it, something that told him people could be happy there. There was no way to be happy in Hell. That was kind of the point. Hell was hot and dirty and blood and pain in the best of times. That was why he'd left, and why he was never going back.

He *did* want to go back to the lake eventually, though. He missed his little house and his books. But living in the city was fun, and Sal had been eating donuts. He loved donuts. What he *didn't* like was the lack of privacy.

He'd been staying at the League's headquarters because he was trying to find the demon who'd almost killed Ilyhas and Esi, and that was easier to do if he was there. He hated not having privacy, though. There was always someone around, talking and making noise. Even though Sal had a bedroom and a bathroom, they were both tiny, and the walls weren't enough to cut off the noise.

Sal didn't like noise. That was one of the reasons he lived alone in an isolated area.

He grumbled and pushed his eggs around his plate as he tried to ignore the group of demons talking and laughing at the back of the dining hall. He could have gone somewhere else to eat, but he didn't want to leave the place, and taking food to his bedroom was out. It had taken two days to clear out the smell the last time he'd done that.

"What crawled up your ass and died there?" Cumar asked as he slid into the seat in front of Sal's with a tray.

Sal wrinkled his nose at the lasagna in Cumar's plate. "How old is that thing?"

"Don't know, don't care." Cumar patted his stomach. "I can eat rocks and have no problem."

Sal didn't have a problem believing that.

"What's up with you, then? Still nothing about that demon you're looking for?" Cumar asked after shoveling a forkful of lasagna into his mouth.

"Nothing. Whoever it is is very good at shielding themselves from me."

"But you're better."

Sal grinned. "Damn right I'm better. I'll find them, and I'll make sure they can't do the kind of shit they pulled again."

Sal fluttered his wings. He was excited about this. The work he usually did wasn't this exciting—healing, finding people who weren't trying to hide very hard, creating spells. He earned a lot of money because he was one of the best, so much so that even humans came to him, but it wasn't exciting.

This was, though. He almost felt like a League warrior, even though he probably wouldn't be able to kick a fly's ass. He looked badass, but he was anything but.

Cumar grinned. "That's what I'm talking about. You need help?"

"Not really, but you can come with me once you're done. I'll try to locate the demon again."

"I don't have anything else to do, so I'm in."

"Where's your better half?" Cumar and Thailor were usually together, at least at HQ. Sal knew both of them had partners—romantic partners—but they were as close as brothers in a way that made Sal's heart ache with jealousy and envy.

His brother had tried to kill him. Twice.

"Hanging out with Chase. I knew I was going to lose him

when Chase agreed to come work here. And hey, I have you now."

"I'm not going to stay. As soon as I find that demon, I'm going home."

Cumar pouted. "Why? Don't you like it here?"

"I *hate* it. There's too much noise, too many people. I can't think with all that mess around me."

"What about Harrison?" Cumar asked, pointing his fork at Sal.

Sal blinked. "Harrison?"

"You know, the cute human guy."

"I know who Harrison is." How could Sal not know him? He'd been the only one who'd taken care of Sal when Sal had managed to find out where Esi had been kidnapped to. Of course, that was because all the others had run to get Esi back, and Sal was used to taking care of himself after doing spells. He always did. It wasn't like his clients were going to hang around to nurse him back to health once they had what they needed from him.

The fact that Harrison was an adorable little human also helped, of course. He was one of the few who wasn't in the least intimidated by Sal and who didn't treat him differently than he did everyone else, including his human friend Jordan. And of course, he was beautiful — and he didn't seem to know it. Sal had been attracted to his messy brown hair, his hazel eyes, and his big heart since first meeting him, but he'd been too busy to try to lure him into his bed. Besides, his neighbors would probably have heard whatever they got up to, and that was the last thing Sal wanted.

"How are you two going to get it on if you leave?"

"We won't." Harrison was cute, but Sal wasn't sticking around for anyone. He wanted his life back.

"I bet he's going to be disappointed. He has a puppy crush on you."

3

"Isn't he too old to have puppy crushes?"

"Not in his case. He's a bit like a puppy all the time. Eager, jumping around, you know. He's slobbering all over you whenever he's next to you."

Sal rolled his eyes. "Are you done eating? I have to go try that spell again."

Cumar pushed a few more forkfuls of lasagna into his mouth, until he looked like a squirrel with puffed-up cheeks, and got up. Sal followed him to drop off their trays, grinning at how Cumar was trying to chew without spitting lasagna all over.

"What's that spell like?" he asked when he finally managed.

Jadon had given Sal free run of the facility, and Sal had found a small, mostly unused conference room. It was more isolated than his guest bedroom was, which was good. He didn't need curious demons stumbling on him while he was working. "It's a location spell, like the one I did to find Esi. I'm using the materials the demon used against Ilyhas to find them, but so far, they've been shielding themselves."

"Aren't they going to continue doing that? It's what I would do if I knew you were coming after me."

"You're right, but they have to renew the spell they're using every so often. The ingredients tend to lose efficacy, especially when I'm battering against them with my own spell. I just need to catch the exact moment the demon is doing it, and I'll be able to tell where they are." It was a bit more complicated than that, but Sal doubted Cumar would understand. He was great at his job—fighting and saving people—but he knew nothing about Sal, and that was okay. Sal knew nothing of Cumar's job, either.

Sal liked having someone watching over him as he did the spell, though. That way, Cumar would be able to help him if he needed it.

He spread the map he'd been using on the floor in front of where he was sitting cross-legged. He kept the ingredients he needed in one bowl and the ones this demon had used against Ilyhas in another. He grabbed the black candle and lit it, putting it onto the map. Then he took the bowl of ingredients and sprinkled them in the other bowl.

"Smells good," Cumar murmured.

Sal smiled. "Salt, garlic, and cayenne pepper."

"And you can use that to do the spell?"

"Yes. It's not really about the ingredients, although picking the right ones helps. It's more about having something to channel my powers. Now shut up. You'll distract me."

Sal closed his eyes. He'd put the bowl with the stuff that had been used against Ilyhas in the crook of his legs so it wouldn't move. He hovered his hands over it and focused on the traces the demon had left on their ingredients, channeling his power through the salt, garlic, and pepper.

He hadn't been lucky yet, but he was now. He might have to keep Cumar around as a good-luck talisman.

The demon's spell had lost enough power that Sal was able to get to them. He knew the demon would redo the spell again as soon as possible, so he needed an address.

He heard the burst of heat on the map and knew he'd gotten one. He let go of his focus. He was tired, but not overly so, thank Satan. And there was only a little blood dripping from his nose, which was an improvement.

"Is doing this hurting you?" Cumar asked. He crouched next to Sal and handed him a tissue.

Sal took it with a smile and pressed it against his nose. "It takes energy, more than I usually use, because this demon is so powerful. I'll be okay, though. Nothing a little rest can't heal."

Cumar was still frowning, but he didn't push. "You know where the demon is?"

Sal and Cumar looked at the map. Sal had no idea if the location was a good thing or a bad one, but from Cumar's expression, he thought it was probably bad. "What?"

"That's a human area. A business one. No apartments or houses. People go there to work and go back home at the end of the day."

"You think the demon is hiding in plain sight?"

"Yes. That means they can pass for human."

And that Sal wouldn't be able to get to them. There was no way he could pass as a human, even in his wildest dreams.

"You busy?"

Harrison looked up from his computer. "Nope."

Jordan arched a brow. "Aren't you doing paperwork?"

"That's what I said. Not busy."

"Someone has to do that paperwork."

"I will. Just not now, since you seem to be needing me."

Jordan chuckled and sat on the other side of Harrison's desk. They shared an office—they'd just started their PI business, and they didn't have much money to spend on rent yet, even with Jordan's second job as a liaison between the League and the city's police force—but Jordan was barely there usually, so it really was more Harrison's office.

"What do you have for me?" Harrison asked. Anything to get away from paperwork. He hadn't liked it when he was a detective, and he didn't like now that he was his own boss. Well, kind of. Jordan was his boss, really, but it felt more like they were partners, even though the business was technically Jordan's.

Jordan tapped his fingertips onto the desk. "I got a call from Jadon."

That made Harrison sit straighter in his chair. He might routinely work with demons now, even though they were wary of him and Jordan since they were humans, but the warriors fascinated him. The fact that Salomon, the demon he kind of had a crush on, was still staying at the League's HQ, didn't have anything to do with his interest.

Maybe.

Okay, it had a lot to do with it, but Harrison just wanted to do his job and help people and demons alike. The fact that he might get to ogle Sal in the process was just a nice bonus.

"What does he need?" Harrison asked.

"Sal finally managed to locate the demon who tried to kill Ilyhas and Esi. It's hiding in a human-only side of town, possibly working alongside humans. When he got the reading, the demon was in an office building, although Sal wasn't able to find out who it was. He was able to pinpoint the floor, though, and it's a law firm."

Harrison frowned. "Why would a demon work in a human law firm?"

"To hide? They have to know the League is looking for them, and we can't get to them there."

"But we can."

Jordan nodded. "We can. Well, *you* can, in this case. I don't have the time to do this. The chief of police wants to see me about something or other."

"About demons?"

"No doubt. That's the only reason I have contact with the police nowadays."

"So I'm in charge of this? I get to find the demon?"

"Yes. You're going to need to work with Sal and a few League warriors, no doubt. Jadon is expecting you tomorrow morning for a meeting. You'll get all the info. I took the liberty of looking up the law firm when he called me. There's a mailman job available. I know a few people there, and I managed to get you hired for the length of the investigation. They weren't happy about finding out that they have a demon in their midst."

Harrison had no trouble believing that. "So I'm a mail boy now?"

"As well as my partner, yeah. Jadon will tell you more, but don't put yourself in danger. Find the demon and report to him and whoever he puts in charge of this. They'll take it from there. They just need to be able to identify the demon."

"Got it. I could go now." It was getting late, but Harrison wasn't looking forward to going home to his empty apartment and eating dinner alone in front of the TV.

"Nah. Jadon thinks the demon is going to stay where it is, since so far, it hasn't been found. Take the night off, take care of whatever you need to take care of tomorrow so you don't have to come back here until the job is over, and go to HQ."

Damn. "Okay. You're going home to Caelan?"

Jordan's usual grim expression lightened, and he smiled the smile that was reserved only for Caelan and any thoughts of him. "Yeah. He's off tonight, so we're going to take advantage of it."

"That's great. Have fun, then. I'll lock up, so go ahead and leave."

"You're sure?"

"Yeah." It wasn't like Harrison had anything better to do anyway.

He smiled when he heard Jordan whistle as he left the office. Jordan hadn't always been so happy. He still wasn't most of the time, but Caelan had a way of making him smile and softening him that Harrison hadn't thought he'd ever see. Jordan was different when he was with his boyfriend, as it should be. Harrison wanted what Jordan had with Caelan eventually, but so far, he hadn't had luck in that department.

Of course, if someone asked his dad, he'd say Harrison hadn't had luck in the job department either. He didn't like that Harrison wasn't a cop anymore, and he didn't waste a chance to tell Harrison how disappointed he was about that.

But Harrison didn't want to think about that right now. No, the only things he wanted to think about was his couch, a cold beer, a warm microwave meal, and a TV series—just not one about cops.

Harrison turned off his computer and left the office, making sure he locked the door. He dragged his ass home after briefly wondering if he should go to a bar. Underworld, maybe? He was human, but they were as welcome as demons at Underworld, even though the place was owned by a half-demon. Harrison wasn't sure he was up for the noise, though, and he certainly wasn't up for the vigilance he'd need to hang out at Underworld. He might be friends with the owner, and humans might be welcome there, but that didn't mean no one was going to try to start something with him. Demons tended to be confrontational even on their best days, and they weren't usually happy to find a human encroaching on what they viewed as their territory.

Home it was, then.

Harrison trudged to his apartment. He had to take the bus, which he hated, but it was nearly impossible to find a parking spot at the office, and the few there were reserved for clients.

The bus stank, though, and it was slow going. When Harrison finally got off, the only thing he wanted to do was take a shower and burrow in bed, so of course, he found Icha waiting for the elevator.

Harrison almost groaned. He liked the oni demon, but Icha was always trying to get into Harrison's pants, and Harrison wasn't sure he had the energy to fend him off tonight. It looked like he was going to have to try, though, because Icha had noticed him.

"Harry!" he crowed.

Harrison glared. "My name's Harrison, not Harry. You know that."

Icha touched Harrison's arm. "I know, but Harry rolls off the tongue better, don't you think? I could demonstrate it to you. It would be perfect for screaming while you're fucking me."

Harrison didn't like the fact that he blushed every time Icha tried anything with him—which was every time their paths crossed. They lived on the same floor, and Icha frequently came around to borrow sugar or whatnot, usually wearing little to nothing. Harrison was perpetually blushing in his presence, and Icha seemed to find it hilarious and possibly arousing. Harrison couldn't stop it, so he tried to avoid Icha as much as he could.

He didn't always succeed.

Icha ran his hand up Harrison's arm. "You know it would be good."

Harrison barked out a laugh. "I don't doubt that."

"Then why don't you give in?"

Harrison had been tempted more times than he remembered. He *could* give in and have sex with Icha. It would be fun and light-hearted because that was how Icha was. And it *would* be good.

But Harrison wasn't a one-night stand kind of guy, and that was all Icha was offering. Even if he wanted more, Harrison doubted *that* would work between them. He didn't like Icha that way, the way he liked Sal, no matter how ridiculous that sounded. There was no changing it, though.

Harrison was relieved when the elevator doors opened. He was going to have to ride up with Icha, but he knew how to keep the demon at bay by now.

Icha squeezed Harrison's ass only twice before the elevator stopped at their floor, and Harrison rushed out. Icha followed him at a more sedate pace, pouting. "When are you going to make me happy?" he asked.

"When are you going to be ready for a relationship?"

Icha grimaced. "Never, I hope. It's just not me."

"And fucking around is just not me."

Icha grinned. "Maybe, but I sure as hell am having fun trying to convince you it is."

CHAPTER TWO

Sal was surprised to see Harrison was at the meeting. Surprised, but pleased. He liked the human, and he liked to see him blush.

He reclined in his seat and looked Harrison up and down. "That's a nice pair of jeans." And an even nicer ass in it, but Jadon was there, and Sal didn't think he'd appreciate where Sal's mind was going.

Sal's words were enough to make Harrison's cheeks blaze. "Thank you. Uh, I like your t-shirt."

Sal beamed. "Thank you. I like it too." It was blue, with a drawing of a fox on it. The phrase said, *Look at all the fox I give*, and Sal found it hilarious.

"Are you two done talking about clothes?" Jadon groused.

Harrison paled a bit, and Sal didn't like that. He understood that they had better things to do, of course, but he wanted time to tease Harrison and see how hard he could make the man blush.

Later. He was going to make sure they had time later.

Harrison sat in the other chair in front of Jadon's desk. "Jordan told me you need a human."

"Did he tell you why?" Jadon asked.

"Something about Sal having found the demon who tried to hurt Esi and Ilyhas?"

"Exactly. Sal will explain things to you in more detail than I can, but he found out the demon is hiding in a human law firm. We have no idea who the demon is or what they look like, and we can't send Sal in there."

Sal scowled and rubbed one of his horns. This was why he spent most of his time in his house. He didn't want to deal with humans who were afraid of him just because he had wings and horns, and okay, the claws were probably scary, but he hadn't killed anyone in decades, and never humans.

Harrison looked at him with wide eyes. "I see, yes." He didn't seem afraid, but Sal didn't have the time to try to read his expression, because he looked right back at Jadon. "Jordan found me a job at the firm, as a mail boy. That means I'll be able to walk around and see a lot. I don't know if it's going to be enough, but it's certainly going to be more than what we have right now. It would be great if you guys had more details about this demon, though."

Jadon looked at Sal. "Sal?"

Sal linked his fingers and leaned back in his chair, laying his hands on his stomach. He didn't miss the way Harrison's gaze lingered on them—or his stomach—but he knew this wasn't the right moment to do something about it. He cleared his throat, smiling at the way Harrison's head jerked up. Harrison was blushing again. "I can't do more. The cloaking spell the demon has been using is in place again. I was lucky they let the cloaking weaken as much as they did. Whoever this is, they're a powerful demon, and they already put up the cloaking spell again."

"So there's nothing at all you can tell me that would help me? I need to have at least a vague idea of what I'm looking for. Is it a male or a female? Do they look entirely human, or have any signs that might expose them as a demon?" Harrison asked.

"I can't tell you anything more. I'm sorry. I haven't been close to this demon, so I can't even use their energy signature to recognize them."

"That means you'll go in blind," Jadon said. "You can't take risks. The last thing we want is for you to get hurt. This is just an exploratory job. Once you locate the demon—if you manage to—you call us, and we'll take it from there."

"You do remember I was a cop, right?" Harrison asked.

His expression was pinched, and unless Sal was wrong, he thought he'd detected a hint of sarcasm in his voice.

"I do, but this isn't a human you're going up against. It's a demon, and from what Sal told me, it's a powerful one. You're also not going to be able to tell who the demon is, so it could take you by surprise. You were a cop, but you're still only human, and that doesn't help you against most demons, let alone a powerful one."

Harrison scowled. "Maybe, but I know what I'm doing, and I *have* had to face demons when I was a cop. I'm not helpless, and while I do understand why I need to let you know as soon as I find out who the demon is, *you* need to understand that I'm not going to back down if this demon attacks me. It's your jurisdiction, so I'll call you in. But don't ask me to turn a blind eye if you're not there and there's something I can do."

Jadon raised his hands. "Of course. I do realize you have training. What I meant is that no one here wants to see you hurt. You're one of the few human allies we have, and we value that. But even if you weren't, the League was created to support and help both demons and humans. We don't want anyone to be hurt if at all possible." He smiled. "And you're a friend, so it's even more important that you make it out of there safe."

Sal loved how fierce Harrison could become. Seeing the fire in his gaze sent a shiver down Sal's spine, and he couldn't help but think about what it would be like to have that fire focused on him, possibly while they were both naked and in bed. Now wasn't the right moment to think about Harrison naked, though. This was a serious situation, more so than anything Sal had been through recently.

He could all too easily imagine what this demon could do. They were in a human environment, hiding because of what they'd done. They had to know that the League would find them eventually, and this could end badly.

Sending Harrison right in the thick of things was a gamble. He could find the demon, but the demon could just as well attack him, and Sal didn't like that thought. He couldn't go with Harrison, but he could do everything he could to make sure Harrison was as safe as possible, considering the circumstances.

"I'll prepare a few spells and amulets for you," he said. He hadn't talked to Jadon about this, but he knew Jadon would agree.

Harrison blinked at him. "Amulets?"

"I know you humans don't have a lot of faith in what demons can do, but—"

"I have complete faith in what you can do, Sal." Harrison's cheeks flushed. "I've *seen* what you can do, remember? And I'm not like other humans." He bit his lower lip. "Okay, that sounded awkward. But I'm not afraid of you or demons in general. I know you guys are dangerous, much more so than humans, but I've met enough of you to be aware of the fact that just like with humans, the majority of you are good. *You* are good, and you know what you're doing. So yes, I'll take whatever amulet you want me to carry. Thank you."

Sal had been grinning for most of Harrison's little speech. "I *am* dangerous."

"I know. I also know you don't hurt people, though. You help them."

"Because they pay me to."

Harrison arched a brow. "Does that mean you expect me to pay you?"

Sal could think of a few ways he'd like Harrison to pay him, and none of them involved money. Jadon was there, though, watching them and probably wondering what the fuck Sal was doing. "No. Jadon is already paying me for my time."

Harrison's little smile fell. "Right. Of course he is." He turned back to Jadon. "How are Ilyhas and Esi?"

Jadon smiled. It was weird to see him smile that way. He and Sal went way back, and Sal couldn't remember a time when he'd seen him as happy as he was when he was with his boyfriends. It was weird, but a good weird. Jadon deserved to be happy.

But watching him talk about his boyfriends, Sal wondered if he would ever have something like that again. He had, several times, but he'd stopped allowing himself to fall in love. He couldn't, not when it hurt so much to have to watch his loved ones age and die while he stayed the same.

Harrison closed Jadon's office's door behind him. He was trying very hard not to look at Sal. He wasn't sure what had happened in the office—he thought Sal had been flirting with him, but that couldn't be right, could it? Why would Sal flirt with him? He was just a human, and Sal, well, he very much wasn't, and Harrison wasn't thinking about his horns and his wings.

There was just something about Sal. He was bigger than life, and it had nothing to do with him being a demon.

"When will you start working at that law firm?" Sal asked.

"Tomorrow morning. I have to be there at seven." Harrison wasn't looking forward to the early wake-up call, but he was used to them, or rather, he'd been used to them when he'd worked as a detective. He didn't have to wake up early nowadays, not unless he wanted to go to the gym before heading into work.

Sal nodded. "I see. Come with me."

Harrison expected Sal to lead him downstairs to Jadon's apartment, where he was staying, but instead, he went to one of the rooms the warriors used when they needed to spend the night — or the day — at HQ. "You're not staying with Jadon anymore?" Harrison asked.

Sal grimaced. "No. He and his boyfriends are very . . . handsy. I've walked in on them one too many times, so even though I hate staying here, it's better. The noises are different, at least. More fighting and less fucking. Isn't as frustrating."

Harrison's cheeks were on fire, but he was determined to ignore it. He stepped into the bedroom after Sal and blinked at the mess. "How long have you been staying here?"

"Huh? About a week, I think."

Harrison blinked. The room was a mess, so he'd expected Sal to say he'd move out of Jadon's place the day after Esi had been recovered almost three weeks ago.

There were clothes — colorful clothes from the entire rainbow spectrum, including several combinations that hurt to look at — everywhere, including hanging from the nightstand lamp. That wasn't the only thing that seemed to have exploded in the bedroom, though. There were also books, maybe even more than there were clothes, and what Harrison thought were ingredients for spells, including a ton of spices, feathers, rocks, and colored candles.

"You can sit down," Sal said.

Harrison didn't think there was an empty spot for him to sit. He could probably clear one, but he wasn't sure he wanted to find out what else was thrown around in the room. "I'll stand."

"Suit yourself. I'm not sure where the amulets are, though, so this might take a while."

"You don't know where you put the amulets you want me to use so I stay safe?"

"Well, I didn't know they were for you, or I'd have been

more careful with them. I thought *I* was going to be the one going after the demon until Jadon informed me that the demon is hiding in a human building."

"But you're not a warrior."

"So? I've been around for a while, way longer than you have. I might not be a warrior, but I could be one if I wanted to." He straightened and poked at his cheek with a green claw. "I don't like that tattoo on their face, though. It would mare my beauty."

"I doubt anything could do that." Harrison realized what he'd said only once the words were out of his mouth. He snapped his lips shut, but it was too late. Sal looked at him from above the mountain of stuff he was digging in on the dresser. "Really? So you think I'm beautiful?"

Harrison rolled his eyes. "Are you fishing for compliments? You know you are."

Sal turned to face Harrison fully. "I don't know. I mean, demons usually like the way I look, yes, but you're not a demon. Even though the wings and the horns don't intimidate you, I wouldn't have thought you'd view me as beautiful."

Harrison wasn't going to start waxing poetic about the way Sal looked, especially not in front of him, but he *was* gorgeous. His leathery wings and his deer-like horns only added to it. His long white hair, blue eyes, and pointed ears gave him an otherworldly appearance that Harrison found more than a little appealing. He'd wanted to stroke Sal's wings ever since the first time he'd met him. "You're gorgeous," he said, looking away.

"Even with the claws?" When Harrison looked back, Sal was wiggling his fingers at him.

"Even with the claws." Although Harrison couldn't help but wonder how *that* worked when Sal was having sex. Not that he thought about Sal having sex. Well, not often, anyway. "They're painted green."

Sal beamed and looked at his claws. "They are. I like this color."

"It's . . . pretty, and it makes them look less dangerous." But no less appealing. Harrison could too easily imagine Sal running his claws down his back—and nope, he couldn't think about that now. "The amulets?"

"Oh, right." Sal turned to the pile again. "I thought I put them here, dammit."

"I could help you look."

Sal grinned at him. "Please. Just start wherever."

Harrison wasn't sure what spot to pick, but since Sal was working on the dresser, he sat on the bed and focused on the chair next to it. Clothes were piled high on it, and he folded them as he removed them. Sal loved colorful rude shirts, and most of them made Harrison smile.

He stuttered when the next article of clothing he pulled from the pile was a pair of lace boxer-briefs. He licked his lips and looked at Sal, who was still working on his pile. He was wearing jeans that showcased his ass, and Harrison couldn't help but wonder if he was wearing a pair of underwear similar to the ones he was holding.

He wasn't sure if he wanted the answer to be yes or no.

He folded the underwear and put it on the pile of clothes next to him. There were a few more, and each of them made his dick harder in his jeans—especially the jockstrap. *Dammit.*

There was a black box at the bottom of the pile. Harrison grabbed it and shook it. Something rattled inside of it. "Sal? Are the amulets in a black box?" he asked.

Sal looked at him. He'd moved on to a pile that was on the floor. Shoes poked out of it, as well as books and what looked like a bundle of cables. "Oh, no. Those are my sex toys."

Harrison dropped the box. "Sex toys?"

"Yes. You can leave the box on the nightstand."

Harrison obeyed and put it there, pushing to the side

several bottles of nail polish, lipsticks, and a palette of reddish eye shadows.

Harrison got up. He needed to get away from Sal's bed before he started imaging what kind of toys were in that box and what Sal did with them. He decided to try the bathroom, although he regretted it as soon as he peeked inside. If the bedroom was a mess, the bathroom was worse. There were what had to be two dozen products on the sink, five hairbrushes, and several nail files. Hair ties were peppered around, most of them dotted with long white hair.

"Found them!" Harrison heard behind him. He was relieved he wouldn't have to search the bathroom.

Until he turned around and found Sal's ass poking out from under the bed. Sal's upper body was half under it, and he held his ass high, in the perfect position to fuck him—or spank him.

Heat flowed in Harrison's body, and he forced himself to look away and stare at the wall. "That's great."

He saw Sal wiggle his way out from under the bed from the corner of his eye and looked at him only once he was standing and brushing invisible dust from his t-shirt.

"I remembered I put them under the bed so I could find them when I needed them."

"I see."

Sal grinned and opened the red box he was holding. "Yep, there they are. Now, I need to rework this one, because it would look weird on you." He held up a leather necklace that displayed what looked like something's—or someone's—claw. "But you can wear the other two right away." He put the claw down and held out a silver chain with a small pouch attached to it. "Want me to explain what's in this and how it works?"

Harrison took the pouch. "No. I wouldn't understand anything anyway. But thank you."

Sal's face was serious when he answered. "I don't want you to get hurt. Jadon is right, you're one of the few humans who's not afraid of us, or at the very least, who doesn't hate us. I don't want the world to lose that. And of course, you're kind of cute."

Harrison groaned. He was never going to make it out of this alive, and not because of the demon he was hunting.

CHAPTER THREE

Harrison had no idea what he was looking for. He'd only been on the job a few days, and he'd kept his eyes and his ears open, but he had no more idea of who the demon was than before he'd started.

Everyone looked human. Even the assholes who treated him like shit because he was a lowly mail boy looked human, and they probably all were. Harrison doubted the demon would try to draw attention in any way, and that included yelling at the mail boy.

Harrison rubbed his face. God, he hated this job. He was lucky it wasn't his real one and that he'd be able to quit as soon as he had what he needed, but damn. Someone else would take his place, and *they* wouldn't be able to quit when they wanted.

"Are you okay?" a woman asked.

Harrison blinked at her. "Yes. It's just, well, I didn't expect to be yelled at for something I have no power over when I signed up for this job."

"Who was it?"

"Uh, Jensen. He wasn't happy that the documents he's expecting haven't arrived yet."

She grimaced. "He's an ass. I'd tell you to ignore him, but that's not exactly practical, with your job."

Harrison smiled at her and rubbed the back of his neck. "You're right, it's not. I guess I'll have to get used to it." He looked around. "Maybe you can give me pointers on who to avoid as much as possible?" He was pretty sure this lady liked him, at least physically. Or maybe she was just nice. He'd never been good at understanding that kind of thing.

She smiled. "I can. I'm Daphne."

Harrison smiled back. "Harrison. So, Daphne. Who should I steer clear of?"

She looked around. "Well, Jensen is one of them, of course. And Sawyer, too. She doesn't like to be disturbed, ever, so if you have mail for her, try to leave it on her desk when she's not there."

Harrison made a mental note of that. He'd already determined that the demon couldn't be any of the people who'd worked there for long. From what Jadon had found out, this demon worked for other demons, making spells and whatnot. That just wouldn't fit with a job in a law firm, no matter how unimportant it might be. No, the demon had to be one of the people who'd just been hired, and Harrison had to find out who those people were.

The easiest way would be to get into HR and find a list of the people they'd hired, but Harrison was only a mail boy. There was no way he'd be allowed to do that, not without a warrant, and he couldn't exactly get one, since he wasn't a cop anymore. Besides, even if he was, no one would have given him a warrant because a demon had almost killed another two other demons. They might have if they'd been sure this demon was posing as a human, but they had no way to ascertain that.

But Harrison wasn't a cop, so he was going to need to find another way to get what he needed.

"Thank you," he told Daphne.

"You're welcome, and feel free to come around for more tips."

"I will." Harrison needed to get her to trust him, and he needed to do it fast. It would sound suspicious if he just came out and asked her who was new in the firm. Hell, maybe *she* was new and she was the demon, although Harrison doubted it. She seemed to know the people who worked there well, since she was giving him tips, and that knowledge only came with time.

Harrison gestured at the cart where the mail was stacked. "I better go before someone else gets angry at me for not delivering their mail fast enough."

Daphne smiled. "You know where to find me. Come by whenever, and I'll tell you everything you need to know to make your job easier."

"Thank you. I'm not sure why you're doing that, but I appreciate it."

Harrison finished his tour of the office, handing out mail and retrieving things that had to be sent out. He was glad to go back to the mail room and hand everything over to the next shift. He wasn't used to this kind of work, and he'd been bored out of his mind the entire time. He also didn't have anything to show for the day of work, although that wasn't surprising. He hadn't expected to find the demon right away, but still. He didn't like the thought of having to come back tomorrow morning. He also had to go by HQ before going home to tell Jadon and Sal what he'd discovered — or rather, not discovered.

He was glad when he got to HQ and the place was mostly empty. It was late afternoon, so it would take a while for the demons to arrive and get to work. That meant no one was gawking at Harrison as he walked in, which was a relief. Harrison didn't have anything against demons, and the warriors seemed to have accepted him easily enough, but he never knew how to behave when he was there. It was their turf, not his, and even though he knew no one would do anything to him, he was uncomfortable.

He found Sal first. He was sitting alone in the dining hall, poking at whatever was on his plate as if he expected it to attack him. Harrison took a moment to observe him.

He wasn't sure why he found Sal so attractive. He was gorgeous, yes, but he was also so very different from the men Harrison was usually attracted to, and not because he was a demon. Harrison had been drawn to demons before, but they often looked more . . . human.

Sal didn't. There was no way that Sal could have passed for a human, which was the reason why he wasn't playing mail boy in Harrison's place.

Sal was nothing like Harrison's exes, but God, he was beautiful. He was so *much*—noisy, messy, but also always happy and bouncy and spreading so much joy around that Harrison found himself smiling every time he was in the same room as him. And he wanted so much more. He couldn't help but think about what his life would be like if Sal was part of it, even though he knew it was a moot point. The reason Sal was still there was that he was looking for that demon. Once he found it, he'd go back to his house on the lake, many hours away from the city and Harrison, and Harrison would probably never see him again.

He cleared his throat and strode toward Sal. "Already awake?" he asked, sliding into the seat in front of Sal.

Sal put down his fork. "The asshole in the room next to mine decided to bring his girlfriend home."

"Oh. They're noisy?" Harrison remembered how Sal had moaned about hearing Jadon and his boyfriends going at it.

Sal glared. "Are two people having sex noisy? Hell, yes. They've been at it half the day. I couldn't sleep."

That didn't make him any less gorgeous. "I'm sorry."

"At least tell me you found the demon. Please. I need something good to start my day."

Harrison shook his head. "Sorry. I've been able to rule out several people, but I haven't pinpointed the demon yet."

Sal sighed. "Damn it. I *hate* having to stay here. It's noisy, and there are too many people."

He looked so down that Harrison wanted to hug him. "I'm sorry. Maybe you could ask Jadon if you can switch rooms?"

"It would be the same. Warriors come and go, and I get it. This is their home, not mine."

"But you're here to help the League."

Sal sighed. "I know, and I'm sure Jadon would do whatever he can if I asked him to. But like I said, this isn't my home, and I don't want to create problems."

"But you hate being here."

"What gave me away?"

Harrison chuckled. He liked Sal when he was happy, but it was nice to see he could also be moody. It made him more human, even though he was anything but. "What can I do to help?"

Sal put down his fork. "Nothing, unless you're offering me a place to stay."

This was a bad idea. Harrison knew it was, yet he was going to do it. "You can have my guest room."

Sal cocked his head. "What?"

"My guest room. It's small, but I'll be the only one to share the apartment with. I'm pretty quiet, and I definitely won't be bringing anyone home."

"But—"

"And the building is demon friendly. My neighbor is an oni demon. He's nice when he's not trying to get into my pants. Not that he's ever going to manage to get in them, of course." Harrison swallowed. He was babbling, and he hated it. "What do you say? Are you going to be my housemate until this is over?"

Sal wasn't sure what to say. "Why?" he asked. It was the fastest way to get the answers to the questions he had.

Harrison shrugged. "Why not? As I said, I live alone, and the building is demon friendly."

"And you saw my room and the mess I make. This is how I am. My house is the same. Your guest room will be the same if I move in there, and there's no telling for how long that will be. I mean, I know you're a cop and that you can find the demon, but since they look human, it's going to be next to impossible to be sure you found them unless they attack you or whatever."

Harrison wrinkled his brow. "Will your mess stay in the guest bedroom? Or will it take over the entire apartment?"

"I can make sure it stays in the bedroom."

"I'm fine with it, then. I assume you'll clean up when you leave?"

"Of course I will. I'm not going to leave my stuff behind." Not when he'd found so many pretty clothes since he was in the city. He was going to need another suitcase to take everything home.

"Then I don't see what the problem is."

"I didn't say there was a problem. I just want to know why you're offering me a place to stay when you don't have to."

Harrison leaned back in his chair. "We're friends."

"Are we?" Sal hadn't been there long, but he hadn't missed the way Harrison sometimes looked at him It was also impossible to forget the way Harrison had taken care of him when he'd had to blast through the demon's spell to find Esi. It was evident Harrison was a caring person, though, so Sal had no idea if that was the reason he was doing this or if there was more to this.

Harrison frowned. "I thought we were. Not close friends, but we could be if we had more time to get to know each other. I know you're going to have to go home sooner or later, but we could keep in touch. And I don't spend a lot of time home anyway, so you'd have the apartment to yourself most of the day. As long as you don't burn it down or something, I don't see why you shouldn't stay with me. It'll be more relaxing for you. You wouldn't find yourself eating breakfast in the middle of the afternoon all alone in the dining hall. I'm not going to force you, though."

Sal smiled. "I know, and thank you. I accept your proposal." Sal wasn't sure it was a good idea, considering how cute he thought Harrison was and the way Harrison looked at him, but he wasn't one to live cautiously, or at least he hadn't been until recently.

Harrison smiled. "Great. That way, I won't have to come back here every day to tell you how the investigation is going."

"Is that why you asked me to move in with you?"

"You're not moving in, just temporarily staying. But no, that's not why. I want you to be comfortable, and it's obvious you're not here. That's all."

Sal propped his elbow on the table and laid his chin on his hand. "You're a nice guy, aren't you?" He'd been there for him when Sal had done the spell, and he was there for him again now even though they weren't friends, not really.

Harrison's cheeks flushed. "I don't know."

"You are. And thank you. You didn't have to help me, yet you are. If you ever need anything, call, and I'll do whatever I can to help you."

Harrison blushed even harder.

Sal didn't want to see him as cute and adorable. He didn't want to see him as a man he might like. Sal didn't do love, not anymore. He was hundreds of years old, and he's lost too many people to want to go through it again. He always stuck to sex only—when he even had sex. He'd learned a long time ago to be alone, and it had worked until he'd had to come to the city to help Jadon.

Now he wasn't sure it still worked. Harrison was a friend,

but Sal knew himself. He knew how easily he could fall for Harrison, no matter how little he wanted to, especially if Sal moved in with him for a while.

Sal was going to have to be careful with Harrison. He didn't want to break Harrison's heart or take advantage of him and his goodness, and he certainly didn't want his own heart to get broken in the process.

CHAPTER FOUR

Sal scowled at the bowl on his legs. He needed to find that fucking demon, for fuck's sake, and not just because he wanted to go home.

He might have changed his mind about that. He *did* want to go back to his lake house, of course. He missed the quiet and space, having all his things there, being able to go outside without anyone staring at him. He liked Harrison's apartment, but it was small, and sharing it with Harrison was somewhat awkward. Harrison was trying hard to make Sal feel welcome and everything, but it was apparent he wasn't quite sure what to do with Sal, and Sal didn't know what to do with Harrison.

Taking him to bed would have been easy. Sal was sure of that. Having sex with a human would be something of a novelty, although not much. Sal tended to avoid humans, but that didn't mean he'd never been with one. He'd even had a human girlfriend a few decades back, although she'd left him before things could get too serious.

And they *would* get serious with Harrison, at least for him. Sal couldn't let that happen, for both their sakes, so the best thing he could do was to find the demon, tell Jadon about it, and go home. That was why he was still there, and once it was done, he'd be able to go home without feeling like he was failing Jadon.

He had to try again. He wouldn't be able to get through the cloaking spell, but maybe he didn't have to. He knew a lot of demons. There were more he *didn't* know, of course, especially since he didn't usually live in the city, but this demon wasn't just a demon. They were powerful, so much so that Sal was having trouble finding them. That probably meant he *had* stumbled onto them before. All the powerful demons eventually either worked together or tried to kill each other, sometimes both. If Sal could recognize the demon's signature, the way their power felt, then he could identify them and make things easier for Harrison.

He just needed to make a small adjustment to the ingredients in the bowl so he could identify the demon rather than find it.

He put the bowl down and grabbed the bag containing his ingredients. He had to take out half of them before he could find what he needed, but he knew it was there. He might be messy about a lot of things, but he always knew what he had to the ounce. He took his job seriously, especially when he was dealing with a dangerous demon.

Once he had everything he needed in the bowl, Sal grabbed it and closed his eyes. He didn't need to look to set fire to the spices, and a few words in his native language were enough to guide him to the demon. This time, he didn't try to batter through the cloaking spell, but rather, he sensed it.

It was good work. The spell was potent, but that meant the demon's signature was strong. Sal only had to find it.

He dropped the bowl when he recognized it. The spell popped and dissipated, and Sal scrambled to his feet. He stared at the bowl and the spices on the floor, trying to process what had just happened.

"Sal?"

Sal jerked. Harrison was standing there, still wearing pajama pants and the old t-shirts he seemed to like wearing in bed. His hair was standing up, and there was a crease on his cheek.

"Sal?" Harrison repeated. He took in the bowl. "What

happened?"

Sal shook his head. He cleared his throat, but nothing came out of his mouth. He wasn't sure he wanted anything to come out. He was going to have to tell Harrison about this, and he didn't like that thought. It was the right thing to do, though, no matter how he felt about it.

"Okay, Sal, you're freaking me out, and I hate freaking out. What happened? Are you hurt? Do I have to grab my gun?"

Sal shook his head. He leaned against the wall and closed his eyes, breathing in and out. He was surprised when Harrison reached for him, but he didn't resist when Harrison pulled him close. He could feel how hesitant Harrison was, but he was glad Harrison didn't back away. He needed to be close to someone right now, and Harrison was there, and he was perfect.

Harrison rubbed the back of Sal's neck as Sal pressed his forehead against his shoulder. "Just breathe, okay? I don't know what happened, but it's obvious you're freaking out, so you need to calm down. Lean on me and breathe, yeah?"

Sal obeyed. Harrison's voice was soft, though worried, and his presence was soothing. Sal knew he was safe, so it was relatively easy to focus on his breathing and his heartbeat.

"Your wings are fluttering," Harrison said in a voice that sounded awed.

"I'm not doing it on purpose."

"I know. I noticed it happen when you're, well, emotional. It's not a bad thing," he added in a rush.

Sal chuckled. "I know. Emotions are good." Except in this case. Sal didn't want to be feeling everything he was feeling.

Harrison was still rubbing the back of Sal's neck. "They are, even when you hate that you're feeling them. You want to talk about what's going on?"

Sal didn't, but he also didn't have a choice. "No."

Harrison chuckled. "All right. You do know that if it has to do with the demon, you're going to have to tell me, right?"

"I know. Can we stay like this for another little while before I have to spill out my feelings to you?" Sal didn't think Shaila would leave. She didn't know he'd identified her, so she still thought she was safe.

"Of course. Anything you need."

Satan, Harrison was too good to be true. Sal had a hard time believing he was as nice as he behaved, but he was starting to see that with Harrison, you got what you saw. He was honest and just *sweet*, which was a change from, well, pretty much everyone Sal knew apart from him.

Harrison continued to rub Sal's neck and back as Sal settled down. He didn't ask any more questions. He didn't push. He just gave Sal the time he needed to wrap his mind around what was happening.

Sal wished he could stay in Harrison's arms forever. It felt good — Harrison was still warm from his bed, and he smelled like sleep and like himself, like home and comfort, and everything good in the world.

But Sal couldn't stay like this, not when he finally knew who the demon was and how dangerous she was. He sighed and pushed away, and Harrison let him go. He didn't leave, though. Instead, he peered at Sal, his forehead creased in worry.

"Are you sure you're okay?" he asked.

Sal nodded. "Yes. I know who the demon is."

Harrison's eyes widened. "You do? That means I can go get him or her."

"It does. But she's dangerous, Harrison. You have to be careful." Sal wished there was another way to do this, someone else to send, but Jadon and his warriors would be of no help in this case. They couldn't go into the building where Shaila was hiding.

"I promise I will. I was a cop, remember?"

"I know, but she's powerful, almost as powerful as me. You can't underestimate her."

"I won't." Harrison hesitated. "You know her well, then?"

"We grew up together. Shaila and I were . . . childhood friends. Our caves were next to each other, and we were together from birth to the moment I left Hell."

"I'm sorry. It has to be hard to see one of your oldest friends do this kind of thing and know you have to stop her now."

"It's even harder because she was the first person I ever loved."

Harrison blinked. "You mean, like *love* love?"

Sal had to chuckle at that. "Yes. We were childhood sweethearts, I guess." Although that didn't fit with what their lives had been down in Hell. Nothing was sweet down there. It was all a mess of heat and blood and violence, and only the strongest made it out alive.

Sal and Shaila both had. He'd thought they'd be together forever, even though that had been a tall order considering they both had thelnyss demons as one parent, and thelnysses lived forever unless they were killed. But they'd both changed, and now Sal was going to have to help the League stop Shaila.

He was *not* looking forward to it.

CHAPTER FIVE

Harrison knew who he was looking for now, and that made his job easier, but he almost wished he didn't. Sal had been distraught this morning when he'd found out about his ex, and now Harrison was going to have to stop her. He wasn't even sure how to do that—there was no way she'd come with him quietly even if he asked. He had to avoid her attacking the humans in the office or taking any of them hostage, and he wasn't sure how to do that. He planned to keep an eye on her now that he knew what she looked like, wait until she left the office, and make sure Jadon had people waiting for her at her place, wherever that was. It was the only way they could make sure the humans involved made it out alive and well, and that was the most important thing—apart from Sal—because Sal was more important than catching Shaila, at least for Harrison.

"Hi."

Harrison had been so focused on thinking about Sal that he hadn't noticed Daphne coming up to him. He forced himself to smile at her. "Hi. I have something for you. Two letters and a package."

He handed everything off to her and leaned closer. "So, do you have time for that chat you promised me?" he asked.

Daphne's smile widened. "You mean the one about the people you should avoid as much as possible."

"Yep, that one. I've been keeping my ears open, and some people warned me about a new lady. Not sure of her name, but she's a stunner, or so I heard." Harrison doubted Shaila was using her real name, but he hoped she hadn't changed her appearance. She wouldn't have had a reason to do it since no one here knew her. Only Sal did, and she thought she was safe from him here.

Daphne frowned. "A new woman?"

"That's what I heard, but I have no idea who's new here."

"Well, there *are* a few new people, or recent anyway."

"Is any of them a woman I should avoid? Because I've heard horror stories already, and I've only been here a few days." Harrison knew he was pushing, but he needed to find out who it was ASAP. The sooner this was over, the sooner Sal would feel better. Harrison wasn't looking forward to seeing him leave, but it was what would happen, and delaying things would be no use.

"Horror stories? I didn't hear anything." There was a gleam in Daphne's eyes, though. "What kind of horror stories?"

Great. Now Harrison had to come up with something. "Uh, I guess mostly stuff flying, you know? That's why I want to know who this lady is. I'd rather avoid having anything hit me. I'm too cute for that."

Daphne giggled. "You are. So, I think there are a few new women around, but since you said she's a stunner, it has to be Shaila Prince."

She hadn't changed her name. "Shaila Prince, huh? I'll stay far away from her office. Thanks."

Harrison hurried out of there, ignoring Daphne's call for him to stop. He needed to find Shaila, but of course, she wasn't in her office once Harrison managed to find it. He asked a few people, but no one could tell him anything—until someone did.

"She left about ten minutes ago, I think," the man said. Harrison had no idea who the guy was, and he didn't care.

"Where did she go?"

"She said she'd forgotten something in her car."

Shit. Harrison ran out of the office. He didn't care about being fired, since this wasn't his real job, and he had to get to Shaila.

Why was she leaving? Did she suspect something? Was that why she was running? Had Harrison done something that had betrayed who he was? Or was it the spell Sal had done this morning? He'd said she wouldn't be able to know who had done it, but he'd been shaken, so Harrison wasn't sure how true that was.

He rushed down the stairs to the parking floor. He hoped to be able to catch Shaila's car and the plate so he could find her again. His car was in the parking lot, too, so maybe he'd manage to follow Shaila to wherever she was going, hopefully her home.

Harrison burst through the door and looked around. He could hear the sound of heels clicking on the concrete, and he hoped it was Shaila.

"Excuse me? Miss Prince?" he called out. She hopefully didn't know him as anything but the mail boy, so she might stop.

She did. A woman with long black hair was standing by a car. She turned toward Harrison, and wow, he could see why Sal had said she was stunning. She had that same other-worldly air about her, even though she couldn't have been more diffcrent from Sal even if she'd tried.

She looked human, while Sal was very obviously not human. She was dark—dark hair, dark eyes, a healthy tan—where Sal had pale skin, white hair, and blue eyes. But still. Harrison was pretty sure he'd have pinpointed her as a demon even if he hadn't known she was one.

"Miss Prince? I'm sorry, I'm the firm's mail boy, and I have something for you."

She narrowed her eyes. "The mail boy?"

Harrison forced himself to smile. "Mailman, I guess."

"What do you want?"

"Just to give you something." He reached for his gun, but before he could touch it, she kicked him in the sternum.

He hadn't expected it, and she was damn fast, faster than any humans Harrison had dealt with had been. He flew back, pain radiating from his chest. He hit the wall with his back, and the air whooshed out of his lungs. He pushed himself up and took his gun out at the same time. He pointed it toward Shaila, but she was gone.

Harrison blinked. "What the fuck?" She hadn't taken a car. He was sure of that. He'd have heard it, and she hadn't had the time. Since when could demons disappear into thin air, though?

Harrison leaned against the wall. "Fuck." He'd messed up, hadn't he? He'd let her go, and who knew if he was ever going to be able to find her again.

He rubbed his face. He needed to call Jadon and let him know what had happened. Hopefully, he and his warriors would be able to get to Shaila before she vanished completely.

It was half an hour before he managed to get home. He'd told Jadon everything he knew about Shaila, and he'd been ordered to tell Sal to call as soon as he walked into the apartment. Jadon was no doubt going to ask him to do the tracking spell again, and Harrison hoped Sal would manage to find Shaila. He knew he'd done everything he could, but he still felt guilty about letting her escape, even though she was a demon and she could no doubt have crushed him with a flick or her finger, or something like that.

He'd been lucky. He was still alive and able to walk and talk. That was more than some people who dealt with demons could say.

Harrison was glad Icha was nowhere to be seen as he walked into the elevator and pushed the button to his floor.

His chest still hurt, and he knew he was going to end up with a bruise there, probably the size of a house, but he could deal with it. Some ointment and he'd be as good as new.

Harrison got out of the elevator, already thinking about the nice shower he was going to take. He froze and reached for his gun when he saw that his apartment door was open. Sal had been home when Harrison had left, and while he was messy, there was no way he'd have left the door open if he'd gone somewhere.

"What were you thinking?" he heard Sal ask when he got closer.

There was someone in the apartment with Sal. Harrison couldn't see who it was from the hallway, but from Sal's tone, he wasn't happy to see this person. Harrison knew Sal was only familiar with Jadon and the other warriors of the League, and from what Sal had said, he didn't have other friends in the city.

So who was with him?

Sal had been stunned to find Shaila on Harrison's couch when he'd left the bathroom ten minutes earlier. He didn't know how she'd found him and how she'd gotten in, but he wasn't about to ask.

She got up. She was wearing a tight black dress, and she was as beautiful as she'd been the last time Sal had seen her, albeit more polished. The village they'd grown up in had been little more than dirt and caves, but Shaila looked like she'd never belonged there, and maybe she hadn't. Sal would have been happy for her if he hadn't been hunting her for almost killing two people he'd come to like.

"I was doing the job I was hired to do," she said. She didn't come closer, and Sal was grateful for that.

"You were hired to hurt people. That's not you. It's not

39

what you do."

Shaila snorted. "Of course it is. I'm a demon. This is what we do. We take what we want, and we don't care who gets hurt in the process."

Sal's chest felt tight. "What happened to you, Shaila?"

"You mean, after you left? What do you think happened? I had to learn to live without the boy who protected me all my life up until then. It wasn't easy, so excuse me if I'm a bit hardened and bitchy."

"You're not—"

"Yes, I am. I don't care anymore, Sal. You're the past. Home is the past. I have a new life here, and I'm living it the way I want. No one is going to stop me, not even you."

"The League will." No matter how much this hurt Sal, it was the right thing to do. He wasn't going to excuse what Shaila had done. She'd been hurt, that much was obvious, and surviving had no doubt been hard on her, but they were demons. *Everything* was hard on them, and it didn't matter if they grew up in Hell or the human realm. Sal was doing his best not to hurt people even with his past, while Shaila had chosen to go the other way and use what she knew to push herself into a better life, no matter who it hurt.

She wasn't the Shaila he'd grown up with anymore. He supposed he wasn't the Salomon she had grown up with either.

Shaila snorted. "The League can try, of course. But you know I'm more powerful than the demons who work there."

"You're not more powerful than me. I managed to find you. I'll do it again."

"Not if I make sure you can't." She reached in her cleavage and took out something. Sal half expected it to be a weapon, but it was a small pouch that no doubt contained the ingredients of a spell she was about to cast.

He didn't have time to think about what that spell might

be, because the door slammed open and Harrison barged in, his gun in his hands, pointed at Shaila. "Drop your weapon!" he told her.

She did, except it wasn't in the way Harrison intended. She looked at Sal, a grin spreading on her lips

Sal knew he was in trouble. He tried to move, but it was too late. Shaila threw what she was holding at him, and since she'd opened the pouch, its contents fell out when it hit Sal's chest.

Harrison fired, but Shaila moved out of the way, faster than Sal had ever seen her move. She pressed a hand to Sal's chest, just where the pouch had emptied itself, and said a few words in their native language, words that terrified Sal.

He pushed back. Shaila stumbled away, but she'd already cast the spell. Sal could feel it. Something was missing. He was different. He *felt* different.

Shaila grinned at him. "Now you *won't* be able to find me again."

"Sal?" Harrison asked. Sal could see his attention was torn between him and Shaila.

"Don't let her get away," Sal said, but he already knew that if Shaila wanted to leave, she would. No one in this room was going to be able to stop her, not anymore.

Harrison turned his attention back to Shaila, but it was too late. She had to be using a speed spell, probably something she'd inked on her body. Sal had one, too, but it wasn't active.

None of the spells on his body were, and that could only mean one thing.

Shaila wiggled her fingers. "I'll see you when I see you, Sal. I won't be holding my breath, since you're not going to be able to find me." She blew him a kiss and turned toward the door.

Harrison raised his gun higher, and from his expression, Sal knew he wouldn't hesitate to shoot Shaila to stop her. "Don't!" he yelled.

Harrison's split moment of hesitation was enough for Shaila to leave. She moved fast, and she was out of the apartment before Sal could blink. Harrison swore and went after her, but Sal already knew it was a moot point.

He flopped to the floor, his legs unable to hold him up anymore. There was a hole in his chest, a black hole that was sucking in Sal's life the way he knew it. He didn't know how to get rid of it, not right now, not with Shaila gone.

"Sal? What happened? Are you okay?" Harrison asked. He holstered his weapon and closed the apartment door behind himself before kneeling next to Sal. He took one of Sal's hands in his, and Sal clung to it. He needed an anchor, something that would keep him in place when he threatened to float away.

"You're freaking me out, Sal. What did she throw at you? Was it a spell? What did she do to you?"

Sal swallowed. "She's gone."

"Yeah, she is. I tried to stop her, but she's too fast."

"She probably has a speed spell inked on her somewhere."

"Okay, that makes sense. Are you ready to tell me what she did to you?"

Sal wasn't. "Did you call Jadon?"

"I called him before coming back here. He and the others were going to try to find Shaila. But you're right. I need to call him again."

Sal expected Harrison to step out to do that, but instead, he sat on the floor next to him. He had to let go of Sal's hand to get his phone out, but once he'd dialed Jadon's number, he wrapped his free arm around Sal's shoulders and pulled him against his chest.

Sal was surprised, but he went with it. He couldn't focus on anything that wasn't the missing part of himself, but Harrison's closeness helped. He was warm and solid, which was what Sal needed right now.

"Jadon? She was at my place. No, she ran away when I tried to stop her, and she was too fast for me." Sal felt Harrison look down at him, but he didn't look up. "I don't know. He's not okay, that's for sure, but I have no idea what she did to him. I don't think he needs a healer, but I'll bring him to HQ as soon as he's able to move. No, it looks more like emotional shock. I know she did something to him, but physically, I'm pretty sure he's okay."

Sal groaned. That was as far from the truth as anything could come. He *wasn't* okay. He wasn't wounded, though, and Harrison was right—nothing the healers at the League's HQ could do to him would help. The only one who could do something was Shaila, and she was long gone.

Harrison hung up and threw his phone on the floor. "What happened, Sal?" he asked, his voice soft and soothing. "I understand if you don't want to talk about it, but I need to know if you're going to be okay. Please."

Sal shook his head, almost clocking Harrison in the face with one of his horns. Sometimes, they were a pain in the ass. "I'm not okay," he croaked.

"Okay. What can I do for you' How can I help?"

"You can't."

"What did she do? She cast a spell on you, didn't she? That's what that thing she threw at you was about."

"She did. She . . ." Sal couldn't say it. The words wouldn't leave his lips.

"She?"

Sal licked his lips. "She locked my powers away. I don't have them anymore. I'm powerless."

CHAPTER SIX

Harrison didn't know what to do or to say. He needed to get Sal to HQ, to make sure he was all right, but he doubted that was the case, even though physically, he was okay.

Harrison couldn't even begin to understand what Sal was going through, and while he wanted to help, he had no idea how. Anything he could say would only turn the knife in the wound.

"We need to go to HQ," he murmured. He didn't want to go, because he didn't think Sal was up to moving right now, but Jadon needed answers, and if there was anything the League could do to help Sal, then it needed to happen.

Sal nodded and pushed away. He looked dazed, and Harrison wasn't sure what to do. Would it be too much if he helped him stand and guided him to the parking lot? Would Sal accept that from him? Or would he push him away? Harrison wouldn't even try to coddle Sal in normal circumstances, but this was anything but normal. Sal was still a demon, but he didn't have his powers anymore, and that had to be near impossible to accept.

Harrison had a lot of questions for him, and so would Jadon, but Harrison's first and primary concern was Sal. If Sal needed to be shielded for a while, then Harrison would be his shield. If he needed to be protected, Harrison would be his protector, even if that meant pitting himself against Jadon.

He didn't think Jadon would hurt Sal, but he'd want answers, and he'd want them fast, because they had to find

Shaila. Harrison wasn't sure if they could or if she'd be able to undo what she'd done to Sal, but that wasn't going to stop him, and he suspected it wasn't going to stop Jadon either. Jadon liked Sal. They were friends. He'd want Sal to get his powers back as much as he wanted his boyfriends to be avenged or whatever.

He got up and held his hands out to Sal. "Come on. You'll be more comfortable on the couch."

"You just said we needed to go to HQ."

"We do, but it can wait for a bit. You need some time, and I doubt there's anything you or I can do to help Jadon right now. You can take a little time to start wrapping your mind around what's happening."

Sal's answering chuckle was dark and not at all humorous. "There's no wrapping my mind around this. I lost my powers. I'm not myself anymore."

Harrison couldn't say anything to that. "I'm sure you'll be okay." He hauled Sal up and guided him toward the couch.

"Okay? I've had these powers since I was born, Harrison. Do you know how long ago that was? I spent hundreds of years training myself to use them, and now they're gone. It would be the same for you if you lost, I don't know, an arm or a leg. Do you think you'd be okay if that happened?"

Harrison's first instinct was to leave so that Sal would stop yelling at him, but he couldn't. Sal was lashing out because he was in pain and feeling lost, and while Harrison couldn't do anything to help him with that, he *could* be there for him and make sure he knew he wasn't alone. "I understand. I'm sorry."

"You *don't* understand," Sal muttered.

"Not what you're going through, no, and I'm sorry if I've been insensitive. I'd promise it won't happen again, but I know better. I don't always think before I open my mouth. I *can* promise you I'm not going anywhere, though. I'm going to help you get your powers back, and if I can't, I'll do whatever I can to help you get used to a life without them."

"I don't want to get used to a life without them."

"I know." Harrison rubbed Sal's back. He wanted to do more, but what? He had no idea, and he doubted Sal was about to tell him. No, there was nothing else he could do for Sal, but Jadon was different. He was a powerful demon. He'd be able to tell Harrison what to do.

CHAPTER SEVEN

Sal needed to stop moping, because that wasn't going to help him regain his powers. He'd known that since he'd felt them disappear, but he'd allowed himself one night of despairing and feeling sorry for himself. That was over now, though. His magic wouldn't come back on its own, and that meant he was going to have to be the one to search for it—for Shaila.

She was the only one who could give him back what she'd stolen. She'd been the one to cast the spell that had blocked his powers. She'd made it so he couldn't access them, which was as good as taking them away and had the same result. Sal was an ordinary demon now, and he couldn't use everything he'd learned over the decades. He could probably still cast some weak spells if he used the right ingredients, but he wouldn't get the results he used to get. He wouldn't be able to find Shaila.

He needed help.

Sal didn't like asking for help, but he knew there was no way out of it in this situation.

"Ready to go?" Harrison asked. He still looked worried, and Sal avoided thinking about the way he'd taken care of him yesterday.

Harrison was a caring man, and he had shown that to Sal yesterday. He'd taken him to HQ to see a healer, but when Sal hadn't wanted to talk to Jadon, Harrison had taken him home. He'd fed him lunch and dinner, had made sure he showered, and had put him to bed. Sal had been in a daze, and he still was, in a way. Losing the powers he'd had since he was born wasn't an easy thing to deal with, but it was easier if he tried to ignore the empty feeling in his chest and focused on a solution.

He got up from the couch and nodded at Harrison. "I'm ready."

Harrison's answering smile was so bright it hurt to see. "Good. Because we can stay, if you'd rather have another day to yourself, but I think Jadon might be able to help."

Sal wasn't sure of that, but he did need to talk to Jadon. Even if he couldn't do anything, he had to find someone who could locate Shaila, and Sal was going to need at least a pair of League warriors to go with him when he went to confront her. Jadon didn't *have* to help him, but he'd lost his powers while helping Jadon and the League. So from Sal's point of view, they owed it to him to do whatever they could to make sure he got them back.

He just hoped they viewed things the same way he did.

He was silent all the way to HQ. What was he supposed to say? Harrison knew what was going on, and he seemed to be at a loss, too. Sal was glad for the silence. His powers had been locked away only yesterday, and he still wasn't used to it.

He didn't use them in his everyday life, but that didn't change the fact that he felt like a piece of himself was gone — an *essential* piece of himself. He'd built a good life thanks to what he could do and the way he could manipulate magic and use it to his benefit. He didn't need to work, not anymore, because he'd been cautious and he'd put enough money away to survive for a long time, but he was immortal, or at least, he suspected he was.

His thelnyss half was strong when it came to that, as the fact that he still looked like he was in his early thirties showed. It was always hit or miss when two kinds of demons had offspring.

But now, he probably wasn't, not anymore. He couldn't be sure that his immortality was linked to his powers, but he suspected it was, because the demons with the most potent magic were almost always immortal.

"I know things are looking dire right now, but you have to believe you'll be okay," Harrison suddenly said.

Sal wasn't surprised that Harrison was one of those people who saw the good side of every situation, or at least they tried to. He couldn't understand, though. "How am I supposed to do that?"

Harrison didn't look away from the road. "I get that it's hard, trust me. It's not the same, but when Jordan left the force, I had to choose if I wanted to go with him or to stay where I was. I've always dreamed of being a cop like my father was. I thought it was the perfect job. It wasn't. I knew things were bad between the force and demons, but what I saw while I was a cop . . . let's just say that it was both a hard and an easy decision to make. But once I did make it, I felt lost for a while, you know? Being a cop had been the only thing I'd thought of for so long, and then I wasn't one anymore. I didn't know what I'd do to earn money, and my father was pissed. He still is."

It wasn't the same, but listening to Harrison's story made it easier to forget Sal's, at least for a moment. "For what it's worth, I think you made the right decision."

Harrison grinned. "Of course you do. But yeah, you're right. And I know it's not the same as what happened to you. I'm just trying to show you that things change, things we don't expect to change, but it's not the end of the world." He paused and frowned. "You're not going to die without your powers, right?"

That made Sal smile, something he hadn't thought was possible in this situation. "No, I won't. I'm just your run-of-the-mill demon without them."

"You will never be that. You're special, even if you can never do another spell."

Sal wanted to believe him, both about that and about the fact that he could find another way to live now that he was powerless, but it was too soon. He *knew* he would survive. That was what he did. But he needed time to mourn his loss, and that wouldn't happen anytime soon, because he was going to find Shaila and get his powers back, dammit.

Harrison didn't push for more, and Sal leaned against the car door. It was awkward, what with his wings squished behind his back and his horns taking too much space, but then, cars weren't made with demons in mind. The time spent driving was maddening, because Sal wanted to get to work right away, to find Shaila and demand she undo what she'd done to him.

Why had she done it? She had to know how hard this would be on Sal. They'd trained together when they were young. And while she'd never been as powerful as Sal — probably because of the mix of genes — she knew what she was doing, and she was good at it. She had to know how horrible this was. Sal was pretty sure he would have preferred it if she'd killed him rather than lock his powers away so he couldn't use them.

Maybe that was why she'd done it.

Sal could admit he'd been a dick when he'd left Hell — and Shaila — behind. They'd talked about running away together, but after Sal's father had beat him almost to death, Sal hadn't been able to wait. He'd tried to get to Shaila, but he'd been chased away, and at only twenty-one, he hadn't had the strength to fight for her. He should have gone back, but he'd heard she'd left only a year or so after him, and while he'd tried to find her, he's never been able to.

He understood how much he'd hurt her, and it looked like she was trying to hurt him now. He didn't blame her, but he knew that talking to her wouldn't help. She'd always been stubborn, and she could hold a grudge for eternity. Even if Sal told her what had happened to make him run, she wouldn't soften. Both their lives had been, quite literally, hell, and when his father had come for him . . .

He'd run.

Jadon was waiting for them when they arrived at HQ. Harrison was always a bit uneasy when he stepped out of the elevator, not because of the demons milling around and looking at him—although they didn't help, why on earth were they always staring—but because he felt out of place. He *was* out of place. He wasn't a demon.

"How are you feeling?" Jadon asked Sal.

Sal looked like he wanted to clock someone in the face, and Harrison didn't blame him. Harrison had done his best to soothe and reassure Sal, but he doubted it had worked. He couldn't put himself in Sal's shoes, couldn't even begin to imagine what he felt, but he wished he could take away Sal's pain. No one should have to go through what Sal was going through, but especially not quirky, gentle, *good* Sal.

"I've been better," Sal muttered. "Can we go to your office?"

"Of course."

Harrison and Sal followed Jadon along the hallways. Harrison leaned closer to Sal. He wanted to do more than attempt to help, but he was just human. He had no idea what was going on and what was going to happen. "No one can tell you're not the same as you were the last time you were here," he murmured. He wasn't sure it was the right thing to say until Sal smiled at him.

It wasn't a big smile. Sal hadn't smiled big since yesterday, and Harrison wasn't offended. He wouldn't have been even if Sal had ignored him. But seeing him smile made Harrison hope that maybe he was starting to see that things weren't as desperate as he'd thought right after Shaila had left.

"Harrison told me what happened," Jadon said once they were in his office. "I'd like you to go back to the healers today."

Sal glared. "I don't need to. They can't do anything for me. The only one who can is Shaila, and that means I need to find her."

"Do you have a plan?"

Sal flopped into one of the chairs in front of Jadon's desk. "No. I have no idea where Shaila might go. We haven't been friends in so long . . . I can't even take a guess. I need a demon who can cast a spell to find her, since I can't."

Jadon sat more gracefully than Sal and crossed his arms over his chest. "And once you know where she is?"

Sal sat up. "I'll need help. Now that I can't use my powers to defend myself, I'm going to be vulnerable, especially to her. I still have the spells on my skin, but they won't work miracles, and depending on where she is and who she's with if she's not alone, well, you can see why I need someone with me."

"Thailor and Cumar have volunteered to help you, and I agreed. They're yours if you want them."

Sal wiggled his eyebrows. "Yeah?"

Jadon rolled his eyes. "Shut it, and yes. I can do without them for as long as you need them, although I'd appreciate being kept in the loop about what's going on. I trust all of you to do the right thing, though, so I'm not too worried about that. Just don't spirit away my warriors without giving me a phone call, and remember that while I can't leave HQ because chaos would happen, I'm here if you need anything."

What was Harrison even doing here? He couldn't do much to help except driving Sal around, which was okay, but not enough.

"As for finding a demon who can locate Shaila, what about Priska?" Jadon asked.

Sal leaned forward. "She's in town?"

"Yes. We went to her first when we were trying to find a way to exorcize Caelan, but she wasn't able to help us."

"Not powerful enough."

"That's what she said, yes. It's the reason I sent Caelan to you. But maybe she can help you with this? I don't know much about the magic you use, since they're not weapons I can wield, but she might be able to do something for you."

"Location spells aren't nearly as hard as exorcisms are, so yes, she might. It depends on Shaila, though. It took me a while to locate and recognize her signature on her cloaking spell, and Priska was nowhere near as powerful as I was the last time I saw her."

"Well, I don't have anything else to offer, unfortunately. But you have me and everyone else behind you. Just tell me what you need, and I'll do my best to make sure you have it. You saved Esi and Ilyhas. I don't know what I would have done without them, and I won't have to find out because of you. Whatever you need, you only have to ask."

There was no way Harrison could compete with that. He was only human, and only one man. But maybe he didn't *have* to compete with it.

Jadon was offering his warriors to help Sal, which was what Sal needed. But it was the only thing he needed? He was lost and alone. He needed someone to take care of him, and Harrison would be more than happy to volunteer to do that. Sal wasn't the kind of person who remembered to eat and sleep regularly, and Harrison didn't have anything better to do. He didn't have anything else to do, period, and even if he did, he'd ignore it. Sal was more important than pretty much anything, even though Harrison wasn't sure why he felt that way. The why didn't matter. Harrison wasn't going any-where, not until Sal was back to normal or told him to fuck off.

Sal nodded. "Thank you. And you don't have to do that if you don't want to. I did what I did because it was the right thing to do, not because I expected you to thank me some-day."

"I know. That's why we're friends. I'm offering help be-cause the League protects demons and because, like what you did, it's the right thing to do." He cleared his throat. "You're going to start with Priska, then?"

Sal pushed away a strand of white hair away from his face. "Yes. I can't make plans if I don't know where Shaila is. Once I do, I'll come back to tell you, and we can make plans with Thailor and Cumar."

"Good. Don't keep me in the dark. I want to help, and I *need* to know you and the others are safe."

Sal and Jadon seemed to have forgotten Harrison was there, and that was okay. It allowed Harrison to start plan-ning. He knew Sal and Jadon wouldn't want him to stick around when they went to find Shaila. They underestimated him all the time. He wasn't surprised, and he knew it would take more than going undercover in a human law firm to change their mind, but Harrison wasn't going anywhere.

He might not be a demon, and he might not know how to fight like one, but he'd be there until he was sure Sal was safe and okay—or as okay as he could be if they never found a way to get his powers back. Harrison had faith in Sal and the warriors, but sometimes, faith wasn't enough, and he'd make sure Sal had someone to lean on if things didn't go the way he needed them to.

CHAPTER EIGHT

There was something wrong with Sal.

Harrison knew it had to be because of his powers, but he didn't like seeing Sal the way he was right now. He was wearing jeans, which was fairly normal, but instead of being of an atrocious color like bright pink or orange with a rude sentence or drawing on the front, Sal's t-shirt was entirely black. His white hair was tied on the nape of his neck, and he didn't have any make-up on. His claws were painted, but Harrison was pretty sure it was because they'd been so when Shaila took his powers away.

Sal looked ordinary, or as ordinary as one might look when being a demon with huge wings and deer horns.

"He's not doing well," Thailor said, leaning toward Harrison.

Harrison had invited himself on the trip to this Priska's store, and since no one had said anything, he wasn't about to leave. "He's not."

"He's still staying with you?"

"Yes."

Thailor nodded. "Good. He needs someone to focus on him and to take care of him, even though he won't ever admit that."

"I'm not going anywhere."

Thailor looked at Harrison. "That's good. Things might get dangerous, though."

Harrison snorted. "So? Why do I always have to remind everyone that I was a cop?"

"Oh, I remember. We're not talking about humans here, though. Even if she *is* hiding among humans, Shaila is a demon, and she's strong and powerful enough to lock up Sal's powers. I'm not even sure *I* can do anything about her, although I'm going to try if she ever crosses my path. But no matter what you used to be, you're still human, and that's not going to change. No one would blame you for taking a step back."

"I'm not going to, and yes, I'm aware of how dangerous this will be. I'm not going to throw myself at Shaila. I'm not stupid. I want to be there for Sal, who's pretty much in the same boat as me without his powers. You and Cumar are the ones in charge, and that's fine. Just don't ask me to go home, because I won't."

Thailor grinned. "Good. You keep an eye on Sal, and Cumar and I will do the rest. Besides, today should be safe enough."

"Yeah?"

"We've already worked with Priska. Jordan can tell you about that. She's an okay demon."

"I'm not afraid of her." Even though Harrison didn't know her.

"Good, because there's nothing to be afraid of. You're safe with Cumar and me."

Harrison glared, but Thailor just winked at him and walked faster, stopping by Cumar to talk to him. They'd had to park a little way away because there weren't any empty spots by the shop.

Harrison didn't mind. It gave him time to think and prepare—and to try to coax Sal out of his foul mood.

"Sal?" Harrison called.

Sal blinked up at him. "Yes?"

"You're okay?" It was a stupid question, and probably one Sal didn't want to hear or answer, but Harrison felt the need to do something. He didn't know what and asking if Sal was okay was better than nothing.

"No."

Well, at least that was honest. "I'm sorry."

Sal sighed. "You have nothing to be sorry about. You didn't do this."

"I should have done more to stop her."

"You couldn't have even if you'd tried." Sal smiled, small and sad. "But thank you. It's nice to know I have someone in my corner."

"You have a lot of people there, Sal. You just need to accept their help."

"I am."

Cumar and Thailor stopped in front of a shop. Harrison would have expected to find an old hippie in it from the way it looked, but he knew better than to focus on appearances. "This is it?" he asked.

Cumar nodded. "Yes." He pushed the door open, and they all followed him inside.

The place smelled of incense, which wasn't a surprise. There were candles, crystals, and rocks on just about every flat surface, and the windows were covered to let in as little light as possible. A cat meowed from somewhere, then jumped onto one of the shelves, almost knocking the crystals on it down. It sat and stared at them, and Harrison looked away.

"Salomon. You look . . . different," a woman's voice said.

The bead curtain tinkled, and she stepped into the space where they were standing. Priska's hair was black, and to Harrison's surprise, she wore pastel colors.

Sal crossed his arms over his chest and scowled at her. "You can tell what happened to me."

"I can tell someone locked your powers up, yes. Who was it?"

"Shaila."

Harrison cleared his throat. "So the two of you know each other?" he asked. He was pretty sure it was the wrong thing to do, but he wanted to move Priska's attention from Sal to himself, because she didn't sound too pleasant, no matter how she looked.

Sal shrugged. "All the powerful demons know each other. We sometimes work together, and we often consult, like Priska had to do when she wasn't able to perform the exorcism on Caelan."

The little smirk on Priska's face vanished. "You did it, then."

"I did."

"And you need my help."

"I just want you to find Shaila."

Priska cocked her head. "Why did she take your powers away from you?"

"Because she's angry, and while I get it, I can't allow her to keep me in this state. She's been killing people, and I can't just let her go on."

"You're not her father."

Sal snorted. "Thank Satan for that. Her father was an asshole. Look, I know the two of you are friends. I know she's still angry with me for the way I left Hell, and I understand it. I'm the first to admit that I should have thought about things and taken her with me. But locking away my powers? Do you know what that feels like, Priska? Can you try to imagine it? It's like I'm missing part of my soul, and I'm utterly helpless to do anything to fix it. I won't hurt Shaila. I only need her to unlock my powers."

"And you'll leave her alone after that?"

Sal looked at Cumar and Thailor. "I will."

Harrison sucked in a breath. He'd suspected that was a possibility, but Sal hadn't told Jadon about it, and Harrison wasn't sure how the demon would take it. Shaila had almost killed his boyfriends, so it wasn't surprising that he wanted her to pay.

No one said anything, though, and Harrison wasn't about to bring it up, not when it could put Sal's chances in jeopardy.

Priska nodded. "Follow me."

She disappeared behind the bead curtain. Cumar went first, followed by Thailor and Sal. Harrison wasn't about to let Sal out of his sight, so he followed him.

The next room was pretty much like the first one, except smaller. There were thick carpets on the floor, and Priska sat there, her legs crossed as she grabbed ingredients from a box and dumped them into the bowl on her legs. Harrison had watched Sal do the same thing often enough that he didn't need to ask what she was doing anymore.

They stayed still and watched her as she lit candles and closed her eyes. The demon language she used was different from the one Sal spoke, less musical and harsher, but it was just as fascinating. Harrison didn't understand a word, and to his eyes, nothing was happening, but to Priska's, it was clearly different.

She chanted and frowned as she did so, and Harrison suspected she was having some trouble finding Shaila. It was a long shot, and they were all aware of that. Shaila had been able to shield herself from Sal for days, and he'd only managed to find her because she hadn't renewed her spell in time. Priska might not be able to find Shaila, but so far, she was their only hope — and chance.

Sal raised his hand to his mouth and bit on one of his claws. He never looked away from Priska, leaning toward her with hope in his eyes, but also wariness, and yes, fear. He chewed on his claw until Harrison reached for his hand.

Sal startled, but Harrison didn't say anything. He took his hand and linked their fingers together, then turned back to

Priska, his heart racing. He wasn't sure what part made him more anxious — the one where Priska might not be able to find Shaila, or the one where he was holding Sal's hand.

"I have her," Priska suddenly said in English.

"Where?" Sal asked.

Priska opened her eyes. "She's in Hell."

They had a location.

Sal didn't have to ask Priska to be more specific. If Shaila was in Hell like Priska said, then there was only one place where she could be. Sal didn't understand why she'd go back, but it made sense.

Thailor groaned. "In Hell? Damn it. I swore I was never going back. I hate that place."

"I doubt it's going to be anywhere near the palace," Cumar said.

"I don't care where it is. It's still *Hell*."

"I can't be more specific than that," Priska said. She put the bowl aside and rose to her feet. "Tracking demons doesn't work in Hell. That's probably why Shaila went there. She knew no one would be able to tell where she was exactly, even if Sal found someone able to track her."

"She was right," Thailor muttered. "What now?" He looked at Sal.

Sal was aware of the fact that his fingers were still linked with Harrison's. He didn't pull them away — why should he — but he did straighten. "I don't need anyone to know where Shaila is. I already do."

Cumar blinked. "You do? Why are we here, then?"

"Because I never thought she'd go back. She hated the village where we grew up as much as I did. I still do, and I doubt her feelings have changed."

"Then why go there?"

"She might have thought I wouldn't think to look there. And I wouldn't have, if Priska hadn't told me she was in Hell."

Cumar didn't look convinced. "Are you sure? Because Hell is damn big. We could wander down there for decades without ever finding her."

"Do you have a better idea?" Sal snapped.

"Hey, I didn't say we weren't going to go. But I hope you know what you're talking about."

"I do. I grew up with her. I know how she thinks."

"It was a long time ago, though, right?"

Sal narrowed his eyes. "Why are you making things so difficult?"

"Because it's my job to think about all the possible outcomes and attempt to come up with a plan for them."

Sal shook his head. He needed air. He needed time to think.

He gently untangled his fingers from Harrison's. Harrison's cheeks were flushed, and Sal made sure to smile to him. He didn't want Harrison to think he was angry with him, or even annoyed, because he wasn't.

Then he turned to Priska. "Thank you for your help."

She snorted. "Oh, I didn't do it to help you. I'm getting paid for it."

Sal hadn't expected anything else from her. They knew each other, had sometimes worked together, but at the root, they were rivals, and she'd never liked being bested by him. The fact that he couldn't use his powers right now was probably hilarious from her point of view, and he wasn't going to stand around waiting for her to tease him some more.

He left the room, knowing that Cumar or Thailor would take care of paying Priska. He was already thinking about what they'd need to go to Hell.

Sal was pretty sure Jadon wouldn't have a problem with him dragging Cumar and Thailor along for the ride. He'd promised he'd do anything he could, and this was something he could do. He had other warriors who could protect the city while they were gone.

"So you're going to Hell," Harrison said.

Sal hadn't realized he'd followed him outside. "I am. We are, Cumar, Thailor, and I."

Harrison scowled. "But I'm not."

Sal frowned and faced him. "Why would you want to come with us?"

"To help you."

"I don't need you to take care of me." Even though that was what Harrison had been doing, and Sal loved it.

"I know you don't. I never said you did. You're an adult, and a powerful demon, even without your powers. You can take care of yourself. That doesn't mean you should, though. Everyone deserves to have someone care for them." His cheeks flushed. "You know what I mean."

Sal wasn't sure he did. "I'm grateful for what you did for me. I don't know what I would have done without you after Shaila locked away my powers yesterday. You made sure I didn't freak out too hard, and that I knew there was still hope. I'll always be grateful for that, and if I had my selfish way, I'd take you with me to Hell. But you're human, and humans can't survive there."

Everyone knew that. Humans weren't made to survive in Hell. The air there, the earth, the sand, *everything*, would kill a human in minutes. Sal was selfish, but not to the point that he'd risk Harrison's life so he wouldn't be alone.

"I know I couldn't survive. I still don't like the thought of you going on your own."

"I won't be on my own. Cumar and Thailor will make sure I'm okay, and like you said, I can hold my own even without my powers." Especially now that he'd stopped moping around and that he was ready to do just about anything to have Shaila unlock his powers.

Harrison nodded. It was obvious he wasn't happy about the situation, but there was nothing Sal could do. It was physically impossible for Harrison to go with him, and they'd both have to get used to that idea.

Thailor and Cumar walked out of the shop. They were already talking about what they'd need to pack to go to Hell, and Sal was eager to start.

"We need to go back to HQ and tell Jadon what happened," Thailor said.

Sal wanted to go to the closest portal and cross it, but Thailor was right. Jadon was helping him, so the least he could do was to do as Jadon asked and keep him up to date. Besides, he'd probably be able to give them whatever they needed for the trip. It had been a while since Sal had left Hell, and he'd never gone back. He doubted things had changed much, but they needed to be ready for whatever they were going to find once they crossed the portal, and just as important, for what would happen when they got to Shaila.

Sal didn't fool himself into thinking that she was going to unlock his powers just because he asked her to. He'd need to find a way to convince her—or to force her, no matter how much he hated that thought.

But whatever happened, he *was* getting his powers back. He wouldn't have it any other way.

CHAPTER NINE

"We need to go to Hell," Sal announced as he walked into Jadon's office.

Jadon was sitting behind his desk. He rubbed one of his horns and arched a brow. "Not even a hello, Sal?"

Sal snorted. He flopped into one of the chairs on the other side of Jadon's desk sideways, his legs dangling off one arm. "Hello, Jadon. We need to go to Hell."

"I'm going to guess you saw Priska and not that you're insulting me."

"I wouldn't have said *we* if I were insulting you."

"True. And I know. Thailor called me when you left Priska's store."

Harrison—who looked like someone had kicked his puppy—Thailor, and Cumar had followed Sal in the office. Harrison had sat next to him, but Thailor and Cumar were standing. They were tense, as tense as Sal felt. Going to Hell wasn't a walk in the park, and he'd never be going back if he had a choice.

But he didn't.

He was glad he wouldn't be going alone. He would have gone on his own if he hadn't had a choice, and he'd probably have been fine. Although, without his powers, it would have been harder. This was better, though. He'd be with two demons he trusted with his life, and that meant something. He'd made the trip to the human realm on his own, frightened and hyper-vigilant. He'd still be hyper-vigilant, but someone would have his back this time around.

"When do you want to leave?" Jadon asked.

"As soon as possible." If Sal had it his way, he'd go right now, but he wasn't so selfish as to not understand that Cumar and Thailor would want to spend some time with their loved ones. Hell was dangerous, and Sal would have prayed for them to all come back if he believed in any God. He wouldn't mind spending some time with Harrison himself, even though they were only friends. He'd miss Harrison if he never came back.

But he'd rather die than be stuck in Hell.

Jadon nodded. "You can, of course, use whatever you need from HQ. Thailor and Cumar have full access to our equipment, and they'll make sure you have everything you need."

"Thank you."

"Give us a few days to organize everything. I know you're eager to go, and if you think Shaila will move, you can go sooner."

Sal wanted to say yes, but he wasn't going to lie. "She's not going anywhere. She knows the village where we grew up is the last place where I'd look for her, or at least that's what she thinks. She won't move from there." Sal felt kind of sorry for her. He could remember all too well how horrible that place was, and he was pretty sure Shaila had never planned to go there again. She wouldn't have if she hadn't blocked Sal's powers. Sal was sure of that.

"Good. That will give Thailor and Cumar some time to organize things. You can stick around, of course, but I'd suggest you get some rest." Jadon looked at the planner he held open on his desk. "The day after tomorrow. Is that soon enough for you?"

It wasn't, but Sal nodded anyway. Jadon was right—a few days wasn't going to change anything. It would be a few more days with his powers blocked, a few more days in which he'd feel lost and empty, but he was the one who had to shoulder that, not Jadon, not Thailor and Cumar.

He forced himself to smile. "I guess that means Harrison is going to have to babysit me for a few more days."

"I don't mind, and I'm not babysitting you," Harrison snapped.

Sal winced—Harrison sounded harsh. He'd know Harrison wasn't happy about how the situation was evolving, but he wasn't sure how to deal with it. Nothing he could do would change the fact that Harrison was human and he couldn't go to Hell. He'd die if he tried—if he breathed the air there—and that wasn't something Sal even wanted to consider. The world would be a worse place than it already was without Harrison in it. Harrison was a bright light, a gentle soul that needed to be protected, and that was what Sal was going to do to the best of his capacity now that he didn't have his powers anymore.

Sal smiled at Harrison. "I know. But I can come back here if I'm too much of a bother. I'm sure you have better things to do now that Shaila isn't your problem anymore."

"She's going to be my problem until you get your powers back."

"But you can't do anything else. You found her, and she's back in Hell. You can't come with us. You should probably move on to the next job." Sal didn't understand why this was so important for Harrison. They were friends, or something close to friends, but he seemed to care too much. Or maybe it was just that Sal wasn't used to having friends anymore and he didn't know how friends treated each other.

Harrison's scowl deepened. "I know I can't go with you to Hell. You don't have to repeat it every chance you get."

"I'm sorry."

Jadon cleared his throat. "I think we're all tired and worried. This is one of the reasons we need a few days to relax and try to focus on other things, and of course, to pack.

Harrison, thank you for your help, and I'm sorry you can't be involved in the rest of this, but Sal is right. Hell wouldn't be good for you."

"I'd die as soon as I step out of the portal. I know," Harrison muttered.

"You would. Your help was welcome, though, and useful. I'll make sure Jordan knows that and that we'll be eager to work with you again if the need arises."

Harrison's nod was hard and quick. "Thank you." He got up and stretched, and Sal couldn't help it if his gaze went right to Harrison's ass. It was a fine ass. "You know how to reach me if you need me," Harrison added.

Sal looked away. He caught Cumar's gaze, who was also staring at Harrison's ass. Cumar grinned and winked.

Sal had to stop himself from laughing. This was one of the things he'd missed while living on his own at the lake. He loved his privacy and being able to walk around his house naked whenever he wanted to. He loved not having to answer to anyone. He loved being alone most of the time, but he did miss having friends, people with whom he could talk and laugh, and share inside jokes. He wasn't sure what would happen once he had his powers back—and he had to believe he would, one way or another—and he went back to the lake. He liked to believe Cumar, Thailor, and the others would keep in touch, but he had no way to be sure of that.

But that was something to think of later, wasn't it? Sal wasn't sure what he'd do if he couldn't find Shaila, or if she refused to unlock his powers. He didn't want to think about those possibilities, not yet, hopefully, not ever.

He still had hope, and until that hope was blown to smithereens, he was going to think that he would get his powers back and that everything would be all right.

"What about Yo'ash?" Cumar asked.

Sal blinked. "What about him?"

"Well, Harrison can't come with us, and I'm sure Thailor and I would be enough to ensure you're safe, but we don't know what we'll be walking on, and Yo'ash has experience. He worked as a bodyguard for my father before he left Hell."

"And he'd want to go back?" Jadon asked.

"He wouldn't be happy about it, but we all know you can't afford to send two teams off, so this could be a way around that."

"And you could fuck your boo while on the job," Thailor said in a grumble of voice.

"I wouldn't fuck him while on the job." Cumar sounded offended.

"Everyone knows you totally would."

"I'll call Yo'ash and check with him," Jadon said, interrupting the fight that was no doubt coming. Sal had been around Thailor and Cumar often enough to know they *liked* fighting and teasing each other.

Sal wanted as few people with them as possible, but if Jadon thought Yo'ash should go with them, then he'd agree. Hell, maybe Priska should come, too. They'd need someone who could do magic to make sure Shaila had gone home and that she wouldn't move, but Sal already had someone in mind, and he was *not* spending more time with Priska if he could avoid it.

CHAPTER TEN

Harrison needed to do something. He couldn't let Sal go on his own to Hell. And he knew Sal wouldn't be alone, since Thailor and Cumar were going with him, but Harrison didn't think it was enough.

They knew what they were doing. They were League warriors. They kicked demons' asses every night, and that was what they were going to do when they were in Hell, but who would take care of Sal? Who would make sure he ate and slept and did everything he needed to do to make it back alive and well?

Harrison was aware that wasn't his job, but he wanted it to be, and in a way, it *had* been while Sal had been staying with him. Sal was going to leave him behind, though, and Harrison didn't like that thought. He *hated* it.

What could he do about it, though? He couldn't follow Sal to Hell. He wouldn't survive. That was the only way he had to make sure Sal would be all right, but was there a chance he could go? He didn't know magic, and even if he did, he wasn't a demon, and he couldn't use it.

But he knew someone who did.

It was a crazy thought, and he knew Sal and everyone else would be pissed if they found out, but Harrison knew he wouldn't be able to rest until he was sure there was nothing he could do to help. He wasn't one to leave things halfway through, and that was what he'd be doing if he didn't help Sal to the end. Besides, the only reason he wasn't part of the group that would be going to Hell was that he couldn't physically survive there. If there was a way around that, then he'd go. He could defend himself against demons, although he wasn't looking forward to it.

He was aware of the fact that Hell was nothing like the human realm, as demons called it. Here, demons tended to stay out of the way of humans because things would end badly for them if they didn't. But in Hell, they probably wouldn't think twice about grabbing him and maybe eating him, or worse.

That didn't mean Harrison wasn't going to do everything he could to go, though.

He shuffled his feet. "I'm going to go."

Sal had been staring at Cumar, but Harrison's words got his attention. "You are?"

"Yes. I'm sure Jordan will be happy to hear that I'm done with this, and that he's already started piling up files for me to review and take care of. The sooner I start, the sooner I'll be done. I'll be home later, though."

"Harrison, it's the middle of the night."

"So? All of you are awake." And hopefully, Priska would be, too.

"But you're not a demon. You're not a warrior. You're human, and you have normal hours."

"I haven't been keeping them with you around." But Priska worked both with demons and humans, so hopefully, she'd still be awake, if not open. Harrison needed to go now, just in case. "It'll be fine. I'll go to the office, check my desk, and call Jordan. He's been keeping weird hours, too, what with Caelan working at the club. Just come home whenever you're ready. Maybe bring food?"

Sal blinked. "Food?"

"You know, from a restaurant. Or you can pick up a pizza. You know I'm not particular." And this sounded like they were living together long term, which wasn't something he wanted to think about.

Harrison rushed out of the office. He hoped Priska would be able to help him, but if she didn't, he was going to have to look for someone else. No one that had anything to do with the League would help, not for this, but they weren't the only demons in town. Harrison knew he'd be able to find some demon with fewer scruples that could help him.

Or at least he hoped so.

The store windows were dark when he got there, but he pounded on the door anyway. He didn't have Priska's number, or he'd have called her. As it was, he was going to have to knock until she opened. From the sign on the door, she'd only closed an hour earlier, so hopefully, she was still there in the store.

"What the fuck do you want?"

Harrison cocked his head at Priska. She was still wearing the clothes she'd had on earlier, but unlike the smile earlier, she looked pissed. He raised his hands in what he hoped was a soothing gesture. "I'm sorry. I just need to talk to you."

She crossed her arms over her chest and peered through the glass door. "What about?"

"Sal going to Hell, for one."

"You're not going to go away until I listen to you, are you?"

Harrison grinned. "Nope. I guess the sooner you let me in, the sooner I'll leave."

Priska sighed. "Fine. But you need to be quick." She unlocked the door and stepped to the side.

Harrison had no intention of staying longer than he needed to, so he went right to the point. "I want to go to Hell with Sal."

Priska stared at Harrison. "You're human."

"I'm aware of that, yes."

"You'd die as soon as you took that first step out of the portal."

"I know that, too. That's why I'm here. I need a way to survive in Hell. Anything. A spell, or a curse, I don't know, and I don't care."

She frowned. "He means that much to you?"

"I don't know what he means to me." That was the truth. "But I do know I can't let him go without me. He needs me." Whatever that meant.

"It's going to cost you."

That was what Harrison had been afraid of. "I don't have a lot of money. I was a cop before, and it's not like we earn millions. But I have some savings."

Priska raised a hand. "Not money. I want a favor."

"What kind of favor?"

"I need more jobs like the ones I do for Jadon. The League pays well, and I need that money."

"Okay. I'm not sure what I have to do with this."

"You know Jadon. You're familiar with him and the League. Can you talk to him?"

"I can try, but if you know him, you know that nothing I can say will convince him to do something he doesn't want to do. Besides, he'll probably be pissed when he finds out you're helping me with this."

"But it will show him the kind of work I can do. I'm tired of doing fake card reading and all that crap."

"I'll talk to him. I can promise you that. I *can't* promise you you'll get what you want, though."

"I can deal with that."

"All right. What did you have in mind? A spell?"

Priska tapped a fingertip on her chin. "I can't make you a demon and making you impervious to the air in Hell and everything else that would kill a human would be too difficult." Her eyes narrowed. "How close are you to Sal?"

"We're friends."

"This should work, then." She turned around and

disappeared into the room where she'd done the spell earlier.

Harrison stayed where he was, since she hadn't asked him to follow her. He could hear her move around, the sound of her footsteps. She lit a few candles from the look of it, then she chanted. Harrison didn't understand what she was saying, and he wasn't sure he wanted to know. He didn't like what he was doing, and he wouldn't be doing it if he had a choice.

But he didn't, not if he wanted to go with Sal and make sure he was okay.

Priska came back, pushing the bead curtain to the side. She was holding something, and she held it out to Harrison. He took it—that was why he was there after all—and looked at it. He hadn't expected *it* to be two bracelets.

They were simple silver circles. When he raised them, he saw that they opened by pushing one of the sides down and sliding the small linchpin there out of the hole where it fit in. Closing them would be as easy as opening them—and as fast. "What am I supposed to do with these?"

"You need to wear one and put the other one on Sal's wrist."

They didn't look like they could do anything. "What will happen then?"

"You need to be sure, because once they're on, only Sal will be able to unsnap them, and we both know he doesn't have magic right now."

That gave Harrison pause, but not very much. "What do they do once they're on?"

"They make you one. You'll belong to Sal, at least in the eyes of the demons you'll encounter. This is something some demons use when they want to keep a human pet. It allows them to share their physiology. You'll be able to breathe as easily as you do here. The only downside is that you'll belong to Sal."

"Will he be able to make me do things I don't want to do?"

"You'll still be you. But there's no going back, not unless he takes them off or one of you dies. That'll be okay if he manages to convince Shaila to unlock his powers, but if he doesn't . . ."

She didn't have to explain for Harrison to know what it meant.

CHAPTER ELEVEN

Harrison swallowed and stared at the guest room door. Sal was in there right now, packing the bag he'd take when he, Thailor, and Cumar went to Hell. He'd been flitting around the apartment since he'd woken up, while Harrison had been waiting and wondering when he was going to put the bracelet on him.

He didn't like feeling like he was betraying Sal, but he was. Sal was going to be angry when he realized what Harrison had done. Was Harrison ready to face that? To face Sal possibly not talking to him again? He could still decide that Harrison needed to stay home in the human realm, even with the bracelets. He'd probably take his off as soon as he managed to get his powers back, or unlocked, however that worked.

This was a stupid idea, but no one had ever said that Harrison was smart.

He raised his hand and knocked on the door. "Sal?"

The door swung open. Sal's hair was loose again, flying around his face as he moved. A strand of it had caught on one of his horns. He was wearing a black t-shirt, but it wasn't plain—a sign that Sal was feeling better. He was doing something, taking action, and he felt better for it.

That was how Harrison felt about the bracelets. He knew it was the wrong thing to do, but that wasn't going to stop him. He needed to go with Sal, whatever the reason he felt that way, and while he wasn't smart, he *was* stubborn.

"Yes?" Sal asked.

Harrison licked his lips. "You're packing?"

Sal smiled. "Yes. We're leaving tomorrow, as you know."

Harrison nodded and looked down. He did know. He couldn't stop thinking about it. "Everything is set, then?"

"Yes." To Harrison's surprise, Sal reached for him. He laid his hand on Harrison's arm and squeezed. "I'll be okay. I'm not going alone, even though Yo'ash said no. Thailor and Cumar will be there. You know that."

This was it. It was the perfect moment, with Sal's arm extended like it was. Harrison wouldn't get a second opportunity, not like this one.

He was holding the bracelet. He'd already put his on, so he only had to snap the other one on Sal's wrist.

His hand trembled when he reached for Sal's hand. Sal's eyes widened, but he didn't move, and Harrison couldn't think about why he didn't, what he thought Harrison was about to do.

Harrison grabbed Sal's hand with one hand, then snapped the bracelet on his wrist. It took Sal a moment to realize what was happening, and it was long enough for Harrison to close the bracelet and let go of him.

Sal raised his wrist. "What is this? What . . . what have you done, Harrison?"

Harrison swallowed. "I went to see Priska last night."

"And she gave you this?" Sal thrust his arm at Harrison. "Do you know what kind of spell she put on this?"

"She said it's used when demons want to take humans to Hell. It makes them one or something."

"It can't be broken, Harrison! The only ones who can do it are you and me, and you're human, while I don't have my powers anymore. This"—he almost hit Harrison in the face while waving his hand around—"this can't be broken. It means that you're mine."

"I know. Priska said you wouldn't be able to make me do things I don't want to do."

"Only because I'm not that kind of person. What were you thinking?"

Harrison caught Sal's wrist. He wasn't sure why he did it, but he pressed his lips against the back of Sal's hand and tried to make him understand *why*. "I can't let you go on your own."

Sal blew out his cheeks. "Why not? We're friends, but we haven't known each other long. You owe me nothing. If anything, *I* owe you. I don't want to see you hurt just because you're too stubborn not to see how dangerous this is."

Harrison twisted their hands until he could link his fingers with Sal's. He didn't want to think about why he was doing it. It didn't matter, not as long as he managed to convince Sal. "I'm coming with you. I can now, and I *can* keep you safe. And I know you'll have Thailor and Cumar with you, and yes, they're great warriors. But I *need* to do this."

"I don't understand why."

Harrison shook his head. "Neither do I." He suspected it was because he was more than crushing on Sal. He'd found Sal fascinating in the beginning, mostly because he was a demon, but he'd quickly seen beyond that. Sal wasn't just a demon, just like Harrison wasn't just a human. Sal was a good person. He was fascinating because of his personality, not because he had horns and wings.

"I could leave you here anyway."

"I know. But that wouldn't change the fact that we're stuck together until you get your powers back. I want to help, Sal. It's the reason I became a cop. I might not be one anymore, but that doesn't mean that instinct is gone, and it's stronger when it's friends I can help. You know what I'll do if I can't come? I'll hang around this apartment and pace until you come back. I won't stop worrying. I won't be *able* to stop worrying about you, if you're okay, what you're doing."

Sal sighed and squeezed Harrison's hand. "I'm still angry,

and I won't stop trying to convince you to stay here."

"I know."

Sal took his hand away, and while Harrison wanted to take it back, to make sure they were okay, he stayed right where he was. Pushing Sal, especially when Harrison himself still wasn't sure what the fuck was going on in his mind, wasn't going to help.

"This is dangerous. Do you know what demons do to the humans who manage to get in Hell and not die right away?"

"No." Although he had a pretty good idea. He might never have worked with demons, but that didn't mean Harrison hadn't seen the worst side of humanity. Some humans were worse than a lot of demons Harrison knew, even though they didn't look like it.

"Priska told you this means you belong to me. I won't use it against you. I won't force you into anything. I'll protect you to the best of my ability, but you have to understand that I'm not myself right now. I can't use my powers to cast spells. That doesn't mean I'm helpless, but you're going to be, once we're in Hell, whatever you think. You're a cop, but that doesn't mean anything in Hell, and you're going to learn that the hard way. There are consequences to every action we make, including this one. I hope you're ready for them."

Harrison wasn't sure he was, but he wasn't about to back down. He hadn't changed his mind. He'd done this to be by Sal's side, and he'd gotten that. *Nothing* was going to keep him back, not even not knowing why he was doing this or not knowing any specifics about the dangers he'd find there.

Sal needed to do something—anything—to get that bracelet off Harrison's wrist. He'd tried calling Priska, but she was conveniently—for her—out of town. Sal could go over to her shop, but he doubted he'd get different results. She'd known what she was doing when she'd agreed to do this for Harrison, and she'd known how angry Sal would be at her. She was probably going to stay out of town or in hiding wherever she was for a few more days, just enough time for Sal to leave for Hell.

He knew he was right to hate her.

She was playing with Harrison's life without remorse. She could have easily said no when he'd gone to her, yet there Sal was, linked to Harrison through a spell. It also looked like Priska had lied to Harrison about Sal not being able to force him to do anything he didn't want. That was kind of the point of the spell she used. It *was* used when a demon wanted to bring a human pet back to Hell with them, but that wasn't the only thing it did. Demons liked to toy with humans, to humiliate them. The spell allowed them to do that, and to hurt them, not physically, but mentally.

Fuck. Sal was in trouble. He'd never do anything like that to Harrison, but he didn't want to have that kind of power over anyone, least of all over someone he liked. Add to that the fact that without his power, he wouldn't be able to protect him as effectively as he could have if he had them. Of course, he wouldn't need to protect him if he still had his powers.

Sal clearly should have stayed home when Jadon had called him to ask for his help.

"I'm *fine*," Harrison repeated.

Sal ignored him and dragged him out of the elevator. He had to hold Harrison's hand to do that, and he tried to ignore how soothing and reassuring that was. "I know. It doesn't mean you'll stay fine, and I need to at least try to find a way to get the bracelets off."

"You're not going to be able to."

"I know," Sal muttered. Harrison had made sure of that, hadn't he?

"Then, why are we here?"

"Because Jadon, and most of all, Thailor and Cumar, need to know about this, don't they? Or do you think we should wait until tomorrow to dump this on them?"

"Okay, you might be right."

"Might be, huh?" Satan, Sal wanted to strangle Harrison, but at the same time, he wanted to kiss him for being so worried about him. When had something like this ever happened to him? When had anyone been so worried about him to do something this huge and stupid?

Sal pushed open the door of Jadon's office without knocking. He didn't even think about it until he was there, standing in the middle of the office, with Jadon peering at him from his side of the desk. "Sal? Has something happened?"

Sal let go of Harrison's hand and raked his fingers through his hair. "Yes, it has. This man is—is an *idiot*. The worst idiot I've ever met."

"I thought we'd already gone over this," Harrison said, sounding both annoyed and hurt.

Sal glared at him. "We have. That doesn't mean I'm not still angry at you, or that you're not an idiot."

Jadon cleared his throat. "Do you mind explaining what's going on?"

Sal stopped pacing. "This idiot went to see Priska instead of going home last night like he said he would. He asked her for a way to be able to go to Hell with me, and she gave him this." Sal thrust his arm toward Jadon.

Jadon cocked his head and gently took Sal's wrist with both his hands. He touched the bracelet, and Sal wanted to pull away as if Jadon shouldn't be touching it. It was stupid, and he held himself still. "What is it?" Jadon asked.

"Priska put a spell on it. The one demons use to take their humans to Hell."

He didn't need to say anything else for Jadon to understand. His eyes widened, but that was the only indication he gave of his surprise. He dropped Sal's hand and looked at Harrison. "Do you know what this does?"

"I do," Harrison said. "Priska told me."

"She also lied to his dumb ass," Sal intervened. "She told him I wouldn't be able to force him to do anything, and that's not true."

"And I don't care," Harrison interrupted. "Because I trust you, and I know you won't do anything to hurt me or whatever."

"Why don't the two of you sit down?" Jadon asked.

Sal flopped into the chair, winced, and wiggled until he found a position that didn't hurt his wings. "He's an idiot."

"You've already said that." Jadon sounded perfectly calm, and Sal wasn't sure how that was possible.

He leaned the back of his head against the chair. "What do we do now? Because Harrison is convinced he's coming with us." And while Sal wanted that, he wanted Harrison to be safe more than he needed him as a security blanket.

"Maybe it's not a bad idea."

Sal jerked up. "Not a bad idea? He's human! He's going to get his sorry ass hurt."

"Maybe, or maybe not. He'll be two more hands to keep you safe, though."

"Against demons?"

Jadon linked his fingers together. "What's going to happen if he stays here? And be honest, Sal."

Sal huffed. "Nothing. He'll be safe."

"But that spell Priska cast feeds on your magic, even though you can't use your powers."

Why was Jadon still talking? "Yes. That's how it works."

Jadon arched a brow. "I know. Harrison doesn't, though."

Of course, that got Harrison's attention. "What's he talking about, Sal?"

Now that he knew, Harrison wasn't going to let this go, so

Sal continued. "It means that the further apart we are, and crossing a portal to Hell means we'll be very much the fuck apart, the stronger the toll this spell takes on me will be. It's fueled by my magic if you will."

"What will happen if it takes too much from you? Because that's what you're saying, right? That it takes energy, or magic, from you to work."

Sal sighed. "Yes, that's how it works. And I'll get weaker the more magic it takes to hold up our connection. The magic it takes when you're right next to me is so little that it doesn't make e difference. But with you here and me in Hell . . ."

"I'm coming with you. I'd already decided that, so it's not like this makes a difference."

"I should have known better than to think you were going to help," Sal grumbled, scowling at Jadon.

Jadon shrugged. "I just thought he needed to know. He was the one who put the two of you in this mess, after all. He needs to know what the consequences are, and I don't want you sacrificing yourself because he didn't think before he acted."

Harrison's expression twisted. "I'm sorry. I didn't know."

Sal sighed. "I am aware of that. You rushed into things because you thought it was the right thing to do. And maybe it was. I don't know. I just know that I don't want you to get hurt, and now that you're going to have to come with us, there's a high chance that's what will happen." And Sal couldn't do anything about that. "And if I never get my magic back . . ."

"Then we won't be able to take the bracelets off," Harrison finished for him.

"Exactly. That means that unless you want to one day kill me, you're going to have to stay with me, as close as possible. Are you ready to do that, Harrison? Are you ready to spend the rest of your life with me?" The question was moot, since they wouldn't have a choice, but Sal needed Harrison to understand what he'd done. He was trying to help, but the path to Hell was paved with good intentions and all that.

Harrison looked guilty, but he didn't hesitate. "I am."

Sal shook his head. "You don't know what you're talking about. There's a reason I live alone."

"But you've been staying with me, and we haven't had problems."

"It's only been a few days. You have plenty of time to change your mind."

"I won't."

Sal hoped Harrison was right, because if he wasn't, he had a big problem on his hands.

CHAPTER TWELVE

Sal was angry. Harrison had known he would be even before snapping the bracelet around his wrist, but he'd thought they'd gotten over it after they'd talked, and after the conversation with Jadon.

He'd been wrong.

Sal had been talking to him then, but he'd stopped when they'd stepped out of Jadon's office. Now he was pouting, or whatever it was he was doing, and Harrison didn't know how to fix things. He wasn't sure there was a way to do that, but he didn't regret what he'd done.

He was going to Hell with Sal and the others, and that was that.

He had things to do before they left, and he'd been more than a little relieved to leave Sal behind, even though it was to visit his family. Harrison loved them, but their family reunions over food had become tense since he'd left the force, and he wasn't looking forward to seeing his father. It had to be done, though, just in case something happened and he never came back.

He wasn't going to tell them where he was going or why. He'd mention he had a job and that they could contact Jordan if they needed anything, but that was all. Jordan wouldn't be able to call Harrison or to contact him in any way, but he could reassure them, even though he wouldn't know anything.

His parents' front door swung open before Harrison could knock. His sister grabbed the front of his t-shirt and pulled him inside. "Thank God you're here. Dad is already driving me crazy," she whispered.

Harrison groaned. That didn't bode well. "What is it this time?"

"He went back to his usual *women should stay at home and men should earn money*. Peter is pissed, but so far, he hasn't said anything."

"And you need me to run interference. You know I hate it when he starts in on me not being a cop anymore."

Helen grimaced. "Yeah, but he's been going on for the past hour. It's your turn now."

Helen was a hot-shot attorney, and she earned enough money that she and her husband, Peter, had decided Peter would be a stay-at-home dad. He did some work illustrating children's books when their kids were at school, but that wasn't enough for Harrison's father. He thought things should be the other way around, and he never missed a chance to let Helen and Peter know that. And when he couldn't grumble about their situation, he turned his attention to Harrison, who right now, was his greatest disappointment.

Just what Harrison needed right now.

There was no way out of it, though. He'd told his mom he'd have lunch with them, so everyone expected him, and Helen had him in her grasp. She pulled him toward the living room, where their father was sitting in his usual armchair, scowling at a glass of water in his hand. Harrison had no doubt his mom was forcing him to drink it. She'd been more careful with his health since he'd retired, and he wasn't happy about that.

"Look who's here, Dad," Helen said, sounding too chipper for the situation.

Their dad looked up. "Your mother said you were coming around, but I didn't expect you to do it."

"I always try to keep my promises."

"Unless you have to *work*." There was a lot of scorn in that last word, but then, there always was when he talked about Harrison's new job.

Harrison wasn't going to get angry. He couldn't afford it, not today of all days. He didn't want the last time—possibly—he'd been with his father to end up in a fight. Even though he was angry and he didn't understand Harrison's choice, his father loved him. He hadn't batted an eyelash when Harrison had come out to him.

He forced himself to smile. "Yeah, well, I don't have to work today, so here I am."

"I suppose we should feel lucky that those demons don't need you today."

Harrison took a deep breath. *Not going to snap.* "I also work with humans, you know. Jordan is the liaison between—"

"The fact that you work with humans doesn't mean anything, not when you *also* work with demons."

Helen hooked her arm around Harrison's. "Come on. I'm sure Mom will be happy to see you. Dad, keep an eye on Erica and Jeremy, will you?"

"They're not even here," their father grumbled. "Your husband took them outside to the garden."

"Good. Then you can rest for a bit before we eat." Helen pulled Harrison along before either he or his father could add anything. Harrison was glad for the reprieve, even though he knew he was going to have to face his dad again once they were at the table to eat.

"You have to ignore him," Helen said as soon as they were out of sight of their dad. Harrison could hear their mom singing in the kitchen as she cooked and the faint sound of the kids playing outside. He and Helene were alone in the hallway, and from the look in his sister's eyes, he knew he was about to be pestered with questions.

He raised a hand. "I know."

"But there's something going on, isn't there? I thought it was weird when Mom said you were coming. You hate spending time here."

"Only because of what he says. You heard him."

Helen snorted. She pushed a strand of hair behind her ear and pushed her glasses up. She wore contacts when she worked, but not when she was with her family. "He's like that with me, too. Why do you think Peter took the kids outside? He'd had enough of having to listen to Dad tell him he's a failure as a man because he's not the one supporting our family."

"He knows that's bullshit."

"Of course he does. That doesn't mean he likes hearing it." She leaned closer and peered at Harrison. "What's going on?"

"Nothing."

"Bullshit. Tell me before Mom realizes you're here and decides she needs you in the kitchen."

"I have to leave for a job tomorrow. I don't know when I'll be back, and I won't be reachable."

Helen frowned. "What if something happens?"

"You can call Jordan. He won't be able to reach me, though."

"Where are you going? Undercover?"

Harrison frowned. Which one would be worse, telling her he was going undercover, or telling her the truth — that he was going to spend some time in Hell with three demons, and that he'd bonded himself to one of them, possibly forever?

"Don't even think about lying," she said through gritted teeth.

Harrison sighed. Of course she'd realized he was going to lie. "One of my friends needs help. In Hell."

Helen blinked. "He lives there?"

"No. He lives here, but he needs to go back to the village where he grew up."

"You're human, Harrison. You can't survive in Hell. Unless the demons have been lying to us?"

"I wouldn't be able to normally, but I had a spell done, so I'll be able to breathe and everything. You don't have to worry about me."

"Not worry? Are you crazy? You're going to *Hell*. I have no way of knowing if you'll make it back, if something happens to you. How am I supposed not to worry?"

"I won't be alone. I'm going with two of the guys I sometimes work with, and with Sal. He's the one who has to go back to his village."

Helen cocked her head. "Sal? Isn't that the demon you were talking about last time? The one with the wings?"

Harrison wasn't going to blush. "Yeah. Like I said, he needs help."

"And the fact that you're going doesn't have anything to do with how pretty you think he is?"

Okay, Harrison was blushing. "No. He needs help."

Helen smiled. She was still worried—Harrison could see it in her eyes—but she knew she wasn't going to be able to make him change his mind. "And you're going to be his knight in shining armor. I'm not surprised."

"He's not a princess."

"Maybe not, but princes also have to be rescued sometimes."

"Sal would hate being called a prince."

"Then don't tell him I did. I'm worried, but I understand why you have to do this. Just, let me know when you're back, okay?"

"I promise. And I promise I'll stay safe. I'm not going alone, and Thailor and Cumar know what they're doing. Hell, even Sal does. They don't need me."

"Why are you going there?"

"Because I can't stay back while they risk everything. I

wouldn't be able to forgive myself if something happened to any of them." But especially Sal. Somewhere along the line, Harrison had started to feel like Sal was his responsibility, his to protect, and Harrison wasn't going to balk at that.

CHAPTER THIRTEEN

"You're still angry?" Thailor asked. He didn't look up from his sword, stroking the edge of it with a rag.

Sal was sitting cross-legged on the table with his wings hanging off behind him. "Of course I am. He's going to get himself killed."

"You'll be free of him, then. Isn't that what you want?"

Sal huffed. "No. I don't want him to get hurt." Somewhere along the line, Harrison had become important to him. He didn't know why or when, and he didn't care. He wasn't going to act on whatever it was anyway. But that didn't mean he didn't worry about Harrison and his safety. He didn't want anyone's death on his conscience, but especially not Harrison's.

Satan, the man was infuriating.

"Well, he's an adult. He knew what he was doing when he went to get that bracelet, and when he put it on your wrist."

"But he didn't. Priska lied to him."

"Only in part, and I doubt that knowing that you could make him do what you want would have even made him hesitate. He's stubborn, and he thinks he's doing the right thing."

"But he's not!" How could it be that Sal was the only one who saw that? "His curiosity and fascination with demons are going to cost him his life."

Thailor put his sword down. "I don't think he's fascinated with demons. He's curious about us, but his fascination is centered on one demon in particular."

And that wasn't something Sal would allow himself to

think about. "He barely knows me. Why would he want to come with me to Hell of all places? In the human realm, I might understand. But the stories humans tell each other about Hell are correct, and Harrison has to have heard them. He has to know he's going to get hurt."

"You'll make sure he's okay."

"I'll have other things to focus on." Like finding Shaila and getting his powers back.

"You can multitask, Sal. Stop freaking out."

Sal glared at Thailor. "You're too relaxed for what we're about to do."

Thailor leaned his hip against the table and crossed his arms over his chest. "I'm not relaxed, trust me. And I've been in Hell before, so I know what we're going to face. I'm not happy about having Harrison with us, but there's nothing we can do about that. The fact that he was a cop means he knows how to defend himself, although we can't know how useful that knowledge will be facing demons. But it's no use obsessing over it right now. It's not going to change anything. The only thing we can do is make sure we're as ready as we can be. That means explaining to him what we're going to find once in Hell and giving him weapons."

Sal pulled on a strand of his hair. "I wish he hadn't gone back to Priska. I'm going to kill her once I have my powers back."

"Are you also going to get rid of that?" Thailor asked. He gestured toward Sal's wrist, and Sal scowled at the bracelet around his arm.

It was pretty, a simple band of silver, but he didn't like what it represented. "Of course I will."

"Is it because you don't want to be bonded to Harrison, or because you think you two shouldn't be together?"

Sal cocked his head. "Why should we be together?"

"Because he's not following you to Hell because he likes

demons, Sal. Or not just generic demons anyway. He likes *you*."

"I don't know what you're talking about."

"Yeah, you do. Everyone knows he has a crush on you. It's as obvious as the nose in the middle of your face."

Sal couldn't say he hadn't thought about it. He barely knew Harrison, yet Harrison had offered him his guest room and had taken care of him when he'd been weak. He was *still* taking care of him. Harrison was powering through Sal's anger at him as if he didn't even notice it. He was still as happy as Sal had always known him, or at least, he'd been when he'd left the apartment while Sal was half-asleep in the guest room. He'd said goodbye as if they hadn't been fighting, which they weren't, not really.

Harrison was a walking contradiction, and Sal wasn't sure what to do with him, not beyond dragging him to Hell because they didn't have a choice.

"Why would he like me that way?" Sal asked out loud. He didn't expect an answer from Thailor, but he got one.

"Why not? You're a good guy. You're eccentric and fun when you're not moping around because of your powers or because Harrison went off on his own and messed things up for you."

"He didn't mess things up. He just made them more complicated."

Thailor smiled. "So you do care for him."

Sal wasn't sure how to answer that. "He's . . . nice."

"That's true. He's one of the few humans who don't act as if we're less than them."

"He doesn't. But he's not Chase, and I'm not you. We don't work that way together." Because once Sal got his powers back, he'd be immortal again. He'd have to watch Harrison age and die if he wanted to be with him, and he couldn't, not again. It was easier to go home and hide in his home.

"Maybe, maybe not. Trust me. I didn't think Chase and I could work together, either. He didn't like me in the beginning, and I thought he was annoying. All high and mighty because he thought I was a killer and nothing more than that. But we fell in love, and we make things work even though no one would have said it was possible. We're as different as they come, but it doesn't mean we're too different to be together."

"It's not that."

"No, it's that you've become used to being on your own. Right? I mean, you live all alone in that house on the lake. It's gorgeous, and I'd love to spend a week or two there, but it's not life. You isolate yourself, and now that you've been forced to reenter the world, you don't know what to do with everything—and with the people. Give Harrison a chance, maybe? He's a good guy, and you could do much worse."

Sal didn't need Thailor to tell him that. He already knew it.

It wouldn't make a difference, though. He'd decided years ago that he was done losing the people he loved, done suffering through that, done leaving pieces of himself behind.

CHAPTER FOURTEEN

Harrison made sure to stay away from Sal but close enough that he could intervene if he needed to. He could do without the glaring on Sal's part, but he'd decided that ignoring it was the best policy, and he'd continue to do that.

"Everyone ready?" Thailor asked.

Harrison looked at their little group. He'd be the one to stick out like a sore thumb between Cumar, Thailor, and Sal, even though he'd made sure to dress down from his usual dress shirt and pants. He'd picked jeans and a t-shirt, but while Sal was wearing the same, they couldn't have been more different. Sal's jeans were black, and they cupped his ass like a thing of beauty, while his t-shirt was orange with some kind of cartoon girls on it. Harrison's niece, Erica, could probably have told him what show they were from, but he had no idea.

But the thing that put Harrison apart the most was that he lacked any visible demon mark. He didn't have wings and horns like Sal, or a tail or claws or marks on his skin. Thailor was the one who looked the most like a human, but no one would have taken him for one, just like no one was going to take Harrison for a demon.

He might be a bit over his head.

Sal's glare got worse. "Yes, we're ready, or as ready as we'll ever be, considering everything and the bad decisions someone made."

"You're about to cross the line from passive-aggressive to plain aggressive," Cumar said. He seemed to think the situation was funny, and maybe it was. Maybe they'd be able to look back at it in the future and laugh about it.

Or maybe they'd all die in Hell.

Harrison cleared his throat. "I'm ready."

Thailor nodded. "Good. Let's go, then. Harrison, make sure to stick close to at least one of us." He cracked a smile. "I'd avoid Sal for a bit if I were you. He looks like he might try to kill you himself if you're not careful."

Harrison rolled his eyes. He was there to protect Sal, and that was what he was going to do. He was armed, although instead of a sword like Thailor had, he had his gun and enough ammunition to last him for a while. He hoped he wouldn't have to use his gun, but he was prepared to. He might be an idiot, but he didn't have a death wish, no matter what Sal seemed to think. That didn't mean he wasn't anxious about passing through the portal, though. He'd tried finding people online who'd done it, but their stories hadn't been nearly as okay as Harrison's was, and the only memories they had of their time in Hell—in the hands of whatever demon had taken them—were, quite literally, hell.

Harrison swallowed and looked at the portal. It looked like an empty doorway, except for the signs carved around it. It was down in the sewers so humans couldn't stumble on it by accident, so they'd already had to walk for a bit, and their journey was only starting.

Cumar and Sal stepped through and disappeared. Harrison tried to ignore the anxiousness that gave him and looked at Thailor. "I'm ready when you are."

Thailor sighed and shook his head. "I hope your crush on Sal isn't going to get you killed."

"It's not." Harrison didn't think telling Thailor he didn't have a crush on Sal would do him any good. He might as well admit it, at least to himself, and right now, to Thailor, too.

"Let's go, then."

Harrison followed Thailor through the portal. He wasn't sure what to expect, but it wasn't what he got. It was like stepping through a door, nothing more, nothing less. Heat slammed into him as soon as he was past the portal, and he started sweating.

He looked around. On this side, the portal was a stone archway that stood in the middle of nowhere. Harrison could see through it now, as if there was nothing there.

The sky was red, a rich blood red that made him shiver. He'd known it would be like this, utterly alien and strange to his human eyes, but it was still a shock. And the red sky and the heat weren't the only things he wasn't used to. All around them stood a forest of what looked like dead trees. They were black, as if they'd been burned down, their naked branches reaching for the sky like skeletal hands. The ground at their feet was just as black, and from what Harrison could see, there wasn't another living being around them.

He'd half expected demons to be crowding the place, but the vast emptiness of it made him just as nervous, maybe more so. He could try to defend himself against demons, while there was nothing he could do about this place and the way it made him feel.

"Goddammit. I hate this place," Thailor grumbled. He reached back and tied his hair away from his face and the back of his neck. Some strands were already curling around his ears and sticking to his forehead.

"Does the sky stay red during the night? Is there a night?" Harrison asked.

"It turns black in this area of Hell," Sal told him.

Harrison was mildly surprised that Sal was talking to him, but he wasn't going to look a horse's gift in the mouth.

Harrison kicked a pebble. The ground was black earth, and it was dotted with stones and rocks, some big enough to hide their four-man team if they needed to stay out of sight.

Harrison didn't like that, because it meant that other people — demons — could hide there as well.

Cumar and Thailor were as tense as Harrison. They had their weapons out, and they were looking around, their gaze moving over the panorama. "We shouldn't linger," Cumar said. "We don't know what else might come through the portal."

"We're not going to, but I'm waiting for—"

Harrison never found out what Sal was waiting for, because someone jumped out from behind the boulders he'd been eyeing. He acted on instinct, taking his gun out and moving his body until he was in front of Sal. He pointed his gun at the intruder. "One more step and you die," he snarled, his heart racing in his chest.

The demon laughed.

Lazarus was laughing in Harrison's face, and Sal didn't like it. He might be angry with Harrison, but that didn't mean he wanted Harrison to feel like he was in danger — or for him to shoot Laz, which was what would happen if Sal didn't step in.

"Stop laughing," he snapped at Lazarus.

Laz grinned at him around Harrison. "But it's funny. *He's* funny. He really thinks he can hurt me?"

"He can if he shoots you in the right place, and he will." That was one thing Sal was sure of. Harrison might not be equipped to deal with demons, but that didn't mean he was harmless to them.

Laz arched a brow. He didn't seem convinced, but he stepped back and raised his hands. Harrison wasn't the only threat to him, of course. He was lucky Thailor and Cumar hadn't skewered him with their swords.

Sal put a hand on Harrison's shoulder. "He's a friend,

Harrison. I promise."

Harrison lowered his gun, but he was still tense, enough that Sal knew he'd shoot Laz if he even hinted at hurting him. That made something inside his chest feel tight and warm, and he didn't want to give in to that feeling.

"Who is this?" Thailor asked.

Sal should probably have warned them that he'd contacted Laz. It had taken him a lot of effort, since Priska was gone and he didn't have his powers anymore, but there were ways. They needed Laz to find Shaila and to make sure she was where Sal thought she was—and that she stayed there. "This is Lazarus."

"Laz," Lazarus said.

"Laz. He's an old friend of mine."

"You grew up with him," Harrison said as he put his gun away.

Sal blinked. "How did you know?"

"You said you hadn't been here since you left when you were twenty-something."

"And you remember that?"

Harrison frowned. "Of course I do."

Sal was *not* going to kiss him or do anything that stupid. He couldn't afford it, especially not now. "You're right. Laz grew up in the same village as Shaila and I."

"And I'm not one bit surprised that the two of you tried to kill each other," Laz said.

Sal glared at him. "Now's not the right moment to talk about that. Have you found her?"

"She's at the village, just like you said." He stepped closer to Sal. "Can I hug you, then?"

Sal grinned. "Of course." They'd been childhood friends, growing in the same dust and pain, and while Sal had never managed to contact Shaila after he'd left, he *had* been able to talk to Laz. They'd stayed friends through the decades. Laz wasn't immortal like Sal, but Sal had made sure he could live as long as he did through spells and everything else he could think of. He hated all the ties he had to this place except for one — Laz. If he could have convinced Laz to come to the human realm with him, he would have. He hadn't managed yet, but he still had hope. And maybe having to be in Hell would make him see that things weren't as bad as he remembered them.

Fat chance of that.

"It was about time you came back," Laz murmured.

Sal patted his back. "I missed you too, asshole. And leave Harrison alone. He takes my protection very seriously."

"I noticed."

They separated, and Sal pushed back his hair. "Sorry I didn't tell you about this," he told Thailor. "I kind of forgot."

"You *kind of forgot?*" Thailor asked. "You know what? Never mind. He's going to help us get to Shaila?"

"He is. You heard him. She's in the village. He's going to make sure we can follow her if she leaves. He can use his powers, so he's going to be useful." Sal looked at their little group. "You know this is Laz. Laz, these are Thailor with the red hair, Cumar with the tail, and Harrison."

"The human," Laz said. "How did you—" His eyes widened, and he grabbed Sal's hand. "What did you do, Sal?"

"*I* didn't do anything." But Sal wiggled his wrist so Laz could see the bracelet. "*He* did. That's why he's here. We'll talk about it later," Sal murmured, looking at Harrison. He didn't look happy, but then, he hadn't looked happy ever since Sal had yelled at him about his stupid life choice.

"We will, Sal. I'm not letting this go." Laz pulled on his white hair. "Fuck. This is a mess."

"But there's no going back. I need to find Shaila."

Laz slapped Sal's back. "Let's go, then."

They took the lead, walking side by side along the panorama where Sal had grown up. Nothing had changed.

Nothing ever changed in Hell. Demons were born and died, they were tortured, and they tortured. Sal had never regretted leaving, and he still didn't. He'd never have come back if he'd had a choice, but Shaila had taken that choice away from him.

"What's going on?" Laz asked once they'd taken a good rhythm.

"I already told you. Shaila locked my powers, and I need her to unlock them."

"That's not what I was talking about. The human. Why did you bond yourself to him?"

"I didn't." Sal sighed. He didn't want Laz to think badly of Harrison, or worse, to realize how Sal felt about him. "He's been taking care of me."

"What does that have to do with the spell?"

"I'll explain, if you let me."

Laz raised his hands and waved at him. "Go ahead. I'll keep my mouth shut."

"Somehow, I doubt that. As I was saying, he took care of me after I'd done a spell. There was no one else, because they'd gone to the rescue of someone. But Harrison stuck around and made sure I was okay. He fed me. And he continued to take care of me after that. He offered me a room in his apartment when I complained that I didn't like sharing the building with the League warriors. And when Shaila locked my power, he ignored my bad mood and tried to find a way to solve it. He came with us to see the demon who found Shaila." Sal wrinkled his nose. "He also went back to her to get the spell on these bracelets. He wanted to come and continue protecting me, and he couldn't without that spell. The fact that she lied to him and made him think that nothing bad would come out of it isn't his fault, although I can't say he wouldn't have done this if he'd known everything. That's just the way he is. He wants to protect everyone, and for some reason, he fixated on me."

"For some reason? Come on, Sal. It's obvious he has some kind of feelings for you."

"They'll fade."

"Maybe, if you leave him behind. He looks like he's a stubborn one, though."

"He is." And that was a problem, wasn't it? Harrison wasn't going to let Sal push him away easily. Sal could try telling him he didn't want him in his life, but even if Harrison believed him, that didn't mean he'd leave. No, he'd want to make sure Sal was okay, that he ate and slept and whatnot. He'd do it in his quiet way, he'd try to stay away from Sal if that was Sal wanted, but he wouldn't just leave. That wasn't him.

But both Thailor and Laz had noticed that Harrison seemed, well, attracted to Sal. He had no doubt Cumar had, too. Maybe Thailor hadn't been wrong when he'd said that Harrison was there with them for more than his fascination for demons and his curiosity to see Hell and the demons who lived there.

Maybe he did have a crush on Sal, and Sal couldn't deny he felt something for him, too. He didn't want to, and he knew he'd have to leave Harrison behind when he went home—because he *was* going home. But maybe they could be closer in the meantime. Maybe that was something Sal could allow himself. He'd have to be careful not to develop feelings for Harrison, and he'd have to be clear that Harrison shouldn't, either, but Satan, Sal was tired of being alone. He'd been on his own for so long, and even though it was his own doing, it didn't make the loneliness easier to bear.

Harrison didn't like Laz. He might not know anything about the demon, and he didn't want to get to know him, but he didn't like him. He wasn't sure why, and he didn't care.

"You're jealous," Cumar said.

Harrison blinked. "I don't know what you're talking about."

"Of course you do." He tilted his chin toward Sal and Laz, who were walking ahead of them, their bodies close enough that their arms and wings brushed together as they walked. They were talking, but Harrison couldn't hear about what. They were keeping their voices low, probably on purpose, so he didn't hear them.

"They're friends," he said.

"They are. Do you think they were more than that? Before, I mean."

Harrison swallowed. "I don't know. But Sal was with Shaila when they were kids, so I don't think so." And Sal had said that he hadn't seen Laz in a while, so Harrison didn't think they'd ever been *that* close. Although, of course, he could be wrong. He didn't know Sal, not really. Maybe he and Laz had been together before he was with Shaila. It wasn't like Sal had told Harrison his life story, so it was a possibility. But even if they'd never been a couple, they cared for each other. They even looked alike.

They shared the same long, white hair and the claws, although Laz's eyes were dark, maybe black, while Sal's were blue. Harrison didn't think they shared the same ascendant, and not only because Laz's skin was a pale shade of blue. It was hard to say, though. Harrison didn't know a lot about the demons who lived in Hell, or even about the ones who lived in the human realm. He could recognize most of those, but he knew that while they stuck with each other in the human realm, in Hell they tended to roam and have mixed children. Sal had told him his mother was a mastema demon while his father was a thelnyss demon. Laz was no doubt mixed race, too.

"You love him, don't you?" Cumar suddenly asked.

Thailor slapped the back of his head before Harrison could answer. "That's none of your business, Cumar, and not exactly the kind of conversation we should have here."

Harrison cleared his throat. He didn't know how to answer that question, and he didn't want to try. "Do you know Laz?"

"About as well as you do," Thailor said, confirming what Harrison suspected.

"He didn't tell you about Laz, did he?"

"Nope. He didn't, so we were as surprised as you were."

"You could just tell him, you know," Cumar piped up.

Harrison sighed. He knew Cumar well enough to be aware of the fact that he wasn't going to let this go unless he had to. "What am I supposed to tell him?"

"That you're in love with him."

"I'm not." Maybe. Or maybe he was. Harrison honestly wasn't sure, and like Thailor had said, this wasn't the right place to do this. He needed time to think, and he wouldn't have that until they were back in the human realm, and maybe not even then. It all depended on what happened here, on whether or not Sal got his powers back.

Because if Sal did, he'd leave. He'd break the bond that kept them together and allowed Harrison to breathe and survive here, and he'd go home. And if Shaila *didn't* give him his powers back, well, Harrison didn't know what would happen. He and Sal would have to stay close, but that didn't mean much. Sal might continue to live in Harrison's bedroom and find himself a job and a boyfriend, or a girlfriend, and Harrison would have to watch.

Because he wouldn't kick Sal out. His guest room—his apartment—was Sal's for as long as he wanted it. Harrison would make sure he was okay, that he made it through if he never got his powers back, or if they had to search for Shaila again.

Harrison was only human. It would be enough if he fell in

love with another human, or with any other demon. Sal was so much, though. He was bigger than life, and he deserved bigger than life. He deserved more than what Harrison could give him, especially long term. Once he got his powers back, he'd be immortal again, while Harrison was just human. He'd get old, and he'd die, and he didn't want Sal to go through that.

Of course, that was only if Sal, by some miracle, felt the same way as Harrison did, and Harrison doubted that.

"You do have a chance with him, you know," Cumar said. His voice was gentler now, less provoking, as if he knew he'd touched a nerve. And maybe he did. He wasn't a bad guy. He was sweet, actually, and caring when it came to his friends. The fact that he hid that under a layer of goofiness and teasing didn't change it.

"You can't know that," Harrison said.

"Not for sure, but I've seen the way he looks at you. Maybe if you talked to him . . ."

"Leave him alone," Thailor said.

Harrison looked at Sal and Laz again. Sal looked like he belonged with Laz, or with another demon. He'd looked like he belonged with Shaila, too. Hell, Harrison wasn't even sure Sal was bisexual. He'd been in love with Shaila, and he hadn't mentioned anyone else that way. As far as Harrison knew, he only liked women and female demons.

He shook his head. "Let's focus on the mission."

The smile Cumar gave him was sad. "All right. But I'm here if you need to talk."

Harrison might have to take him up on that offer once they went home.

CHAPTER FIFTEEN

Harrison wasn't sure how long they'd been walking when Laz and Sal decided it was time to stop. Nothing around them had changed except for the portal they'd arrived from. It wasn't behind them anymore, but everything else looked the same — dead trees, a red sky, black earth, and no movement around them.

Harrison had expected Hell to be different. It was hot as, well, hell, and the panorama *was* like something he might have expected, but he'd thought there would be more demons around, more blood and fighting. Instead, there was nothing around, not even animals. Harrison wasn't even sure if there were animals in Hell. He was glad things weren't more like what he'd imagined, though. He'd been distracted since they'd arrived, and he had only himself to blame for that. He needed to get his head back in the game before something happened, and he needed to do it ASAP. He was there to protect Sal. That was the whole point of him coming here.

"Laz needs to cast the spell again, just to make sure we're still going in the right direction," Sal said. "Shaila doesn't know we're coming, but she has to know I'm after her. She'll be careful and ready to run at the slightest hint that something is wrong. We just want to be sure she's still where she's supposed to be."

Cumar dropped his backpack to the ground, raising a small cloud of black dust. "Great. We can drink some and rest. I don't know about you, but I'm not used to walking such distances anymore."

Harrison had never been. He went to the gym and ran as often as he could, but this was different. The heat felt like it sank into his pores and sapped his energy. It was a feeling he wished he could shake off, and he couldn't wait to go home and take a shower, or even better, a cold bath. He would have paid pretty much anything to do that right now, and they hadn't been there much more than a few hours.

Harrison looked around and found a rock he could sit on. He dropped his backpack and took his water out, keeping an eye on Laz, who was now sitting on the ground. Harrison had already seen Sal casting that kind of locating spell, so he knew what Laz was doing. He had a rudimentary map that looked handmade spread in front of him, and he was gathering herbs and spices into a bowl.

"How are you feeling?"

Harrison snapped his head up at the sound of Sal's voice. "I'm fine. You?"

Sal shrugged and sat on the boulder next to Harrison. There wasn't much space there, so they were flush against each other, closer than they'd ever been. Sal's body was warm and damp, and he smelled of sweat and herbs and *Sal*. Harrison leaned closer without realizing it, and when he did, he stayed where he was. If this was all he could get of Sal, then he'd take it.

"I've been better," Sal said.

"Bad memories?"

"Yes. There's a reason I left this place."

"Oh, you mean you didn't leave because of the terrible weather and the dirt?"

That got a smile out of Sal.

Harrison smiled back.

"I can't say I enjoy the heat. I'm much happier when I'm at the lake. I love watching the rain coming down, the sound of it and the smell."

"Doesn't look like there's a lot of rain here."

"There isn't, and when it does rain, it's not water, but acid that comes down."

Harrison grimaced. "I see. Let's hope it doesn't rain, then. I didn't pack an umbrella, and even if I had, I doubt it would be much use."

Sal bumped their shoulders together. "You're right, it wouldn't."

Harrison brought his attention back to Laz. He was done dumping stuff in his bowl and had lit a tiny candle. There was no breeze, so the flame didn't waver.

"He's using the same spices I used when I did it in the human realm," Sal said. "Salt, cayenne pepper, and garlic."

"How does it work?"

"It's hard to explain. The spices in themselves are just spices. We use them to focus our powers, our magic. Different spices focus the magic in different ways."

"What about the candles? Do their colors mean anything?"

"It depends on what was used to give them their color. Usually, some of the spices we need for the spells are used in the candle, so it's not the color but what's inside the wax. And again, that's just a way to make our job easier. Laz could cast this spell even without all of that, but it would take a lot more energy from him, and he can't afford that, not right now. Besides, why would he want to tire himself when there's a way for him not to?"

Harrison nodded. He was surprised that Sal was telling him all this. "Why are you explaining this to me?"

Sal shrugged. "Because I know you're curious about it. I noticed you always watch when magic is involved."

"You didn't have to explain, though."

"You're right. I didn't have to. I want to, though."

Harrison wasn't sure what to make of that. Did it mean Sal had forgiven him for the bracelets and the spell? Harrison had thought he had once already, but then Sal had started ignoring him, and he'd realized he'd been wrong. What was different now? Was it because they were in Hell and Sal had given up hope that Harrison would go with them? He had to have known that Harrison would as soon as he'd found out that not coming would weaken Sal—hell, as soon as he'd decided to visit Priska and ask for her help. "I didn't want you to do this alone," he began. He wanted Sal to understand why he'd done it, why he'd bonded them.

"I know. That doesn't change the fact that it was a stupid idea."

"I'm not going to deny that. I did the only thing I could do, though. I couldn't have stayed back while you were here looking for Shaila and going through God knows what."

Sal patted Harrison's knee. "You're too caring for your own good, Harrison. You're going to get yourself killed one day. You can't let that happen. You're too good for the world to be without you."

Harrison's chest felt like it was about to burst. He turned toward Sal and reached for his hand, but before he could say anything, Laz exclaimed, "I've got her."

Sal got up and strode toward him, each of his footsteps raising dust. Harrison sighed and watched him go.

That could have gone better. He wished it had, because he didn't like the thought of Sal being angry with him. It looked like things were improving, though. It gave him hope that they could fix things between them, whatever those things were. He needed Sal to trust him if he was going to protect him, and that was why he was there.

"Is she still in the village?" Sal asked as he crouched next to Laz.

Laz blinked. "Yes. She's still there, and she isn't cloaking herself."

"Why not?" Harrison asked. He'd wondered about that a

few times before, but he'd never asked.

Sal looked at him. "She probably doesn't expect me to be here. I'd say she *definitely* doesn't. She doesn't know I had Priska find her, and holding up cloaking spells can become taxing."

"Can't she tattoo it on her skin? You mentioned something about that."

Sal got up and, to Harrison's surprise, raised his t-shirt. He pointed at an intricate tattoo on his hip. "This is a cloaking spell. It's not working at its full potential right now because it feeds on my magic, on my powers. The same goes for Shaila. If she does have one and if she's planning to use it, she has to be careful not to overuse it. That would tire her too much, and being so tired that you don't react fast can be dangerous here."

"Does every tattoo on your skin work as a spell?" Harrison had seen Sal bare-chested a few times, so he knew he had more.

"Yes. Casting a spell makes the tattoos stronger, but they can work without it, too." He dropped his shirt. "We should go. We need to find a safe place to spend the night."

Harrison wanted to ask more questions, but he knew better. He'd gotten all Sal was going to give him already.

Sal could see Harrison had more questions. He always seemed to have more of them, about everything he could think of. He was especially interested in demons, and apparently, in their magic and in what Sal could do. Sal wished he could cast a hundred spells and explain all of them to him, but he couldn't do that until he got his powers back, and they *did* need to get off the road before it got dark. Hell was never a pleasant place, but it became especially bad at night, because that was when the worst demons came out. Things seemed tranquil right now, but it wouldn't last.

"Is that tavern still there?" he asked Laz as they got back on the road.

"It is. It's as bad as it probably was when you came around the first time."

"And only. I wasn't looking forward to spending another night there."

"I don't think anyone is. It's not a great place, but they have food, and we'll be safer than if we stay out here." He looked back. "Well, we will. I'm not sure about your man, though."

"He's not my man." The denial came out of Sal's lips before he could think about it.

Laz rolled his eyes. "Tell that to someone else. But okay. Let's pretend you're not already halfway in love with him. He's not going to be safe when we get to the tavern. You've been there. You know what kind of demons hang around there since you've spent a night there. He's going to be a target."

Sal held up his hand. "He's bonded to me, though. They're going to respect that."

"Maybe. Probably. *Hopefully.* But what if they don't? You can't use your powers."

"That doesn't mean I'm helpless." No demon was, and Sal had been in his fair share of trouble and fights. It hadn't happened in a while, but he made sure he was trained and that he could defend himself if he needed to. Most of the time, the people who hired him just wanted to heal from whatever they suffered from or find people or things. Sometimes, they were assholes who wanted to hurt people, and when Sal refused, they tried to hurt *him*. That never went well for them. Sal made sure of that.

"I know you're not, and your reputation has preceded you back. I don't think anyone is going to try anything with you, but you never know. Of course, the fact that you're traveling with two League warriors will also help. But there are always idiots who don't think before they act, and those who drink too much before they do. We have no way to know what's going to happen, and I suggest you stick close to Harrison, just in case. We all will, although I'm pretty sure he'd rather it be you."

Sal couldn't resist peeking back to check in on Harrison. He was walking and looking around as if he weren't already tired of seeing the same things all over the place. His eyes still had that excited glimmer, even though he was dead tired like all of them, and no doubt scared shitless. He didn't belong, yet he was there, for Sal. When had anyone done something like this for him?

Never. Sal didn't have to think about it to know it.

"I'll protect him." He'd do it even if it was the last thing he ever did. Harrison deserved no less.

And how could Sal continue to deny, at least to himself, that Harrison *was* important to him? How could he continue to deny he was halfway in love with the man when the proof of that was staring at him in the face, when his heart felt lighter and his life easier when Harrison smiled at him?

Sal was in trouble, in more ways than one.

Chapter Sixteen

When he saw the quirky building in the distance, Harrison was so happy he could have cried. His feet hurt, he felt dirty, and he needed more water than he'd packed. He'd tried to drink slowly, but it was too damn hot, and whatever he drank poured out of him minutes later in the form of sweat. Then the black dirt caked onto his skin, and now he probably looked like he'd rolled on the ground rather than walking.

"There it is," Laz said from in front of Harrison.

They'd been walking pretty much in the same formation as they'd started. It appeared that Sal and Laz had a lot of catching up to do, and they'd talked the entire time.

"Thank fuck," Cumar murmured. "It's about time."

"You knew what you were going to find when you agreed to come," Thailor pointed out. His ponytail was dripping, and like all of them, he looked like he could use a bath.

"I suppose we should be lucky there *is* a tavern. Remember when we had to get to my father's palace? That was a few days in the desert where I thought I'd die and become a mummy."

"If the demons hadn't eaten you first."

Harrison ignored the two. They'd been talking around him most of the day, and that was okay. Even though he'd become bored with the panorama, he didn't have much to add to the conversations. It was his first time in Hell, and he didn't know much about demons and whatever else they'd been talking about. Besides, he'd needed all his breath to continue walking. The air wasn't only hot as fuck—it was also dry, and so

112

much so that Harrison felt like his mouth would dry up if he opened it to talk. It had certainly felt that way the few times they'd stopped.

"Harrison?"

That was Sal. "Yes?" Harrison croaked.

Sal let Laz walk ahead and waited for Harrison, Thailor, and Cumar to get to him. Then he moved next to Harrison. "You'll need to be extremely careful once we're there. The demons are going to think, well, to be honest, that you're my slave, with all that implies. They're probably going to either ignore you or treat you like they do me because the bracelets mean we're one in their eyes, but I want you to be aware that some of them will see you as nothing more than a servant, or worse. One of the reasons demons like to toy with humans is that they like to humiliate them, and I don't have to tell you that one of the most humiliating things that can be done to someone is rape."

Harrison blinked. "They're going to think you keep me around for sex."

"Pretty much. Now, I hope you know I don't see you that way."

Harrison was *not* going to let the pain those words caused show on his face, because it was ridiculous. Sal wasn't saying he didn't see Harrison as a boyfriend, or whatever Harrison was hoping there could be between them. He was saying he didn't see him as a sex toy, and that was good. "I know."

"And I'll try to treat you with as much respect as you deserve, but I don't have my powers, so I won't be able to defend you to the best of my abilities if one of the demons decided he wants a piece of you. You *have* to stick to our room or with at least one of us. I wouldn't forgive myself if something happened to you tonight, or any of the other nights we'll spend in Hell."

"It would be my fault, though. I insisted on coming, and I

went to Priska."

"I'm not denying that, but it doesn't mean I want you to get hurt, especially when I know *exactly* what can be done to you."

"I promise I'll be careful. I might have wanted to come, but I don't have a death wish."

Sal nodded. "Good." He looked as gorgeous as he always did in Harrison's eyes, but Harrison couldn't deny he was as rough as the rest of them tonight. His white hair had become gray with dust, and there were patches of black dirt on his skin. His wings drooped a bit, enough to tell Harrison how tired he was.

They all needed a good night's sleep, food and water, and possibly, a shower.

They all became tenser the closer they got to the tavern. Now that Harrison could see it better—the sky was pitch black, but the tavern was well-illuminated, no doubt to attract clients—he realized it wasn't as much of a dump as he'd expected it to be. He knew some demons like to live in luxury, like Cumar's father, but he hadn't thought that would be the case here, in the middle of nowhere. The structure looked like several buildings of unrecognizable style had been stuck together, but it was clean, almost blinding white in the darkness, and it was well-kept.

Harrison stuck as close as possible to Sal as they walked to the front door and pushed it open. They filed in, and Harrison couldn't help but look around.

It was *nothing* like what he'd expected.

There was some black dust, but then, they were in the middle of a freaking desert of it. The tavern was clean, though, cleaner than some of the demons sitting at the tables drinking whatever it was they were drinking and yelling at each other.

They all stopped talking when they heard the door and

noticed Harrison's little group.

Harrison had always disliked being in the spotlight, but this was by far the worst. He didn't know what most of the demons watching him were, and he didn't want to find out. Some of them looked like the stuff nightmares were made off, like the one that seemed to only have a wide mouth as his face in the corner.

A warm hand on the small of his back startled him, but he didn't let it show, and he leaned closer to Sal. "Just walk," Sal murmured.

Harrison wasn't sure where to walk, so he followed Laz toward the counter. Behind it sat what Harrison thought was a female demon, although he wasn't a hundred percent sure. She did seem to have breasts under the tunic she was wearing, but she didn't have hair, and she wasn't particularly feminine. Harrison supposed he needed to ditch the preconceptions of what was feminine and masculine in Hell. Sal had longer hair than most of the demons in the room.

"What do you want?" the lady demon snapped. She was cleaning wooden mugs, and she set down the one in her hand so hard on the counter that Harrison wondered if that was why they didn't use glass.

"How many rooms do you have?" Laz asked.

She eyed them. "How many do you need?"

"Three, but we can do with two."

"I have three."

Laz nodded and took out a pouch from his shirt. "Half now, half tomorrow after we've had food."

"That's not how it works."

Laz leaned over the counter. "It is for me."

"You could always sleep outside."

"But then you wouldn't get paid."

She hesitated, her red eyes narrowing as she looked at their group again. "What about him?" she asked, tilting her chin toward Harrison.

Sal wrapped his arm around Harrison's neck. "He's with me. I need a room with a bath."

Harrison swallowed. He didn't know if Sal wanted the bath for his benefit, but it was a nice gesture anyway.

"They all have a bath. You think I want people as dirty as you hanging around here?" She turned around and grabbed three keys from their hooks. She dumped them onto the counter. "There." She pushed one of them toward Sal. "This one has the bigger bed."

Harrison didn't need to ask why she thought Sal wanted to know that. The thought made him queasy in more ways than one. He wanted to share a bed with Sal, and he wanted to have sex with him, but he disliked what everyone but the people they were traveling with thought would happen. Sal might look scary for most humans, but he was a gentle and eccentric soul. He wouldn't hurt Harrison even if it made his life easier. Harrison was sure of that.

"So we're sharing a room?" he asked in a whisper as Sal steered him toward the stairs on the right of the door they'd just walked in through.

"We are. You're mine, aren't you? Anything else would raise suspicion."

Of course *that* was why they'd be sharing. Had Harrison expected anything different?

Sal wasn't looking forward to going down to dinner, even though he was starving. He hadn't missed the way every single demon in the tavern had eyed Harrison when they'd walked in. There was no hiding the fact that Harrison was human and that he was utterly out of place in Hell and this tavern.

"Ready to go downstairs?" he asked.

He and Harrison were sharing a room. It made the most sense, but Sal couldn't help but wonder what it would mean for what was growing between them. Would one of them have the courage to take the last step that separated them, or would they have to go through an awkward night until they were ready to leave? Sal wasn't sure which one was the wiser — actually, that wasn't true. He *knew* which option was wiser , but it wasn't what he wanted.

"I'm not sure it's something to look forward to, but sure. Let's go downstairs," Harrison answered.

"You need to eat."

"I know that. Couldn't you bring me something when you come back?"

"I could, but I don't want to leave you alone." He wished he could, because Harrison looked so comfortable spread out on the bed. They'd washed up, and his skin was pink with the heat of the water. He appeared as tired as Sal felt, and while Sal wanted to let him rest, he didn't trust anyone in the building except for Laz, Thailor, and Cumar. He wouldn't be surprised if someone managed to sneak into the room to get to Harrison, and he wasn't going to allow that to happen. "I could stay with you," he suggested.

Harrison sighed and pushed himself up. "No. Let's go eat. Am I'm going to be able to eat the food here? I was wondering if it was the same food we have in the human realm."

"I don't know if it's going to be good, but you can eat it. Demons usually stick with meat, though, so you should get ready for that."

"That's fine. I like meat."

Sal didn't tell him he wouldn't find pork or chicken on the table. Harrison probably knew that.

They met the others in the hallway and headed down. Sal was tense, more than he would have been if Harrison hadn't been there. He needed a good night sleep, but he wasn't sure he'd be able to get it, not when he was worried about Harrison.

"I'll put a spell on your door when we come back upstairs," Laz said.

Sal blinked. "Did I say that out loud?"

"No, but I can tell you're worried, and while I know you're worried about Shaila and getting your powers back, Harrison's situation is more urgent. I'll put a spell on the door so you can be sure no one will try to get in. The spell on the bracelets should be enough to keep everyone away, but you never know."

Sal was grateful, and he hoped Laz knew it, because he couldn't say it, not when they were walking into the tavern's main room. There were even more demons there now, but the demon who'd given them the keys waved them toward a table in the back. It was big enough for the five of them, and Sal gently steered Harrison toward it. He was glad they'd be able to sit with their backs to the wall. Laz wouldn't mind not seeing the rest of the room, and while Cumar and Thailor wouldn't be happy about it, they could deal. The important part was that Harrison would be boxed in and kept safe.

They sat down, Harrison between Sal and Thailor facing the room. The demon at the counter came over to ask them if they wanted to eat—they didn't get a choice of *what* to eat, and Sal hoped that whatever ended up in front of them would be something Harrison could eat. Some of the meats that were served were poisonous to particular demons, and would be to a human, too.

The food was steaming when the demon dropped the plates onto the table. Harrison reached for it, but Sal grabbed his wrist, shaking his head, and turned to the demon. "What kind of meat is this?"

"Dagon."

Sal let go of Harrison's wrist. "Thank you." He turned to

Harrison. "You can eat."

Harrison was frowning, but he didn't ask questions. Instead, he reached for a bit of the meat and poked at it. Thailor was grimacing at his plate and doing pretty much the same thing. "I've seen one of those in action. I'm not sure I want to eat it. They're ugly."

"But tasty," Harrison said. His mouth was full, and he swallowed. "I wasn't sure what to expect, but it's good. What's a dagon demon?"

"Trust me. You don't want to know," Thailor said. He picked up a bit of meat and put it into his mouth. His frown smoothed out. "Okay, it's not bad. Better than I thought."

They all fell quiet after that, focused on their meal and on filling their stomachs. That was why Sal didn't notice the demon until he was right at their table, his gaze fixed on Harrison.

Harrison's back went ramrod straight, but he didn't even look up, focusing on eating instead and letting Sal deal with this. *Smart man.*

Sal looked up. "Yes?"

The demon—an alu that had to crouch to avoid hitting his head against the ceiling—rumbled. "How much for the night?"

"I'm sorry?"

"With your human. How much for the night?" He grinned, exposing his fangs. "I promise not to be too rough."

He wouldn't have to be to hurt Harrison, not with how big he was. Alu demons often reached ten feet, and while this one might not be that tall, he wasn't far from it, either. Sal didn't even want to think about what the alu would want to do in bed, especially not to a human—to Harrison. "He's not for sale," he snapped.

Laz, Thailor, and Cumar were still eating, but Sal could tell they were ready to act if anything happened. It would take all three of them to subdue the alu, while Sal would focus on keeping Harrison safe.

"I'll pay whatever you want." The alu licked his lips. "It's been a while since I've had a human. They're always so tight."

Harrison shuddered next to Sal, and his head snapped up. Sal grabbed his hand and squeezed it, silently telling him to be quiet. Harrison gritted his teeth, and Sal turned his attention to the alu. "I said, he's not on sale."

He'd hoped that would be enough, but it wasn't. The alu demon reached for Harrison and grabbed his wrist. Harrison pulled back while Sal rose from his seat and punched the alu right on his little bat face.

The alu jerked back and let go of Harrison. He glared and reached again, but Cumar and Thailor rose from their seat and unsheathed their swords. Sal thought they were going to have to hack the alu to pieces, but the demon at the counter intervened before blood could be shed. "He said the human's not for sale, so sit your ass down back in your chair, unless you want me to kick you out of here," she snarled right in the alu's face.

The alu raised his hands, the flaps under his arms moving. "No need to kick me out." He had blood dripping from his nose, and Sal's hand hurt, but he stayed right where he was until the alu was back in his seat grumbling about uptight demons and their human whores.

Sal flopped back in his chair and checked his knuckles. Some had the skin broken, but there was barely any blood. He'd survive, and things could have been so much worse. If the alu had wanted to, he could have killed half the demons in the room and taken Harrison.

"Thank you," Sal told the demon — the owner, maybe?

She nodded. "Everyone needs to follow my rules in here. That includes you, so no trying to kill that asshole in his sleep."

Sal grinned. "I promise I won't."

"Stick with your human. I can't promise the alu won't try anything else."

"We will." There was no way Sal was letting Harrison out of his sight right now or for the rest of their stay in the tavern. He was too precious for Sal to risk losing him.

Harrison was jumpy, but then, who wouldn't be after what had happened at dinner? He could too easily imagine the kind of damage that huge demon could have done to him — and had probably done to the humans he'd hurt — and it made him want to throw up.

"You're okay," Sal murmured as he gently pushed him up the stairs.

"I know. Thank you."

"I didn't do much."

"You punched that demon in the face."

"It wouldn't have helped much if the owner hadn't intervened. She's the one who did all the work, really."

"I don't know. Thank you, though." Harrison cleared his throat. "I knew this place was going to be a mess, and that it was dangerous, but I didn't expect it to be so . . . much, I guess. I didn't think you'd have to go around punching demons to make sure I made it out in one piece." Harrison was an idiot. He'd been warned Hell wasn't a place for humans, but he'd ignored it. He hadn't realized that insisting to come along might put Sal in more danger than he would have been if he hadn't been there.

He should never have gone to Priska. He'd have gone crazy with worry waiting at home, but at least Sal would have been safe — or safer than he was right now anyway.

"I'm sorry," Harrison said as soon as they were in their bedroom. He could hear Laz softly chant something outside the door, and he knew they'd be safe for the night. "I shouldn't have come. I shouldn't have asked Priska for that spell. I was an idiot."

Sal leaned against the roughly made piece of furniture that might be a dresser. "You don't have—"

"I *have* to apologize. You warned me this was a mistake, and you were right. I wanted to protect you, but I'm pretty sure I put you even more at risk than you were before instead. I was stubborn and didn't stop to think that what I was doing might hurt you instead of keeping you safe, and that's not right. I wanted to protect you, but I also wanted to soothe myself. I'd have gone mad with worry if I'd stayed home, and it was selfish of me. I focused on my feelings instead of your safety. That wasn't right."

Harrison raked a hand through his damp hair—there was no air conditioning in the tavern, and the night was as hot as the day had been. His skin felt sticky with sweat already, even though he'd cleaned up before dinner.

He'd been an idiot, and he wasn't sure Sal would forgive him. He probably wouldn't if their roles were reversed.

"Are you done freaking out?" Sal asked.

Harrison stopped pacing and faced him. "I wasn't freaking out. I was trying to apologize."

"That sounded more like you were beating yourself up for something you can't change any more than an apology."

Harrison huffed. It *was* true that he was freaking out now that he'd finally realized what he'd done. "I'm sorry. I'm sorry I forced you into a bond we might not be able to break. I'm sorry I forced you to take me along on this trip. I'm sorry you have to protect me instead of focusing on finding Shaila and getting your powers back. I'm sorry I was a selfish asshole who didn't listen to you and decided I knew better than you what was happening and what we'd find here."

"Done now?" Sal asked.

Harrison nodded. He flopped onto the bed and breathed out. He was relieved he'd finally got all of that out, but it wasn't going to change their situation. They were still in Hell, and Harrison still had to be protected. He had his gun and his training, but that wasn't enough, not here, not when he had no idea how to deal with the demons of Hell.

Sal crouched in front of Harrison. "You're right, I don't need protection, not from you. You're like a child around here, vulnerable and weak, and I could have done without having to keep an eye on you. But that's not why I didn't want you to come. That's not why I tried to convince you to stay back even though being that far away from you would have hurt me."

Harrison blinked. "No? Well, if I hadn't put the bracelet on you to being with—"

"Then I could have come without you. You were wrong when you did that. There are no two ways about it. But I understand why you did it. I'm not angry, not anymore, not now that I know."

"Know what? I've always told you the truth and that I wanted to come to protect you."

"Why do you want to protect me, though? Why would it have been hard for you to stay home while I came here? To think about what was happening to me?"

Harrison couldn't answer that question. He shook his head, hoping Sal wasn't going to push.

Sal didn't. Instead, he said, "Hell is dangerous to everyone who spends any length of time there, but especially for demons. I hate knowing that you of all people are vulnerable, and I hate that I can't focus on your safety because I have to make sure I find Shaila and convince her to unlock my powers."

Harrison nodded. "I know. I can't apologize enough for all of that." He cleared his throat. "I should go to bed. We both should. We need to be rested for tomorrow."

He moved to stand, but Sal stayed right where he was and cupped a hand behind Harrison's neck. Harrison just had the time to open his mouth to ask what he was doing before Sal pressed their lips together. He didn't hesitate, didn't ask Harrison if he could kiss him. He just did, and Harrison melted into it.

It felt cheesy and like a romance novel line, but that was exactly what it felt like. Harrison's body relaxed, and he leaned toward Sal, his limbs feeling like all his strength had leaked out of him. Sal's body was warm and strong, solid, and Harrison knew he could hold him up.

It was weird to kiss Sal, though. Incredibly good, but weird. He had fangs he used to nip at Harrison's lips, and there was no ignoring his horns, because they were right *there.*

Harrison raised a hesitant hand and skimmed his fingers along one of them. Sal groaned, but he didn't move away, and Harrison couldn't tell if he'd felt that or if he just wanted Harrison to stop it and focus on their kiss.

"What are you doing?" Sal murmured.

Harrison snatched his hand away. "I'm sorry. I didn't know I wasn't supposed to touch them."

"You can if you want to, but they're not sensitive, not like my wings, for example."

Harrison grinned. "Does that mean you want me to touch your wings?"

"Well, if we're doing what I hope we're doing . . ."

Harrison wasn't used to dealing with wings and horns when it came to sex, and that made it hard for him to get Sal's t-shirt off him. He managed, though, with Sal's help, and he threw the t-shirt to the side. Things would be easier if he lay on his back with Sal over him, so after he got rid of his clothes — without looking at Sal because he needed to focus and not be enthralled by Sal's body — he stretched out and watched.

Sal was gorgeous. Harrison had known that since the first time he'd seen him, but he hadn't fully realized until now. Now he had him naked in front of him, and God, he'd never seen anything as beautiful.

Sal was thin and bendy, and his black wings contrasted with his pale skin and the black tattoos he'd placed on it. His white hair tumbled over his shoulders, and his entire body gleamed with sweat and a light that was uniquely his. He still looked otherworldly, and he was. But Harrison was being given a chance to touch him and to make him his, at least for one night, and he wasn't going to back down.

He couldn't have, even if he'd wanted to, and he didn't.

He opened his arms, and Sal crawled into them. He pressed their bodies together, sliding against him, their cocks brushing against each other. *That* was one thing Harrison knew how to deal with, and he had no trouble wrapping himself around Sal — being careful of his wings — and pushing their groins together, rubbing against Sal.

Sal whimpered and pushed even closer, or at least he tried to. Harrison didn't think it was possible, though. They were as close as two people could be, and damn, it felt good.

"Wanted to do this forever," Sal grunted as he moved.

"Why didn't you?"

"You're human. I'm not."

Harrison squeezed his eyes shut. "You don't like sex with humans?"

"I love sex with you. It's complicated."

Harrison hooked his hand behind Sal's head and pulled it down. "Then stop talking. We can do that later." Tomorrow, possibly, after having sex all night.

Harrison had no idea what was waiting for them tomorrow, or the day after that, how long it was going to take them to find Shaila and be able to go home, but right now, none of that mattered.

No, what mattered was how damp Sal's skin was, how choppy his movements were, how he sounded when he came against Harrison, how he held Harrison through his own orgasm, how he felt in Harrison's arms.

Everything else could — and would — wait.

CHAPTER SEVENTEEN

When Harrison woke up, he and Sal were still wrapped around each other. The light that came in through the window was red and dull, and he had no idea what time it was. He could probably find out, but he wanted to stay around Sal a bit longer.

What now? Harrison had no idea what last night had meant to Sal. They'd had sex—repeatedly, loudly, and enthusiastically—but it might have only been sex for Sal. It hadn't been for Harrison. He had feelings for Sal, feelings that went back to the first moments they'd spent together, but he had no idea what Sal thought or felt. He couldn't read him, even with his experience as a cop. Of course, there hadn't been much to read while they'd been having sex except pleasure.

Harrison rolled his head on the pillow and looked at Sal. He looked gentle when he slept, relaxed. He was on his stomach with his wings spread over himself and part of Harrison, and he had one arm swung over Harrison's stomach. The bracelet there glimmered under the light that came from outside, and its sight made Harrison wonder if it had anything to do with last night. They were bonded through the spell that was on the bracelets. Did that bond influence the way they thought? The way they felt?

Harrison really should have asked more questions before taking the bracelets from Priska.

He tried to breathe, but the thought of Sal having sex with him only because of the bond between them made him sick. He felt like he'd forced him to do it, and he didn't like that

127

idea. It made his skin crawl. It made him no better than some of the monsters he'd arrested.

He had to get out of there.

He wiggled his way to the edge of the mattress, freezing when Sal groaned. Harrison managed to push his pillow into Sal's arms, and Sal wrapped himself around it and smiled in his sleep. He looked happy, but Harrison had no way to know if it was because he was glad to be in bed with him or because he was dreaming.

Harrison rolled to the floor and took a breath. Sal was still asleep, and Harrison was still freaking out. This wasn't how he'd imagined this morning going, but he supposed it could have been worse. It might still be, once Sal woke up, and Harrison needed to get out of the bedroom. He wasn't sure he could face Sal if he woke up and realized that he hadn't wanted what they'd done.

Something banged against the door, startling Harrison—and waking Sal up. Sal jerked into a sitting position, using his wings to keep his balance.

"Guys? Are you awake in there?" Laz asked from the hallway.

Harrison groaned and closed his eyes. He was going to have to kill Laz before he went home, dammit.

"We're up!" Sal yelled. "I think. Harrison? What are you doing on the floor?"

"I fell," Harrison muttered.

Sal's head appeared above Harrison. "Are you all right?"

"Yes."

Sal smiled. He leaned closer and kissed Harrison. Harrison blinked, not sure what to do, but Sal disappeared before he could kiss him back.

"Good morning," Sal said.

"Good morning?"

Sal laughed. "That sounded like a question. I can see why,

I guess. We can't know if it's going to be a good morning or a good day. I hope so, though. If Shaila is still at the village, we'll see her this afternoon, and I can't wait to get my powers back." He sighed and kissed Harrison's forehead. "I feel weird without them, like I'm not myself."

What was Harrison supposed to say to that? What was he supposed to do? He'd expected Sal to wake up horrified at what had happened, yet he was behaving as if they'd been waking up in the same bed for years, as if they did this every day.

Sal got out of bed and stretched, exposing every inch of his body—the body Harrison had licked and touched last night. "I'm going to go wash up. The others will probably be already on their way downstairs." He turned to wink at Harrison. "But then, they probably had the time to rest last night, something we didn't do."

Harrison watched Sal stride toward the bathroom.

He was lost.

He and Sal probably needed to talk, but they weren't going to do it right now. They had to eat and leave the tavern if they wanted to make it to Sal's village as soon as possible. They could probably talk while walking, but Harrison doubted Sal would be in the mood for that.

It would have to wait, and while he was anxious to know what the fuck was going on, he didn't mind waiting.

Sal wasn't hopping as he walked downstairs, but it was a near thing. He couldn't help it—everything was still a mess, he didn't have his powers back, he was in a place he hated, but he'd had phenomenal sex last night, and it was impossible for him not to feel happy.

So he liked Harrison. He'd known that for a while, but he hadn't expected Harrison to like him back. He'd had a puppy-like excitement when it came to Sal and demons in general, but Sal hadn't been sure it would translate to what had happened last night.

It had.

"What happened to you?" Laz grumbled as Sal slid into the seat next to Harrison's. "This isn't a happy place. It's *Hell*. It's not as fun as you seem to think it is."

Sal grinned at him. "But it's going to be a good day. We're going to find Shaila, and I'm going to convince her to unlock my powers." He reached for the bread in the middle of the table and broke a piece off. He put the piece on the plate in front of Harrison, then grabbed the bowl containing the deimur eggs. He tried to dump a spoonful of them into Harrison's plate, but Harrison held a hand up.

"What's that?" he asked.

"Deimur eggs."

Harrison leaned closer and wrinkled his nose. "They're green. They can't be eggs."

"They're not chicken eggs. That doesn't mean they're not eggs, though. Deimur demons have eggs. That's how they reproduce."

Harrison looked a little green—just like the eggs. "I think I'll stick with the bread."

Sal shrugged and filled his plate with the eggs. He took another piece of bread and started eating, but he could feel Laz's gaze on him. He knew his friend had questions—he'd always been a gossip—but Sal didn't want to answer them, not right now. No, right now he wanted to eat, take care of Harrison, then leave the tavern and find Shaila.

Laz cleared his throat. "I cast the spell earlier before leaving my room. She's still at the village."

Sal grinned. "Great. She doesn't expect me to find her. She has to know I wouldn't come back for all the gold in the world."

"But you *did* come back," Harrison said. He was nibbling at the bread, and Sal looked around for more food Harrison could stomach. He wouldn't get anywhere with only a few bites of bread in his stomach. He needed his strength for the day's events.

Sal waved. "Because it's the only way I can get my powers back. She doesn't know I know she's here, though, and she no doubt thinks it's the last place I'd look."

"But she has to imagine you're going to try to find her, even without your powers. You're not the only demon who can cast a locating spell."

"No, but Priska is her friend, or she was, anyway."

"Why did she agree to help you, then?"

"Because she lives in the human realm, and even though we're rivals when it comes to business, I've sent a fair share of clients her way. I can't always handle the amount of work I get requests for, so I give my clients other names and suggest they find another demon. She's on top of the list because she's good, and she can't lose that part of her business, not if she wants to keep her shop."

Sal waved at the tavern owner. She glared at him, but she trotted toward him. "Yes?"

"Is there some meat left from last night? My human doesn't like the deimur eggs, and he needs to keep his energy up."

She arched a brow. "I wonder why that is. I'll go get the meat. But you'll have to pay extra."

"That's fine."

Laz was looking at Sal with his head cocked as if he was trying to understand what had happened. Harrison, on the other hand, looked like he wanted to hide under the table. "Why did you do that?" he asked in a whisper, his gaze moving on the other three men at the table.

Cumar looked like he was still sleeping, while Thailor was wolfing down the eggs as if he wouldn't get to eat anything else today. And maybe he wouldn't. They had no way to know what they'd find when they got to the village, and with the way Sal had left, he doubted his mother would welcome him with open arms, since he'd basically disappeared during the night and had never contacted her again.

Sal leaned closer to Harrison and smiled at him. "Because you need food, especially after the night we've had."

Harrison's cheeks flushed, and he looked at the others again. Cumar was still seemingly sleeping while eating, but Thailor was looking at them now, his head cocked as he watched them. Laz had gone back to his breakfast, but there was a satisfied grin on his face, and when he noticed Sal looking at him, he winked.

"What happened last night, Harrison?" Laz asked, drawling his words.

"Nothing."

"Didn't sound like it, from what Sal said."

Sal kicked Laz under the table. "Leave him alone." He turned his attention back to Harrison. "You do need to eat, though. We have a tiring day waiting for us, and you're only human. You're not as sturdy as us." But he'd been sturdy enough in bed, that was for sure.

Harrison crossed his arms over his chest. "I might not be a demon, but I think I kept up well enough yesterday."

"You did." Sal patted his knee. "I'm just worried." He wouldn't force Harrison to do anything he didn't want, even though he had the power to, but they couldn't afford anyone to lag, so when the tavern owner came back with a plate of meat, Sal placed it in front of Harrison. "Eat."

Cumar blinked and reached for the meat, and Sal slapped his hand away. He wiggled his finger at him. "You can have what's left if there's anything once Harrison is done."

"If you two are done playing love birds," Laz said loudly, "I'd like to plan how the day is going to go."

Sal turned his attention to Laz, but he kept an eye on Harrison. "What is there to plan? You said Shaila is still at the village, so we're going to walk there, and I'll ask her to unlock my powers."

Laz leaned back. "And you think she's going to obey? Just like that?"

Sal knew it wasn't going to be that easy. If he'd had his powers, he could have tried casting a spell to make Shaila more compliant, but he *didn't* have them. He had no idea how he was going to convince her to do anything, let alone give him his powers back. She knew how important that was for him, which was no doubt why she'd locked them away. Getting them back wasn't going to be as easy as Sal was making it sound, and everyone around the table was aware of it.

He was relieved when no one brought that up, though. Being without his powers was frustrating enough. He couldn't rely on the spells he'd normally cast—compliance, location, even healing and taking the pain away from Harrison's feet after the walk they'd had yesterday. Sal had caught himself reaching for his ingredients more times than he was ready to admit, considering that even using them wasn't going to work. He wanted to be the one to find Shaila, but then, he wouldn't be here right now if he could do that, would he?

"Do you have a plan?" Laz asked.

Sal forced himself to smile. "Of course I do. Don't I always?" There was no way to force Shaila to unlock his powers except by threatening her, and Sal wasn't the best with weapons. He wasn't a violent man. He didn't *like* violence. But he had to get his powers back, one way or another, and he was ready to do just about anything to make sure that happened.

He wasn't himself without them. He wasn't complete, whole. He wouldn't be able to get back to work without them, but that wasn't the important part. No, the important part was that he'd had his powers all his life, and he didn't want to have to learn to live without them.

Harrison was confused. He always felt that way when he was with Sal, but even more so today.

He'd expected Sal to ignore him, or maybe to go back to the relationship they'd had until yesterday — if what they'd had could even be called that. They'd been somewhat friends, and Harrison had had a massive crush on Sal. He still did, but now, his feelings were all over the place because he'd had sex with *Sal*.

"Everyone ready?" Thailor asked.

They were standing in front of the counter after having handed out their keys to the owner, each of them holding their bags. They *were* ready to go, even though Harrison didn't want to leave the tavern. As horrible as the evening had been last night, with that demon trying to drag him off, the night itself had been magical. Harrison wasn't sure it would happen again, and while he knew that staying at the tavern wouldn't make it so, it kind of felt like it. There was no hanging back, though. Sal needed to get to his village, and he needed to get there fast.

"Let's go," Sal said. He walked out the door, and they all filed behind him.

Harrison hung back with Cumar and Thailor while Laz walked next to Sal the way he had yesterday. Harrison was relieved to have a little time away from Sal. He liked Sal, was falling in love with him, but he had no idea how to deal with him, especially not after last night.

"Okay, what happened?" Cumar asked as soon as they were on the road.

Harrison didn't look at him. "What happened when?" He knew what Cumar was asking, but he didn't know how to answer. He didn't owe anyone the truth, but it was going to be near impossible to hide that he and Sal had slept together when Sal was all touchy-feely. It was obvious something had changed between them, and Cumar probably suspected what that something was, even though he was giving Harrison the benefit of the doubt.

"It looks like Sal just realized he was in love with you."

Harrison stumbled. "He's not in love with me."

"Okay, not love, but definitely lust. You two had sex, didn't you?" Cumar wiggled his eyebrows. "So *that's* what the noise was last night. I thought we had demons on the other side and that they were making all that ruckus."

Harrison was never going to stop blushing. "Will you stop teasing if I admit to it?"

"You know me better than that. Of course I won't, and you don't have to admit anything, because we know."

"Was it just sex?" Thailor asked, his tone less excited and gentler than Cumar's. "Because the way he's behaving this morning . . ."

"I know what it looks like, but I have no idea what's going on. We didn't . . . talk."

Cumar barked out a laugh. "Of course they didn't. They were too busy."

Thailor slapped him on the back of the head. "Shut it. Can't you see how confused he is?"

Harrison was, and very much so. "Whatever conversation we need to have, it can wait until we're back in the human realm. Sal has other things to focus on right now."

"He does, you're right. That doesn't mean he can brush you off or play with your feelings."

"He hasn't brushed me off." It was the opposite, actually.

"All I'm saying is that you should talk to him. You're not wrong when you say it can wait, since hopefully, Sal will have his powers back by the end of the day, but whatever happens, don't let him push you away. Be honest about the way you feel . . . however that is. I don't know you that well, but what I do know is that you're kind and, well, that you care for people. It's obvious you care for Sal. Don't let him trample you just because of what he's going through."

"I won't." But Harrison wasn't sure that whatever he was feeling would be enough. He doubted it. Sal probably had hordes of humans and demons throwing themselves at his feet, or he could have them, anyway. The fact that he lived alone in his house on the lake was an indication that he enjoyed being alone, but that didn't mean he didn't get all the sex he needed, or that he wasn't affectionate with the people he took to his bed. Harrison had no doubt been convenient for him. He'd been right there in the same room—in the same bed—and Sal knew Harrison had a crush on him. He had to have realized it. Why else would Harrison have gone to the length he'd gone to come with him to Hell?

Besides, what could Harrison give Sal, even if Sal did like him the same way he liked Sal? Harrison was human. He only had a job because Jordan had given him one when he'd left the force. He could as easily have said no, and then Harrison would have had to choose between staying a cop even though he didn't share the values of most of the people he worked with, not when it came to demons, or quitting and finding something else.

There were too many obstacles between Harrison and Sal, not least the fact that Sal could have better. He was a powerful demon, even without the use of his powers. He was immortal. Harrison didn't want to think about the possibility of him never getting his powers back and growing old, even though it was there. It would give him too much hope that maybe, just maybe, there *could* be something between them, something that would make both of them happy. But if Sal didn't get his powers back, then it would be hard for him to accept that idea, and Harrison doubted he'd be able to do anything to help.

He would try, though. Even if nothing ever happened between them again, even if last night had been an exception, a lovely interlude, Harrison would be there for Sal. They were friends before they were anything else, and that meant something to Harrison. He valued his friends, and that included Sal.

He hoped Sal would give him a chance to be there for him — and that maybe they *could* be more than friends once all of this was over.

CHAPTER EIGHTEEN

It was too hot. Sal hated the heat. He hated sweating and the way the dust clung to his damp skin. He hated the feeling of being thirsty all the time. He hated the dirt and the red sky and everything else there was to Hell. He hated Shaila for forcing him to come back. He'd done so much never to have to, yet here he was, panting and sweating and swearing about everything.

"God, you've become bitchy and attached to your comforts," Laz teased.

"There's more than one reason I left this place. The weather, for one. It's awful."

"Never said it wasn't. But you were used to this once."

"Once. Not anymore. It's been too long since I was here, and I'm not happy to be back."

"I noticed. You've been whining since you crossed the portal. And what about that human?"

Sal bristled. "What about him?" There was only one human Laz could be talking about, and Sal didn't like it.

"Is this why you brought him along? Because you wanted to bed him?"

"No. What happened last night wasn't planned, and you know how he ended up here. I told you about it yesterday."

"You probably shouldn't let him distract you."

"I'm not."

"Are you sure?" Laz paused, seemingly to gather his thoughts. "Look, I want you to be happy. We grew up together, and that means something to me, even though I haven't seen you in decades. But you need to focus on Shaila right now if you want her to unlock your powers. You know she's not going to go down easy, or as easily as you seem to think she will."

Sal sighed. He wiped the sweat from his forehead, unsure how to answer that. "I know," he said, deciding to go with the truth. "She was always stubborn, and I know she's angry with me."

"She's right to be. You just disappeared one night, and no one ever saw you again."

"I tried to contact her, just like I did with you. She never answered any of my messages."

"Well, you and I were just friends. She loved you. Maybe she still does, as much as she hates you. She always felt strongly about everything, but especially about you. She locked your powers for a reason. She could have done several things to get away from you, but instead, she chose that. She *planned* it. Asking her to please unlock them isn't going to work. She could always hold a grudge, and I wouldn't be surprised if she held this one to the grave."

Laz had just said what Sal had feared all along. He'd tried not to think about it. He didn't *want* to think about it. Without the use of his powers, he couldn't take Shaila on, and he couldn't force her to unlock his powers. She could make it so that he was never able to use them again, that he'd grow old and die while she watched on.

He swallowed. "I'll find a way."

Laz stared. "I hope you do, Sal. But would it be so terrible not to get them back?"

Sal blinked. "What?"

"I'm not unhappy because I don't have powers."

"You never had them, though. You don't feel like you're hollow inside because you don't have them."

"You're right, I don't. I'll never know how that feels, and

I'm not going to pretend I understand what you're going through. But not having your powers isn't going to be the end of your life, and I do think you should at least think about what's going to happen if that's the outcome. But that's just me, and you've never listened to anyone's opinion if they were different from yours."

Laz hurried his steps, putting some distance between him and Sal. Sal watched him go. He knew he was uncompromising sometimes, and he supposed that living alone for so long hadn't helped with that. He never had to listen to what other people wanted or thought, and he never had to make concessions. Laz wasn't wrong, even though Sal didn't want to think about that right now. He didn't want to think about it until—if—he had to.

"What did you say to piss him off?" Cumar asked as he got closer to Sal.

"He just needs some quiet."

"From you?"

Sal scowled. "We're not used to spending time together anymore."

"And you're in a bad mood. I thought all the sex you had last night would keep you happy."

Sal flapped one of his wings in Cumar's face. Cumar yelped and jumped back, almost losing his balance. "Hey!"

"Don't mess with me. You'll regret it."

"Your friend is right. You *are* grumpy," Cumar muttered. He walked past Sal toward Laz and fell into step with him. That left Harrison and Thailor behind Sal, and Sal slowed down, allowing Harrison to catch up with him. Thailor just nodded at him when he noticed him looking. He didn't try to rush, meaning he was sticking to the back so he could protect them.

"How are you feeling?" Sal asked Harrison. Harrison's face was flushed, and he was sweating heavily. There were traces of white where he'd put on sunscreen, and he glared at Sal.

"How do you think I'm feeling? It's hot and dusty."

"As well as I feel, I see." Sal tried to make his voice light. He didn't want to push Harrison's mood even lower than it already was. "You're quiet. Is it because of the heat?" Harrison hadn't shut up one second yesterday. He'd had questions about everything they saw—the sky, the dust, the trees, the demons and why there didn't seem to be any around, Sal's village. Sal had been slightly annoyed, but he hadn't realized how soothing and distracting Harrison's constant talking was. It gave Sal something to focus on, something that wasn't Shaila and what she'd do.

"Well, it would be easier to talk if I didn't have to focus on breathing and walking. I don't think I've ever walked this much, not even when I was a street cop."

"I'm sorry."

Harrison shrugged. "Don't be. I put myself in this situation, as we agreed last night." His cheeks flushed. "You should probably go back to your friend. I'm sure you want to catch up with him."

"We've already caught up enough that he's bored with me. Didn't you see him running away?"

Harrison finally smiled.

Sal's heart felt lighter.

"You're right, I did. What did you say to make him run?"

"Nothing important. So, do you have more questions? You had enough of them yesterday, and I thought you'd want to know about last night since we haven't had the time to catch up on that yet."

"La-last night?"

"Yes, at dinner. Don't you want to know what kind of demons were there? Or maybe about the demon meat you ate? Or why that tavern was there, right in the middle of nowhere?" Sal wanted a bit of time to forget what would happen by the end of the day. Whatever way it went, it wasn't going to be good, not unless Shaila just gave up and unlocked his powers, and there was no chance that would happen.

"I thought I was bugging the bunch of you with how much I was talking."

"You're not."

"You want to answer my questions?"

Sal grinned and fluttered his wing close to Harrison. "Of course." It would be better than to think about Shaila, or the heat, or how much Sal hated Hell.

Harrison frowned. "What are you doing, Sal?"

"Talking to you."

"You know that's not what I meant. Yesterday, you were angry with me. You told me as much. Then you — you kissed me." Harrison's cheeks flushed even more, and this time, the heat had nothing to do with it. "And we had sex."

Sal knew he shouldn't tease, but he couldn't help it. "All night long."

"Yes. And today you're behaving as if we're, I don't know, boyfriends? Or maybe even just more than friends. Not that you were ignoring me before, but you're being affectionate, and I'm not sure what that means." He huffed. "I don't like not knowing things, Sal. I don't like having to guess why people do the things they do, especially when those people are important to me. So why did you do everything you did? Why are you being all nice and everything? Why are you behaving the way you are?"

Harrison could see he'd stunned Sal. That wasn't something that often happened, from what he knew, and he found it amusing. Not that he was going to tell Sal that. He wanted answers, but not to the questions Sal had thought he had. No, there were much more important things he wondered about.

Sal blinked. "I just want to spend time with you."

That didn't answer any of Harrison's questions. He knew he should wait until this was over — until Sal knew what was going to happen, but Sal was right there, looking for the world like he *wanted* to spend time talking with Harrison, and Harrison *needed* to know why. Not knowing was frustrating. He didn't know how to behave, if he should act as if last night hadn't happened or if he should follow Sal's lead and behave as if they were in love.

That was too close to the truth, or Harrison's truth anyway. He didn't want to act like a couple if they weren't one, or at the very least, he wanted to be aware of things so he wouldn't build things up in his head and delude himself that he meant more than he actually did to Sal.

Harrison had never been good at relationships, and with Sal, things were even harder, because Harrison had no idea how to deal with him. He wasn't human, and he was a walking contradiction. He'd never hinted at wanting anything more than friendship with Harrison, yet last night, he'd been the one who kissed Harrison. Harrison hadn't protested — why should he have — but it had left him wondering what was happening and what he should do.

"*Why* do you want to spend time with me?" Harrison asked. He wasn't sure he wanted to know the answer, but he supposed he was about to find out.

"Because I like you."

Harrison's breath stuttered, and he almost threw himself at Sal. Then he thought better of it. Sal had said he liked him, but that might not mean what Harrison had understood. There were plenty of people he liked, but that didn't mean he wanted to have sex with all of them, and he certainly didn't want a relationship with all of them, not the way he wanted one with Sal.

He cleared his throat. "You like me."

"I thought that was obvious. I don't usually have sex with people I don't like." Sal extended his wing. It brushed against Harrison's arm, and it was too easy for Harrison to remember what Sal had done with his wings last night.

He couldn't think about that, though. He couldn't make himself vulnerable, not yet, not when so much was at stake. "So you like me as a friend?"

Sal cocked his head. "Do you have sex with all your friends?"

"I . . . what? Of course not. I'm not—"

Sal laughed. "That's what I thought." He sobered, and his laughter turned into a small, too small, smile. "I know you don't give your heart easily, even though you're a loving man. I like you, Harrison, and I don't mean as a friend. But I can't make any kind of promises to you, not right now."

"What do you want, then?"

"For now? A repeat of last night would be nice."

Harrison couldn't help but smile at the humor in Sal's voice. "Only one?"

Sal's grin was roguish. "Well, *several* repeats of last night. One every night, possibly."

"And when we're back home?"

"Even then, at least until I go back to the lake house."

Of course. Harrison should have known. "And you're planning on going back soon after we're back in the human realm?"

"I honestly don't know. I wish I could say no, but I have no idea what's going to happen today with Shaila, and I don't want to lie or make plans I won't be able to keep. You deserve better." He sighed. "I want to believe that I'll be whole again once I talk to Shaila, but she's not an easy person to get along with, and I hurt her, more than she deserved. I protected myself and hurt her, and while I still don't think there was another way out of this, I do know I could have done things differently. I wish I had. I was young and stupid. I'm still stupid sometimes, as I'm sure you're aware of."

"You're a good man."

"I try, but I wasn't always one, and no matter how hard I try, I still make mistakes."

"Maybe, but what Shaila did to you wasn't right. She knows how important your powers are to you. She was trying to hurt you."

"And I was trying to arrest her, or at least, to find her so Cumar and Thailor could arrest her."

"You were, and once again, you were in the right. She was the one who hurt Esi and Ilyhas, even though she was hired to do it. She could have said no and walked away. You would have. She chose to stay and do it, and in my book, that makes her a bad person, especially coupled with what she did to you."

Sal frowned at Harrison. He stared until Harrison felt his cheeks heat even more than they already were. "What?" Harrison asked.

"You feel strongly about this."

"Of course I do. You didn't deserve what she did to you. It wasn't fair, no matter how much you hurt her."

"I don't think anyone's ever been so incensed about anything that happened to me. People usually say it's my fault. Laz certainly thinks so, after what I did to Shaila."

"Then he's not your friend." No matter how wrong Sal had been all those years ago, he wasn't this time. Harrison suspected that while Shaila had locked away his powers because it gave her a chance to escape, she'd chosen that particular way to get rid of Sal because she knew how hard it would be on him, how much it would hurt him.

She was a cruel bitch, and Harrison knew he'd have thought that even if he hadn't been halfway in love with Sal.

"I think you might be biased," Sal said.

"I don't think so."

"Of course not. *That's* why you're biased. Even though you were a police detective, you see the best in people. Or perhaps you only do it with me, but I doubt that. I'm thankful for your presence in my life, Harrison. Knowing you believe in me makes me believe in myself."

Harrison wasn't sure what to say to that—which seemed to be something that often happened around Sal. Harrison was left speechless, or rather, he was left feeling unstable, uneasy on his feet. He didn't know what to say, so he kept quiet.

He didn't have any more answers than he'd had before, not when it came to how Sal felt about him. Sal had admitted he saw him as more than a friend, but that didn't mean he wanted more than a friendship with benefits from him. Harrison wasn't sure what he was ready to give, and he needed time.

He didn't know if he'd have it. Sal was about to face his ex-girlfriend and try to get her to unlock his powers. Harrison didn't know Shaila, but from what he'd seen, she was stubborn, and she wouldn't just give in and do what Sal asked. No, they'd have a fight on their hands, and since Shaila was the only one who could unlock the spell she'd put on Sal, they needed her alive.

Harrison couldn't help but wonder if she was spiteful enough to kill herself or let herself be killed rather than give Sal what he wanted.

CHAPTER NINETEEN

Harrison peered at the city in front of him. Or at least, he thought it was a city. It looked a bit like the tavern, like several buildings had been smashed together without thinking about what it would look like. It was big, though, much bigger than he'd expected any settlement in Hell to be. He wasn't sure why he'd thought all he'd see here would be dust. The tavern had shown him otherwise, yet he hadn't been prepared for this.

He didn't know whether to call it a small city or a big village. There had to be thousands of demons who lived there.

And that freaked him out.

Harrison's encounters with demons had been okay, most of them even nice, up until last night with that alu demon. Now, he wasn't looking forward to spending more time in the company of demons he didn't know and who weren't his friends. "Is Shaila here?" he asked. "I thought you said you grew up in a village." Although since Sal hadn't been there for decades, maybe even hundreds of years — Harrison hadn't yet managed to convince him to tell him how old he was — things might have changed since then.

Sal pushed a damp strand of his hair away from his face and glared. "No. This isn't the village. It's the city closest to it. I'd hoped we could get to the village by the end of the day, but we were too slow."

Harrison knew it was mostly because of him. The other four in their group were sturdier, and even though they were hot and tired, they'd walked on like troopers. Harrison, on the other hand, had felt faint for the last few hours and he'd had to slow down. He would have told the others to go ahead, but he didn't want them to leave him behind, alone in a Hell desert, or rather, without them. Harrison hadn't yet seen signs of other demons in the desert, but he wouldn't have sworn there weren't any.

"Our village is in those mountains behind the city," Laz explained. "We lived in the caves there. We'll get there tomorrow, but it's dangerous to stay around at night."

Harrison nodded in thanks. He wasn't sure he liked Lazarus, even though the demon hadn't done anything to get Harrison to dislike him.

"I want a comfortable place," Sal muttered. "Laz, take us to the classiest one."

Laz blinked. "Classiest? Sal, you're in Hell. There's nothing classy around here."

Sal huffed. "The most expensive one, then. I have enough money to pay for it, and since we have to stop for the night, at least we can do it in luxury."

The tavern last night had been more luxurious than Harrison had expected anything to be, even though he knew Cumar had grown up in a palace. It had been rustic, but that didn't mean it hadn't had charm, and he'd slept well. Of course, that probably had more to do with the fact that he and Sal had tired themselves out and had slept wrapped around each other.

They started moving again, trudging toward the city. It blazed with light, reminding Harrison of the city he'd left behind in the human realm. He couldn't say he missed that already, but he did wish the temperature was more similar to the human realm. He felt like he'd gone through the wringer and back, and he couldn't wait to drink half his weight in water and spend a few hours in a bathtub.

He stumbled and scrambled to stay on his feet. A hand

wrapped around his arm and squeezed, holding him up until he regained his balance. He smiled at Sal, cautious and unsure. He could tell Sal was angry—they all could, it would be impossible to miss with the way he'd been grumbling and bitching—but he hoped it wasn't with him, even though he was the main reason they were slow.

"Okay?" Sal asked.

Harrison nodded. Sal took his hand away, and Harrison regretted the distance between them right away. "I'm sorry."

"What for?" Sal asked without looking at him.

"Slowing us down. You'd have been at the village already if I hadn't forced you to drag me along."

Sal sighed. "It's fine."

"It's not. You were hoping to get to the village today and get your powers back, and here we are."

"The fact that we have to stop isn't a bad thing, Harrison. I *am* impatient to get to the village, of course, but stopping makes more sense than hurrying on. I don't know what we'll find when we get there, but Shaila isn't going to roll over and do what I ask of her. I'm going to have a fight on my hands, so it's no doubt better that we have to stop. A few good meals and good night sleep will help immensely and give me a stronger fighting chance than I would have had if we'd gone straight to the village. I knew that all along, but I ignored it because of how much I want things to be over already."

Harrison hadn't asked Sal a lot of questions, not when it came to his power—or the lack thereof. Sal had been down right after it had happened—he'd barely left his room, had only eaten when Harrison had forced him to, and he'd dressed without joy. Things were better these days, now that Sal had an objective in mind, but Harrison still noticed things he didn't like. Sal was more subdued, quieter, and Harrison didn't like it. "How are you feeling?" he asked, hoping Sal wouldn't snap at him. He was genuinely worried, and he wasn't trying to remind Sal what he was missing.

Sal looked at Harrison. "You're worried."

"I am."

"No one has worried about me in decades."

"I don't know if that's true, even though it probably felt like that to you. But yeah, I'm worried about you."

Sal shrugged. "It's like a hole, you know? Or maybe you don't. I doubt you've ever lost something as important and as much a part of yourself as my powers are a part of me. I feel *lost.*"

"Like you lost an arm or a leg?"

"Possibly. It's inside, though. The pain and the emptiness."

Harrison smiled in what he hoped was a reassuring gesture. "We'll get your powers back. Having to stop for the night won't change that."

"I know."

"Laz can cast that spell again tonight to make sure Shaila hasn't moved, and maybe tomorrow morning. We'll all be rested and better equipped to face whatever is going to happen."

The city was bustling with noise and smells, most of them unknown to Harrison. He didn't know where to look, but he decided that down would be the best idea when his gaze crossed with a demon's and the demon licked his — hers, possibly — lips, leaving Harrison no doubt as to what it was imagining. He didn't know if this demon was as evil as the alu from last night, but he wasn't ready to find out.

To Harrison's surprise, Sal wrapped his arm around his shoulders and pulled him close. He glared around as if to tell the demons that Harrison was his, and Harrison relaxed. He should probably be offended by the fact that Sal didn't seem to think he could defend himself or stand his own against the demons, but Sal was right. Harrison was in way over his head, just like he'd been ever since he'd crossed the portal. He wasn't going to let his pride kill him.

"This okay with you?" Laz asked as they stopped in front of a building.

The tavern had been cozy and rustic. This was a different kind of place.

The walls were blindingly white, even though the place was only illuminated with torches and lanterns. The door and window frames were made of dark wood and decorated with intricate gold designs that left Harrison wondering how much they could be sold for. Probably enough to pay his rent for the entire year.

Sal grinned. "Perfect." He steered Harrison inside, keeping him close.

They got three rooms like they had the night before. Harrison couldn't stop looking around — there was a lot of white, wood, and even more gold, but it was classy looking rather than tasteless. Even the demons walking around were dressed better than Harrison had ever seen, with flowing tunics and light pants that wouldn't keep the heat close. The place even smelled good, like flowers and spices, and when Sal ushered Harrison into the room he'd chosen for them, Harrison's eyes bugged out at the sight of the bed. It was bigger than any bed he'd ever seen, and it was all too easy to imagine him and Sal rolling around on its white sheets.

"You can send your human down to the kitchens to pick up your meal," the demon who'd walked them to the room said. She was hovering outside the door.

Harrison opened his mouth, to say what, he wasn't sure, but Sal beat him to it. "He's not that kind of slave," he told the demon. Harrison was pretty sure he'd *winked*, but he was trying not to say anything stupid, so he didn't look up.

"I understand. I'll have someone bring it up, then."

"Thank you."

Harrison heard the door close. He took a deep breath and shrugged Sal's arm off his shoulders. "That's something I hope won't ever happen again," he grumbled.

Harrison was annoyed. That was obvious. Sal knew why, so he didn't turn the knife in the wound. Harrison knew he'd been wrong when he'd put the bracelet on both of them to follow Sal to Hell. He'd admitted as much last night.

"Come on. Strip," Sal told him.

Harrison blinked at him. "What?"

"I said, strip."

"I heard you the first time. I'm just not sure what you mean."

Sal pulled Harrison into his arms and smacked a kiss on his lips. "There's a reason I wanted to stay the night in this kind of place."

Harrison still looked confused. "And that reason is . . ."

Sal turned Harrison around and gently pushed him toward the bathroom. He'd never stayed in this building—he'd been in a rush when he'd left, and he wouldn't have had the money anyway—but the taverns in this part of Hell all shared one thing—bathtubs. The dirt and heat made it so that everyone wanted a bath once they arrived in a place where they could rest. Sal hoped that this tub would be bigger than the one in the tavern where they'd stayed last night because he couldn't wait to get Harrison in there with him.

They walked into the bathroom, and Sal grinned. The owner had had someone fill the tub already, and perfumed steam rose from the water. Although, calling it a tub was an understatement. It looked more like a small swimming pool.

The large bath was sunken in the floor, with steps that went down and a tiled bench that ran along its length. It was big enough for the five people in their group to bathe together, not only Sal and Harrison—not that Sal was going to ask anyone else to bathe with them.

He reached for the bottom of Harrison's t-shirt and pulled it up. The skin of Harrison's arms was streaked with dirt and damp, but his stomach and his back were pale and invited kisses.

So Sal kissed the back of Harrison's neck before pulling his t-shirt over it. Harrison batted Sal's hands away and turned to face him, holding his t-shirt to his chest. "What are you doing?"

"I thought it was obvious. I'm getting rid of your clothes. We can probably hand them over and have them clean before we leave tomorrow, now that I think about it."

Harrison glared. "*Why* are you stripping me? I can do that on my own."

"I'm aware of that. You did it last night." Sal only said that to see the blush on Harrison's cheeks, and he wasn't disappointed. Sal couldn't resist leaning forward and kissing the red flush. "We both need a bath. The water is warm. The tub is more than big enough for both of us."

"So you want to take a bath with me?"

Sal grinned. "That's *exactly* what I want, yes." He hoped Harrison would say yes. He needed him to. He might be trying to act as if he didn't have a care in the world, but they both knew that wasn't true.

Harrison licked his lips. "Shouldn't we focus on more important things? Like what you're going to do tomorrow?"

"But I don't *want* to focus on that right now. I've been thinking about nothing else since Shaila locked my powers, and we're so close to finding her and getting them back that I even dream of it. I want a few hours of peace." He put his hands onto Harrison's hips. "With you. You were good at distracting me last night."

Harrison looked away. "Fine. Let's get in the bath."

Something was wrong, but Sal couldn't tell what it was. Was Harrison annoyed because the demon who'd showed them the room had thought he was nothing more than a slave? Was he afraid that Sal would do something like that to keep up appearances? That's he'd send him down to the kitchens to fetch dinner? "You're not my slave," Sal told him.

Harrison frowned. "I know that."

"The people around here, the demons, they think you are because they can sense the spell on the bracelets. They think I forced you to wear it so I could keep you with me while I travel. That's why that demon asked if you were going to go get dinner. She thought you were my slave and that I was going to force you to do it, that I think you're nothing more than that, but it's not true. You're a good man. Someone I care about, and I don't look at you differently because you're human."

Harrison's shoulders slumped. "I know that, and I'm not angry with you. I guess it's just, well, offensive, even though I know why it's happening, and I know there's nothing you and I can do to change it. I'll be fine. Don't worry about me." He turned toward the pool. "I guess we should take advantage of this since the water is warm."

"That's what I was saying." Sal took off his t-shirt and dropped it to the floor. "Come on, before it gets cold."

"I doubt it's going to become cold anytime soon," Harrison murmured.

Sal had no problem being naked in front of Harrison, but he could tell Harrison was more hesitant. He hadn't been last night, but they'd been in the throes of passion, like Sal's favorite romance books called it, so he probably hadn't thought about it. He was thinking now, though, and doing his best not to be entirely naked in front of Sal.

Sal left him behind to make him comfortable and slid into the water, entirely submerging himself. The pool was big enough that he wouldn't hurt his wings, and there was a seat in the middle of it where he could settle, and where his wings would be free to move in the water.

He kept his eyes closed and followed Harrison's movements through the sounds he made. He smiled when he heard the splash of Harrison entering the water and opened his eyes to find Harrison sitting on the bench in front of him. He was still flushed, but it wasn't because of the embarrassment now. Water drops glittered on his skin, clinging to the hair on his chest, magnifying the freckles that dotted his shoulders and his pectoral muscles. He was beautiful, more so than Sal had ever found any other human.

Harrison cleared his throat and reached for the pile of washcloths waiting to be used. He grabbed one, then the soap next to it, and slathered the washcloth. "What are you going to do once we're back in the human realm?" he asked.

"I don't know. It depends on what happens tomorrow."

"If everything goes well?"

Sal relaxed. "I'll go home. I don't want to have anything to do with the League anymore, not after what happened. Give me nice, boring humans every day. They never want much more than locating their runaway spouse or to find out if they're being cheated on. Newsflash—they usually are."

"So you won't look back once you're ready to leave."

Harrison sounded sad. Sal wasn't sure why, and he wasn't sure what he could do to change it. "Why should I? I'm not a League warrior. I might be a powerful demon, but I've stayed out of the loop for too long, and I have no will to get back into it. I like my quiet life."

"I see."

Sal frowned. "What do you see? I don't understand what you're asking."

"Obviously." Harrison put down the soap and the washcloth. "What about me?"

"What about you?"

"You can't wait to go back home to your lake, yet you told me you wanted to continue being with me even when we got back to the human realm. Which one is true, then?"

"Both. We can have sex until I'm ready to leave."

Harrison crossed his arms over his chest. "So that's all I am to you? A convenient body? Or am I more? What am I to you, Sal? What do you want from me? Do you want more than sex, or is that all there is to me in your eyes?"

Sal wasn't sure how to answer that, but now that he knew what was on Harrison's mind, he understood where he'd gone wrong. He'd told Harrison he liked him as more than a friend, and he did. He'd told him he wanted them to have sex again, and he did.

But he hadn't thought about how Harrison might feel about that. Now that he did, he realized that Harrison wasn't the kind of man who wanted just sex. It had been evident since the beginning that he liked Sal, but Sal had never allowed himself to think of how *much* Harrison liked him, or the way he did.

"I like you," Sal finally said because he had to say something, and he didn't know what else.

"I know you do, and I like you too. Are we . . . exclusive, though? Or are we free to have sex with other people? Other demons?"

The thought of Harrison being fucked or fucking someone else made Sal want to hit something—preferably, the someone Harrison was fucking. "I'd be more comfortable if we were . . . exclusive." Sal didn't want to think about why that was.

Harrison slowly nodded. "I see. Does that mean we're together, then?"

"Together?" Sal knew very well what Harrison was asking. He didn't want to answer. He was afraid he'd lose everything if he did.

This wasn't how he'd wanted the evening to go, dammit.

"Like Thailor and Chase. Cumar and Yo'ash. You know what I'm talking about. Don't act as if you don't."

Sal sighed. "You're right, I do know."

"I take it the answer is no, then?"

He looked so hurt. He'd clasped his hands together under the water, and his shoulder drooped, his head hung. Sal hated that he was the one doing this, but he didn't know how to get out of it, how to make things better. He wasn't sure there was a way. "That's not what I said," he found himself saying without meaning to.

Harrison looked up. "What *are* you saying, then?"

Sal swallowed. "I've been in love a few times over the decades. There aren't many demons who are immortal."

"Yet Shaila and Laz are."

"Laz isn't, no. I work very hard to make sure he's going to live as long as I do, but it's not something I can do for humans. Only demons, and only if they have certain characteristics."

"Have you tried? With humans."

Sal nodded. "I have. You're not the first human I . . . liked, Harrison. I've lived most of my life in the human realm, and I've fallen in love with some of them. I've had to watch as they aged and died. It was either that or break up with them, and I loved them. I couldn't do that. But watching them die . . . you can't even imagine how hard it was, how much it hurt. And to have to go through that again and again, every time I fell in love? There is more than one reason why I moved to the lake house. There I can be alone, and I don't risk falling in love again."

"So you've closed yourself off because you don't want to be hurt."

"Exactly." Sal was relieved to hear that Harrison understood. He hadn't been sure he would. He was human, so he couldn't fully grasp what it meant.

"That's stupid."

Sal blinked. "I'm sorry?"

Harrison grabbed one of the towels at the edge of the pool and rose, hiding his body. "I said that it was stupid. How many years were you happy with those people? With the people you loved? From the sound of it, it was years, right? Decades?"

"Yes, but—"

"I understand how hard it was for you to lose them, but would you rather have never met them? Have never felt as happy as you were with them? Because that's what you're saying. You'd rather not be happy because you don't want to get hurt."

"You don't understand."

Harrison shook his head. He climbed the steps and wrapped the towel around his lower body, hiding from Sal's sight. "You're right. I don't. I've never lost anyone I loved, not to death. That doesn't mean I haven't been in love, though, and that I haven't lost the people I loved. They're not dead, but they're not in my life anymore. It hurt, but that doesn't mean I decided to retire in a house by the lake and live the rest of my life alone."

Sal watched Harrison leave. The water was cooling, but he didn't want to leave the bath yet. How had what he'd expected to be a nice, relaxing bath, with maybe some sexy time, turned into a fight over Sal's ability and willingness to fall in love?

Sal had no idea, and he didn't know where he and Harrison would go from there—if they could go anywhere at all.

Harrison was an idiot. He was aware of it, and he didn't like it. He hadn't been able to resist telling Sal exactly what he thought, though. How could he have? Sal was playing martyr, putting himself in the role of someone Harrison should feel sorry for. And he *did* feel sorry for Sal, but not for the reason Sal thought.

Harrison didn't like the thought of Sal isolating himself and living the rest of his life—his immortal life if he got his powers back—alone. That was a long time to be alone, and fear of losing someone would only push him for so long. When he realized he'd been wrong, he'd still be alone because all his friends and the people he could have loved would be long dead.

Loving someone and losing them hurt. Harrison knew that as well as anyone else. Sal had lost more people that Harrison had, but that didn't mean his emotions and feelings were more important or more right than Harrison's.

"Harrison."

Harrison swallowed at the sound of Sal's voice behind him. He'd hoped that Sal would stay in the bath long enough for him to dress and to eat the meal someone had placed on the table by the window. He didn't want to discuss this any longer than they'd already done. He didn't want to fight with Sal. He wanted to go to bed, do what they needed to do tomorrow, and go home where he could mope for a bit and get over Sal and his broken heart.

But Sal wasn't going to let him do that, was he?

"Harrison?" Sal said again.

Harrison sighed and turned around. "Couldn't you at least give me time to dress?"

Sal smiled sadly. "I enjoy looking at you half-naked."

"I'm sure you do."

"I just want you to understand, please. I can't lose someone else."

"But you'll lose me either way, won't you? You don't want to fall in love with me, or with anyone else. That means you're going to lose me when we go home. You'll go back to your lake, and I'll stay in the city."

"But it'll hurt less."

"Because you're not in love with me." Harrison *really* hadn't needed the confirmation of that.

"I could be, so easily. I can't allow that to happen, though."

"So you'd rather live the rest of your life alone, without love in your life."

"It's easier."

"And so much sadder. Never loving anyone, never letting anyone take care of you the way you deserve."

Sal shook his head. He'd wrapped a towel around his waist, but he was still wet. His hair hung over his shoulder, dripping on his skin, and his wings were heavy with water. The black tattoos he'd given himself stood there, a stark contrast with his skin, and he looked oddly vulnerable in a way Harrison had never seen on him. "You don't understand, Harrison. You can't. You're human."

"Well, you are too now, aren't you?" Harrison snapped. "You won't live longer than me or than any other human."

Harrison regretted the words as soon as they left him, but there was no taking them back. Besides, they were true right now. He could have said it differently, and they might be a moot point if Sal got his powers back, but still. Harrison hadn't lied. He hated the way he'd thrown the truth out there, but he hadn't lied.

He still expected Sal to be angry, though. He wouldn't have been surprised if Sal had stormed out.

He *was* stunned when instead of doing that, Sal sat onto one of the stools at the table and sighed heavily. "You're right. Right now, I have the same life span as you."

He sounded sad, and Harrison didn't like feeling like he was inferior just because he wouldn't live forever. He didn't *want* to live forever. He'd never want that. What purpose would life have if he knew it would be forever?

"But it won't be for long," Sal continued. "Tomorrow we'll find Shaila, and one way or another, I'll convince her to give me my powers back. And once I have them, I'll be immortal again, and I'll go home." He got up again and reached for Harrison, but Harrison stepped away. Sal stared at him. He didn't try to touch him again. "I'm sorry, Harrison. I never meant to hurt you. I should have known—"

"You couldn't have. *I* was a fool to think the sex meant more. I should have known better. But I do now, and I don't want to be bit of fun for you until you get your powers back and lock yourself up in your ivory tower again." Harrison was in pain, but he still had his dignity. This was the least he could do for himself. He needed to be strong. He needed to leave Sal behind because that was what Sal would do as soon as he could.

Harrison swallowed and tried to ignore the way his eyes burned. "I'll help you until we get back to the human realm, just like I said I would. I'll keep you safe." But he needed to close his heart off if he wanted to have any of it left by the time this was over.

Chapter Twenty

Harrison snuck out of the bedroom, leaving a sleeping Sal behind. He'd been warned not to walk around on his own at the tavern, but this place was different, and he hoped no one would try to drag him to a dark corner. With how annoyed and frustrated he felt, he'd probably kick that demon's ass anyway, but he'd rather not have Sal tell him *I told you so* again, especially not after last night.

Harrison sighed and rubbed his face. He and Sal had shared the bed because there was only one, and even though they'd started as far away from each other as possible, when Harrison had woken up this morning, he'd been half under Sal. He didn't know who had moved, and he didn't care. He just wanted to get as far away as possible before he had to face Sal.

He was going to have to, sooner rather than later. They needed to leave for Sal's village as soon as possible, and no one wanted to delay that. Harrison wanted nothing more than to go home so he could lick the wounds Sal had inflicted last night and hide for a bit with the excuse of needing rest.

Harrison walked into the room the demon at the entrance had told them hosted the dining room and stopped. All the demons already there, every single one of them, had looked up to look at him.

He swallowed and took another step forward. He was safe. He was bonded to Sal, so no one would do anything.

Right?

"What are you doing here?" a demon wearing what

Harrison thought was the tavern's uniform asked.

"I wanted to have breakfast."

"Not in this room, slave. You don't think we'll allow you to mingle with us, do you?" He — or she, Harrison was rarely sure — grimaced. "You need to leave."

"He's with me."

Harrison could have kissed Thailor, but he didn't think the demons around them would have been happy at the sight.

The demon turned to him. "I understand, but — "

"But nothing. He's bonded to Salazar, one of the strongest demons who've decided to live in the human realm. I'm sure you won't want to offend him."

The demon hesitated. "I know who Salazar is, of course."

"And this is his human. Do you want to tempt fate and see what happens?"

The demon's shoulders slumped. "No, of course not. Please, take a seat. Not too close to the other tables, possibly."

"That won't be a problem." Thailor wrapped a hand around Harrison and pulled him forward. "Come on."

Harrison kept his gaze down. He could feel the demons watching him, though, and he wondered if this was what the demons in the human realms felt like. He always tried to be nice to everyone, humans and demons alike, and he wasn't afraid of them like a lot of humans were, but he couldn't deny that their living conditions were awful. He wanted to change that, and he'd left his dream job because of the way he'd been forced to treat demons when he was there. He wanted to do more now, though. He'd been in their shoes, was being treated like they were, and it was horrifying.

"Why are you here on your own?" Thailor asked as he pushed Harrison into one of the seats against the wall.

The demon at the table closest to them snarled and got up. He rose from his chair and spat at the floor next to Harrison's table before leaving the room without finishing his food.

"That was . . ." Harrison started. He wasn't sure how to finish it, though. Offensive? Ridiculous? Both of them?

Thailor shrugged. "It is what it is. You'll survive."

"I know that. I just hate the fact that demons are treated this way back home."

Thailor smiled. "That's one of the reasons I like you. You're not like other humans."

"Neither is Chase."

Thailor's smile grew. "You're right. He's *definitely* not like other humans." He frowned. "But what were you doing down here on your own? You know you shouldn't walk around alone."

"I thought it would be safe since this place is nicer than the other one. And it's not like anything happened. They just stared, and one of the hotel's people told me to fuck off, but then you arrived."

Thailor peered at him. "Okay. *Why* are you here on your own, though? Sal should be with you."

"He was still sleeping."

"And you didn't wake him."

"I didn't want to talk to him." Not after last night. He wasn't sure where they were, but he suspected that the least they talked, the sooner he'd get over his stupid heartbreak.

"Why not? He wouldn't want you to walk around alone like this."

Harrison snorted. "Right. He can't wait to get rid of me. I guess if I was killed, he'd be sure to get that even if he doesn't get his powers back." Because if he didn't, he and Harrison would be stuck together forever, and Harrison wasn't sure how to deal with that. He supposed he could ignore that fact until he found out what was going to happen with Sal's powers, though.

Thailor leaned closer. "What are you talking about?"

Harrison sighed. He didn't want to tell everyone what had

happened last night, but Cumar and Thailor knew he and Sal had been something, whatever that was, and they were going to be surprised when they noticed Harrison wasn't talking to Cumar today. "We had a fight."

Thailor grimaced. "Want to talk about it?"

"Not really, but okay. He's going to go back home to the lake once he has his powers back. He doesn't want a relationship because he's immortal. He doesn't want to get hurt."

"I see. And you wanted one."

"Well, I thought that was the way things were going. I guess I was stupid not to realize that Sal and I didn't want the same thing. It's okay. I need a few days to get over it, but I'll be fine."

"But that's not going to be easy when you have to stick with him for the time being. He won't be able to release you from the bond for at least a few days, even if he does get his powers back. You'd die."

"I know. I'll deal with it."

Thailor nodded. "I expected something like this to happen."

Harrison frowned. "You did?"

"I've been through something like this with Chase. I'm not immortal, but it wasn't easy to get over our differences. And I can kind of see Sal's point. He's already been through this enough that he doesn't want to experience that heartache again."

"But that's not life. He can live for another two hundred years, or however old he is, and he's going to be alone all that time? How is that a life? Or at least, one worth living?"

Thailor cocked his head. "That's not your question to answer, is it? He knows what he's been through in the past and whether he can handle it again, not you. You're not the one who's had to watch your loved ones die of old age without being able to help them."

"That doesn't mean I never lost anyone."

"You're right, it doesn't. That also doesn't mean you know what it's like to watch the person you love die, though. You're not the one who's going to have to go through it in this case, either. It's easy to want to try when you'll be the one to die."

That hurt, and Harrison didn't want to think about it, because he suspected Thailor wasn't entirely wrong. He'd only thought about things from his point of view because he couldn't think about them from Sal's. Was the pain of losing someone really worth going through life without love, though?

"Harrison!"

Harrison jumped. Sal barreled toward the table, Cumar, and Laz on his heels.

"Why didn't you wake me?" Sal demanded.

"Why should I have?"

"Because you can't go around on your own here. You'll get hurt, or worse."

"He was with me," Thailor intervened.

Sal's shoulders slumped. "Still. Do you know how scared I was when I woke up and you weren't in the room?"

Harrison scowled. "I don't see why you should be scared since you don't care about me." That was petty and hurtful. It was Harrison lashing out because he was in pain. "Sorry," he muttered. He should probably stay away from Sal for the rest of the trip. He didn't want to hurt Sal, no matter how angry and disappointed he was, and that was going to happen if he was forced to talk to him.

They'd already talked, and Sal had been clear. He didn't want Harrison in his life. It would be best for everyone if Harrison took a step back and left it, then.

That hurt, but Sal understood. Harrison was lashing out

because *he* was hurt, and Sal wanted to tell him everything would be okay. He wanted to throw caution to the wind and try again, fall in love again.

But then he remembered the pain, and he knew he couldn't do it.

That didn't mean he wasn't going to do whatever he had to do to protect Harrison, though. Of course, that would be easier to do if Harrison stopped being an idiot and wandering around on his own. So when Harrison got up to go back to the room they'd shared to get his bag, Sal followed him. He stopped him outside the dining room and leaned close. "Harrison."

Harrison didn't look at him. "What?"

"We need to talk."

"I promise I won't go around on my own again. Nothing happened anyway."

"That's not what I meant."

"We have nothing else to talk about. We did all the talking we needed to do last night." He opened the door and snuck into the bedroom, and Sal couldn't do anything but watch him go.

He pressed his forehead against the cool wall. He wanted to sort things out with Harrison, but he knew he had more important things to focus on. They'd get to the village today, probably this morning, and he'd have to face Shaila. He wasn't looking forward to that.

He wanted his powers back. He wouldn't be whole without them. He didn't want to hurt Shaila to get them back, though. No matter what had happened between them, how long it had been since he'd last seen her, he still loved her. He wasn't in love with her anymore, but that didn't change the fact that he cared for her. He hated what she'd done, that she'd hurt people, and he did think she should pay for that. He wasn't going to drag her back to the human realm, though.

That wasn't his job. It was Thailor's and Cumar, and while Sal wasn't privy to what Jadon had ordered them to do, he hoped they wouldn't have to make the return trip with her. He might hate what she'd done, but he couldn't deny he still had a soft spot for her, and he doubted that would ever change.

They left the tavern, and Sal couldn't avoid thinking about where they were going anymore. He hadn't been at the village since he'd left when he was barely more than twenty, and he wasn't looking forward to being back.

The village wasn't a pleasant place to be born or to grow up in. Most of the demons there belonged to different species. They'd always been a rag-tag group, mostly of females who found themselves having to raise offspring they didn't want or hadn't planned. Not all demons were domestic. Only a few of them were. But most of them were violent and cruel, and they didn't hesitate to torture, rape, and threaten to get what they wanted. Sal was the fruit of one of those situations, and his mother had never missed a chance to let him know what she thought of that—and him. Sometimes, he wondered why she hadn't just abandoned him somewhere instead of raising him and making sure he made it to adulthood. Maybe she'd cared more than she'd ever shown or said, although Sal doubted it.

He supposed he might find out once he got to the village, though.

He couldn't find a reason for Shaila to want to go there. Her early life had been as bad as Sal's had, so it didn't make sense. He had no idea what had happened to her after he'd left, though, so maybe things had gone better than he expected. Maybe this *was* home for her, even though it wasn't for him, not anymore.

Harrison was walking ahead for once, and to Sal's surprise, he was with Laz. It was a relief to see he wasn't rushing on his own, especially since Sal suspected something had happened this morning. Harrison was too worried for it to be just that, even though they hadn't been okay when they'd gone to bed.

Sal wanted to make things right with Harrison. He wanted to put a smile back on Harrison's face. Maybe thinking about that rather than Shaila and what awaited at the village would help.

Sal moved forward to catch up to Harrison and Laz, but Thailor grabbed his arm and pulled him back. "Don't."

Sal frowned. "Don't what?"

"Leave Harrison alone, Sal. He doesn't need this. He's already in pain, and I know you want to fix things with him, but I don't think it's going to be possible."

"What?"

Thailor sighed. "Harrison told me what happened."

"What?" Sal sounded like a broken record.

"Last night. He wants a relationship with you, but you can't wait to go back to your lake house and be alone again. I'm not saying he's right in wanting to push you. I might not have been through what you have been through, but I understand, probably better than Harrison. That doesn't mean you can keep on doing whatever it is you were doing with him, though. He's hurt. That's not going to change, not unless you change your mind. If you only want to fuck, if you only want him because he's convenient, then stop. Let him go."

Sal wasn't going to punch Thailor, but he sure felt the need to do it. "I care for him. It's not just sex."

"I know that. It's pretty obvious. But you're not going to stick around once we get back. That's why you need to let him go. I don't know if he's in love with you or if he just has a crush or whatever, but it's obvious he cares, and if you're not going to love him back, you'll only hurt him by staying with him and wanting to continue what you're doing. The sooner you let him go, the better it will be for both of you, but especially for him."

Sal's first reaction was to tell Thailor to fuck off, but he forced himself to think about what he'd said. He knew he wasn't the most objective of men, especially when it came to matters of the heart.

And that was what was involved when it came to Harrison, wasn't it? No matter how hard Sal was trying to resist, as soon as he'd allowed himself to kiss Harrison, he'd started falling for him. The thought of not having him in his life made Sal want to cry, but what alternative did he have?

Sal turned his attention back to Harrison. He was talking with Laz, which was surprising, since Sal was pretty sure Harrison didn't like him. Apparently, though, that was better than talking with Sal, and now that he'd let himself think about what Thailor had said, Sal understood why.

He didn't like it. He *hated* it.

He wasn't sure what to do about it, though. He knew what he wanted, or at least he'd thought he did. But no, he found himself conflicted. He wanted Harrison in his life for as long as he could have him, but that might mean losing him to death, and he didn't know if he was strong enough to go through that again.

"So you grew up with Sal," Harrison said. He could have asked Laz as a question, but he already knew the answer.

"I did."

"The three of you grew up together."

"If you mean Shaila, yes, we did."

Harrison was mildly surprised Laz was talking to him and answering his questions. He knew he hadn't been welcoming when it came to Laz. He'd been tense and angry when he'd first arrived in Hell, and Laz's laughter at his attempt to protect Sal hadn't helped.

But they'd been walking together for several days, and

Harrison had observed Laz. He cared for Sal. There was no denying that. "Why are you still here?" he asked.

"Where else should I be?"

"Sal left for the human realm. So did Shaila. You stayed."

"You mean, I came back. Because I've been to your human realm, you know. I go there regularly when Sal needs to do some of his magic on me. He wants me to live as long as he does, and I can't say I mind. He's my best friend. My brother. I don't want to leave him alone. But I don't like your human realm."

"I can't say Hell is a nice place to live."

Laz chuckled. "You're right, it's not. Everyone tries to kill everyone. It's easy to die if you're not careful. It's too hot and dusty. But at least I know what the demons in front of me will do, what to expect of them. I don't trust anyone, and they don't expect me to. You humans, though, have become good at hiding your emotions, and you're as treacherous as demons are. You're better at hiding it, though."

He wasn't wrong. One of the reasons Harrison didn't have any people in his life was that he didn't trust easily. "You'd just have to be aware of the fact that you can't trust us."

"Maybe. But I've seen Sal trust several of your kind over the years. Sometimes it went well, and sometimes it didn't. There was no way to be sure, though. I'd rather know right from the start what I'm going against."

Harrison hesitated. He wanted to ask another question, but he didn't want to encroach into Sal's privacy, and he wasn't sure Laz would answer. He supposed he was going to find out. "You knew some of the people Sal loved?"

Laz looked at Harrison as if he were trying to read right through him. "He told you about them?"

"No. He just said that he'd loved people and that he'd had to watch them die of old age."

"He did. He loved them. He wasn't going to leave just

because they didn't look the way they had when he'd first met them. The last of their lives was when they needed him the most, and he was there for them." Laz eyed Harrison. "It's no wonder he doesn't want to go through that again."

Harrison swallowed. "He told you about that?"

"No. He hasn't told me much about you, not anything private. But I know him, even though I don't know you. I can see how much he cares for you." Harrison snorted, but that didn't stop Laz. "He does. That doesn't mean he's not wary of going through that pain again. You'd be, too, if you were in his place."

"I wouldn't want to live without ever loving anyone again, and that's what he's doing."

"Only because he doesn't want to be hurt when it ends."

"Isn't it worth it, though? The love he felt for so long, wasn't that worth it? The memories?"

"Would your memories with him be worth it? Because it looks to me that you're doing the thing you berate Sal for doing."

"I'm not!"

Laz arched a brow. "Are you sure? Sal doesn't want to fall in love and be with a human because it would hurt him too much when it ended, when that human, *you*, died of old age. You don't want to be with him because it would hurt too much when he finally went back home. It seems to me that you're both pulling back because you don't want to feel that pain, and I get it. I just think it's a bit hypocritical of you to be angry with Sal for something you're doing, too. You could be with him until you get back to the human realm and he leaves. You could be happy and make memories. Instead, you're pushing him away."

Laz shrugged and walked away, leaving Harrison behind. He wasn't worried about getting lost or attacked. Laz was in front of him, Thailor, Cumar, and Sal behind him. He'd be okay, at least physically.

He wasn't sure about the rest, though. Laz had forced him to think about the situation differently, and now he understood Sal better. If he wasn't ready to make that sacrifice, to take what he could have with Sal and live with the memories and the pain once it was over, why should Sal do it?

Sal flopped on the black dust, not caring that he was getting his favorite pair of pants dirty. He could see the village from where they'd stopped, hovering in the distance, so close that they'd be there in half an hour. That was why they'd stopped. They'd only been walking a couple of hours, but it would be better for all of them to rest before confronting Shaila.

"How are you feeling?"

Sal jerked at the sound of Harrison's voice so close to him. "What?"

Harrison smiled. It wasn't a happy smile, but it was a smile, and Sal wasn't sure what to make of it. "I asked you how you were feeling. I know how important this is to you."

"It is. I'm nervous, I suppose. Not looking forward to confronting Shaila." If anything because he still had no idea how he was going to convince her to unlock his powers. She could always hold a grudge, and this time wasn't going to be any different. Sal couldn't use his powers to force her to do anything.

He had no way to be sure she'd give him what he wanted. He *knew* she wasn't going to without a fight. Sal hated that he'd have to let Cumar and Thailor fight for him, but he didn't have a choice. He knew how to defend himself and how to kick ass, but he couldn't do it, not with Shaila, no matter what she'd done.

Sal should have thought about what he was going to do a lot sooner. He doubted he'd have found an alternative, though. There wasn't one.

"I wanted to apologize," Harrison said.

Sal frowned. "What for?" he was surprised Harrison was talking to him after last night, especially now that he understood what was happening better.

"For the way I behaved last night. For what I said."

"You mean for calling me a coward for not wanting to be hurt again? For protecting my heart?"

Harrison opened his mouth, then shut it again. "That's not exactly what I said, but yes. I understand better now. I can't blame you for not wanting to be hurt."

Sal smiled. "You're lying."

"What? I'm not."

It was fun to see Harrison sputter, but Sal didn't want to hurt him. "You're not. You still think I should give us a chance. And maybe you're right. Maybe I should. Being with you would be a dream. But I can't afford to think about that right now."

Harrison nodded. "That's okay. That's what I was trying to say. You don't have to think about it. I'm not going to continue pushing. We can stick to sex and go our own way once we get home. It's fine with me."

Sal narrowed his eyes. He knew Harrison was lying. Harrison wanted everything—sex, yes, but also love, someone to care for and who would care for him, someone to maybe have a family with, no matter if that family was made of children or a group of people to love. And he deserved all that. He deserved someone who would dedicate themselves to making Harrison happy, and Sal didn't think he was the right man for that.

Thailor was right. Sal couldn't continue to hurt Harrison the way he had. It would be selfish, and he'd already been selfish enough. It was time to stop. "I can't—"

"Ready to go?" Thailor asked.

Sal was so glad for the interruption that he could have kissed Thailor. He rose to his feet and brushed the dust off his ass, briefly wondering how many times he was going to have to wash his pants for them to be presentable again. "Ready."

Thailor didn't look convinced. "You sure? This isn't going to be easy."

"I know. Nothing ever is with Shaila. But it needs to be done." Sal wanted to go back home. He needed to. It was the only place where he felt like he could think, where he could make decisions.

Like the one about Harrison.

Once Sal had his powers back, he'd be immortal again. He'd never die, not unless someone killed him. Harrison was human, and his death was inevitable. Sal didn't think he could stand watching it happen, but could he stand knowing that Harrison was out there, living his life and being happy with another man? A man who wasn't Sal?

CHAPTER TWENTY-ONE

"She's still here, although I can't tell you where exactly," Laz said as he rose from the ground. He'd cast the spell again now that they were at the village entrance, and it seemed they hadn't walked all this way for nothing, although Harrison wasn't sure how he felt about that.

He wanted Sal to get his powers back, but he didn't deny that the thought didn't make him happy. Sal would go back home once he did, and everything would be over.

Sal watched the village. "I don't need you to be more specific. We both know where she is."

"You think she went home?"

"Where else?"

Harrison looked in the same direction. He wasn't sure what to think about this place. Sal had told him how unhappy he'd been there, but that didn't change the fact that this place was beautiful in a desolated kind of way. There wasn't much to the village, or not much that was visible anyway.

Everywhere Harrison looked, he saw the black dust of the ground and the red of the stone that rose on both his sides. A path snaked through between the two mountains, and holes had been cut into the stone. They looked deep, and from what Sal had said, that was where the people lived. It was probably cooler to live and sleep there than it would be outside, but not seeing any sign of life was strange, and it didn't help make Harrison feel like this wasn't a dead space.

They walked along the path. Sal seemed to know where he was going, and no one came out of the caves to stop them or talk to them. Sal stopped in front of a cave and faced it. Harrison moved to stand by his side, but Laz extended an arm to stop him and shook his head.

"He needs help," Harrison murmured.

"Not right now. He wants to try talking to her first."

"I know he does, but we're all aware that it's not going to work. He doesn't expect it to."

"That doesn't mean he's not going to try."

"Or that he's not going to get himself killed," Harrison muttered.

The heat felt even worse here, with the two walls of stone surrounding them, boxing them in and making it hard to breathe.

"Shaila!" Sal called out.

At least Cumar and Thailor were right there behind him. Harrison wasn't so stupid that he couldn't admit they'd do a better job than him in this case. Still, his gun was ready for him to use, even though he hadn't touched it yet. He didn't want to provoke anyone or anything, and he had no idea what the demons who lived there would think if they saw him walking around with his gun in his hand.

"I didn't expect you to come all the way here," a woman said from inside the cave.

When she stepped out, Harrison recognized her. She wasn't wearing a slick suit anymore, and her black hair was spread over her shoulders. The tunic she wore was loose, and Harrison could see the black designs on her skin, similar to the ones Sal was marked with.

"Of course I came. You knew I would, whatever you're saying," Sal snapped.

"Who helped you find me?" Her gaze moved over their little group and stopped on Laz. "Ah. I can't say I'm surprised. You two were always thick as thieves, although I'm not sure why Lazarus has forgiven you for what you did."

"It took him a while, but he allowed me to explain. You didn't."

"Because I don't care why you left, only that you did, and that you abandoned me here."

Sal shook his head. "I had no choice."

"There is always a choice."

"My father came, Shaila."

Harrison had no idea what Sal was talking about, but Shaila paused. "And?"

"He wanted to take me away. He said that as the eldest, I needed to go with him. He was going to make that happen one way or another. I couldn't let him do that. I couldn't stay. I knew you and Esau would be safe—"

"Safe? Here?"

Sal frowned. "Please, Shaila. I only want my powers back. I won't take you to the human realm or punish you for what you did. I don't care about that."

Shaila snorted. "Oh, I suppose I should be grateful, maybe even thank you."

"You can thank me by giving me my powers back."

"I don't think I'll do that."

Sal reached for her, and Harrison knew something was going to happen before she did anything. Sal didn't seem to, though, and he grabbed Shaila's arm.

She punched him. There was no way she was as strong as that punch made her, so Harrison suspected she was using a spell. Sal flew back. He was lucky Thailor and Cumar didn't step away, catching him and holding him up instead.

Sal got back on his feet and shook off their hands. Harrison could tell this wasn't going to end well. Sal reached for Shaila again, but someone behind her cleared their throat, and Harrison's eyes widened. Cumar dragged Sal back as three demons stepped out of the cave and bracketed Shaila.

Shaila smiled. "Did you really think I'd be alone? Why

would I come home, Salazar? I knew I'd have my family's support. Not that I need it, but it would be nice to watch them beat your ass into the sand."

Shaila stepped away from the cave and started along the path between the mountains, dancing away when Sal tried to grab her arm. "Come find me tomorrow. We'll talk," she said.

Sal reached for her again, but before he could touch her, one of the demons—Shaila's brother perhaps, or her father, Harrison had no way to know—punched him in the face. Sal's head jerked back, and blood spurted. Cumar and Thailor reached for their swords, and Sal took advantage of that to try to go after Shaila again. One of the three demons noticed him, though, and he threw something onto Sal's leg. Sal yelped in pain, and Harrison couldn't stay back anymore.

He took his gun out and stepped toward Sal, but before the demon could hurt Sal again, another one came out of one of the caves beyond them and punched the demon in the face, knocking him out.

Sal dropped to the ground. Blood dripped from his thigh, and he clutched it as he looked up at the demon who'd just saved him. Thailor and Cumar were done with Shaila's brothers, cousins, or whatever they were, and Cumar stood behind Sal, his swords out and dirty with blood, while Thailor had gone after Shaila. Laz had hung back the entire time, but Harrison couldn't. He knelt next to Sal and reached for his thigh to check the wound, but he couldn't look away from this new demon, because he didn't know if they could trust him. He'd beaten the one who'd hurt Sal, but that didn't mean he was on their side. Harrison might have never been to Hell, but he wasn't stupid enough to trust anyone he didn't already know here in Hell.

"He almost killed you," the demon said. "You *let* him do it."

Sal twisted to sit, and Harrison helped him. He didn't like

how much blood was coming out of the wound, but he was pretty sure Sal wouldn't let him help, not right now, not more than he was already. "I didn't exactly have a choice," Sal said. His voice was rough, no doubt with pain.

Thailor came back, alone. Harrison didn't know what had happened with Shaila, and he wanted to know, but he was more worried about Sal right now.

"You could have kicked his ass instead of going after Shaila. I thought the two of you were done, but maybe she joined you in the human realm."

"Are you going to help me, Esau?"

Esau crossed his arms over his chest. "Why should I?"

"Why did you help me just now?"

Esau looked down at the demon he'd knocked out. "Because he was going to kill you, and *I* am the only one who can do that. That's my job, asshole."

Sal wanted to kill his brother, but he needed Esau right now. "You can kill me later."

"Oh?"

"You don't want to kill me while I'm weak. You wouldn't be happy with that. You want to kill me while I'm as strong as you, and that'll only happen after I take care of the wound in my thigh." And after he got his powers back from Shaila. He still didn't know why she'd told him to meet her tomorrow, but he wasn't going to let her get away.

He tried to get up, and Harrison was there, helping him and steadying him. Sal hated feeling weak, but he knew he needed Harrison, and he couldn't find it in him to push him away and hurt him even more.

Esau snorted. "Come on. I'll take care of that wound."

Sal moved to follow him when he turned and headed to his cave—the cave where they'd both grown up in—but Harrison stopped him. "He wants to kill you."

"He's always wanted to kill me. Tried a few times, too."

"And you're going to follow him? Just like that?"

"I am. You heard him. He's not going to kill me, not when I can barely defend myself."

"How do you know you can trust him, though?"

"I know I can't. But he's my brother, and I know him better than anyone else in the world."

Harrison's jaw dropped. "Your *brother*?"

"Yep. That's Esau, my younger brother. Well, younger only by a handful of minutes, since we're twins."

"You two don't look alike."

"What can I say? It's a good thing I don't look like him, since I'm the prettiest one."

Harrison gave Sal a strange look. "You are. And you're crazy, but I don't think we have a choice, not if you're going to meet Shaila tomorrow."

"I won't wait until tomorrow." Sal took a step, but his thigh hurt, and his leg buckled under his weight.

Harrison snorted. "Yeah, I can see that." He helped Sal hop and hobble into his brother's cave.

Thailor and Cumar came closer. "We should go after Shaila. She's wounded."

Sal blinked. "She is?" He'd been busy getting wounded and hadn't realized that.

Thailor nodded. "I got her with my sword, in the calf. Went straight through, not touching the bone. She won't make it far. We can get to her."

"No." Sal swallowed at the pain in his leg. "You'd get lost in the desert. Shaila is used to this place. She knows it. She'll be able to hide right in front of your nose, and you wouldn't see her. I need to go with you, and I can't do that until I take care of this wound." It was kind of fitting that both of them had been hurt on the leg, though.

"Are you sure?" Cumar asked. "Because we're used to fighting demons."

"I'm sure. I'm not going to lose anyone here."

They nodded, and Harrison gently pulled Sal toward the cave again. Thailor, Cumar, and Laz were right behind them, muttering to each other. Sal couldn't hear what they were saying, but he suspected that Laz was informing Cumar and Thailor that Esau was Sal's brother and that while he was an asshole, he wasn't going to hurt him—yet.

The cave was dark and cool, and Sal breathed easier. There was dust in the air, and everywhere else, but it was familiar, and something Sal had never thought he'd see again.

"Dump him over there," Esau said, waving toward the bundle of fabric he probably used as a bed. There was only one of them, Sal's long gone, no doubt, but the sight made him frown.

"Where's Mother?" he asked as Harrison lowered him to the cloths.

He smiled at Harrison, and his chest tightened. Even after everything that had happened between them, everything Sal had put Harrison through, Harrison was still there, taking care of him and making sure he was okay. Sal hadn't asked it of him, and he wouldn't have, but he knew that telling Harrison to stay back wouldn't help. Harrison did what Harrison wanted, nothing more, nothing less.

There would be no living without him, would there? No matter how hard Sal tried, he couldn't stop thinking about Harrison, thinking about his life without him. Even if he did go back home once all of this was over, there was no coming back from this. Sal wouldn't forget Harrison. He never would. He was in love, even though he'd tried to avoid it as hard as he could.

"Stop gaping at your slave," Esau said, dropping next to Sal. He cut open Sal's jeans with a knife and peered at the wound.

"He's not my slave," Sal told him. He didn't want anyone to think Harrison was his slave, but especially not his brother.

"Whatever. Is he your human, then?"

"It depends what you mean by that. And where is Mother, Esau? Don't think I haven't noticed you didn't answer."

"She died a few years ago."

Harrison gasped softly, and that was more reaction than whatever Sal was feeling. "I see," Sal said.

"Yeah. You'll live, though." Esau poked the wound. "Just a scratch."

It didn't feel like a scratch, but there was no way Sal was going to show how weak he felt to Esau. "That way, you'll be able to try killing me again."

"Damn right. Unless you let Shaila kill you tomorrow."

"I'm going today, as soon as you're done."

Esau arched a brow and pointedly poked a finger right onto the *scratch*. Sal had to grit his teeth not to scream at the pain. Esau grinned. "That's what I thought. That bastard used a poisoned knife. You're lucky it barely touched you, or you'd already be dead, and I'd have to kill him. I can give you the herbs to counteract whatever poison is in the wound, and once it's out, you won't feel that much pain anymore. It's going to take a few hours, though, so you should probably spend the night here, or at least a few hours."

Sal didn't want to waste even more time than he already had. He needed to get to Shaila. He couldn't even be sure that she was at what had been their place when they'd been young and in love. He couldn't think of a good reason for her to go there, but he didn't think she expected him to roam the desert until he found her.

And why did she want to see him? To torture him over the fact that he didn't have his powers anymore? That she was the only one who could give them back? He wouldn't have thought that of her before, but now, he realized he didn't know her anymore, and he couldn't put it past her.

"I'll stay a while," he conceited. "Just long enough for the pain to fade." Hopefully, that would only be half an hour or so.

Esau nodded. "Good. You're not as stupid as I remember you being, then."

"Shaila is wounded, anyway. She won't go far." She couldn't, not when there was a desert around them. The closest city was the one they'd left behind that morning, and she'd run away the other way. There was only dust and heat there, and she knew it. They both did. She couldn't be far, and Sal was going to make sure she didn't get any further without having unlocked his powers.

Harrison was horrified. "Your mother died?" he finally blurted out, since Sal wasn't talking about it. How could Esau tell his brother about their mother the way he had? Harrison would be breaking down if he had to talk about his mother's death, and she *wasn't* dead.

Sal frowned. "That's what Esau said."

"I'm so sorry, Sal."

Esau snorted. "Why are you sorry?"

Sal glared at him. "Humans aren't like us when it comes to parents. We might not care what happened to our mother, but Harrison loves his. That's why he's aghast at the way you told me and at the fact that I didn't react the way he thinks I should have."

Harrison still didn't understand. "But . . . she was your mother."

Sal patted Harrison's hand. "She was, in the sense that she gave birth to us, yes, and that she made sure we didn't die as newborns. There's a lot of that around. I suppose we should feel lucky, and I do. But she was never a mother in the sense you're thinking of or in the way your mother is to you. She loves you, doesn't she? She raised you with that love. Our mother was different. We had to fend for ourselves as soon as we were able to. We shared this cave, but that's all there was to our family. There was never love between us. *She* tried to kill both Esau and me a few times, just like Esau tried to kill me. This is just the way families, if you can call them that, work here."

Harrison felt even worse now. What had he expected? He should have realized that even though that woman had given birth to Sal, she'd done little more than that. This was Hell, and Harrison didn't know it as well as he'd thought he did.

He swallowed. "I'm sorry I assumed . . ."

Sal smiled at him and took one of his hands, squeezing it. "That's okay. The demons you know in the human realm don't behave like most of those who are here. That's one of the reasons they fled to the human realm, isn't it? Because they were too similar to humans in their affection and in how they see the world to be able to survive here. You're not going to find loving relationships here. Just look at Esau and me."

"No one could love you," Esau answered. He didn't sound angry, and Harrison was more puzzled than ever by his relationship with Sal.

They were brothers, *twin* brothers, but that didn't seem to have the same meaning it had in the human realm. Esau had stepped in when that other demon had reached for Sal again, but he'd said it was because he wanted to be the one to kill Sal. Was that true, or was it only what he wanted Sal to think? Or maybe a facade he needed to keep up? He didn't live in the best of places, even for Hell, and Harrison suspected that any hint of weakness, be it caring for someone or anything else, would get him killed, or worse.

"I beg to differ. I have plenty of people who love me," Sal

said.

Esau was teasing him — possibly — but he was also preparing some kind of mixture with the herbs he'd gathered. He'd added water to a small bowl, and he was grinding and mixing stuff into it. "Yeah? Are they all human? Because that would explain why they love you. Only humans can. Mother certainly didn't."

"Because she loved you? Tell me, how did she treat you after I was gone? I was always her favorite."

"Her favorite to beat, sure." Esau dipped his fingers into the bowl and slathered some of the paste he'd made onto the wound in Sal's thigh.

Sal hissed and tightened his hold on Harrison's hand. Harrison squeezed back. It was slightly painful, but nothing he couldn't stand, especially not when it came to helping Sal.

"Still her favorite," Sal said through gritted teeth.

Esau rolled his eyes. "Before you left, maybe, but trust me, she didn't like you very much after you did."

"I would have thought she'd have been happy to have one less mouth to feed."

"She'd have gotten that anyway if our father had taken you away like he wanted to, but with one less beating."

"Why didn't he take you instead?"

Esau added water to the paste in the bowl and mixed it with a finger. "Because I hid until I was sure he was gone. Almost died of thirst, too. It took him three days to give up, you know." He thrust the bowl at Sal. "Drink."

Sal wrinkled his nose, but he took the bowl. Harrison wouldn't have touched that thing, not with the way Esau had used his hands and fingers to make the mixture, but he supposed that in this desert, every drop of water was precious, and none of it was wasted to wash hands.

Sal drank down the mixture, sputtering and spitting, but he kept it down. He was still grimacing when he handed the now empty bowl back to Esau. "Thank you. I need to go after Shaila."

He tried to get up, but Esau pushed him down with a hand on his shoulder. "Stay."

"I'm not your pet, Esau."

"Mmm, no, you're not. You'd obey me if you were. But you need to give the herbs the time to do their job. You saw what I put in it?"

"Of course I did. I needed to make sure you wouldn't try poisoning me."

"Then you know that as well as something to make sure you didn't get an infection, I added some painkillers. Once they're active, you won't feel a thing, and you'll be able to go after her. And by the way, what's that about? I was surprised when she arrived a week ago, and even more to see you here. What did she do to you?"

Sal slumped against Harrison's side. "As if you didn't hear us talking. I bet you were hiding in here listening to our every word."

"Of course I was. I needed to know if I had to intervene. Like I said, I'll be the one to kill you, no one else."

Harrison was even more confused than he'd been ten minutes earlier. From the way Sal and Esau spoke, they didn't seem to care for each other, but Harrison was pretty sure that wasn't right. Esau could have left Sal to his fate outside the cave with that other demon, or he could have refused to let them in and to help with whatever herbs he'd put together. No matter what he was saying, Harrison suspected he cared for Sal more than he showed, and the same went the other way. Sal might have never mentioned his brother, but Harrison could see he cared for him in the way he behaved. Their back and forth was nothing more than teasing.

Esau flopped next to Sal and crossed his legs. "Come on. What did she do to you? Or better yet—what did *you* do to her?"

Sal didn't want to explain himself. He already knew Esau was going to laugh in his face, and that was the last thing he needed right now. He couldn't move until the herbs took effect, though, no matter how much he needed to go after Shaila. She was wounded, at least. She wouldn't go far, and the herbs were decently fast acting.

"I was hired to find the demon who cast a spell on the two boyfriends of the League leader to kill them. I didn't know she was the one behind that. When I located her, she found me, and she locked my powers."

Esau's eyes widened. Sal waited, and sure enough, Esau's lips stretched into a grin, and he started laughing. "So you don't have access to your powers right now?"

Sal wanted to slap him. There was little he wanted more. "No. She ran away, and while I wanted to go after her right away—"

"You couldn't, because she would have kicked your ass."

Sal reached out and slapped the back of Esau's head. "Yes."

Esau glared, but he didn't retaliate, maybe because of the others who were there. Thailor, Cumar, and Laz were sitting against the wall, still talking, probably about Shaila and what it was going to take to find her. They couldn't do it in Sal's place, though. They'd never be able to convince her to unlock his powers.

"And she fled to Hell," Esau said.

"She did. I had another demon I sometimes work with locate her, and Laz has been helping since we crossed the portal."

"What are you going to do to her to have her unlock your powers? Because somehow, I doubt she's going to do that willingly. I might not know her as well as you do, but I remember her well enough, and she's always been as stubborn as you, and much more cruel. Are you going to tie her up and torture her? Because that's what it's going to take, and we both know you're not up to doing that."

He was right. Sal had never been as strong and as ready to do whatever it took as Esau was. Even if he hadn't shared a past with Shaila, he wouldn't have been able to hurt her. He'd never had that ability in him, the ability to cause pain to get what he wanted. "I'll do whatever needs to be done," he said.

They both knew it was a lie, and Sal hoped Harrison did, too. He didn't want Harrison to think he was going to torture Shaila. He'd never be able to raise a hand on her, except maybe to protect himself or someone else.

It would be easy to let Esau do it for him, though. It would be easy to look the other way and let his brother avenge him, get him his powers back.

"The pain is gone," he said, rising. The room tilted around him, but he managed to get to his feet without face-planting, mostly because Harrison was helping him. And once he was upright, it was easy enough to stay that way.

Esau huffed and got up. "You should probably wait a while longer."

"She might get away."

"And to go where? She went toward the desert. There's nothing there, Sal. There never was, and there never will be."

"So she might die if we don't go after her."

Esau grinned. "She probably would rather die than talk to you or give you your powers back, to be honest."

"Don't be, please. You never have, and I don't need you to start now." He looked at Laz. "Can you do the location spell again? Maybe try to pinpoint her exact location this time? A vague spot won't be of much help."

Laz scowled. "I grew up here, too, remember? I know this place, and I know how to deal with it. I'm aware of all the problems not finding Shaila's exact position would give us. Sit your ass down and let me do the job you hired me to do."

Sal nodded, but he didn't sit. He wasn't sure he'd be able to get up on his feet again if he did.

"You should bandage the wound," Harrison said gently.

Sometimes—most of the time—he wondered what he'd done to deserve the devotion Harrison had for him. He didn't feel worthy of it, and he wasn't sure what he could do to become worthy, or if it mattered. Harrison was a man who gave his heart freely, much more so than anyone else Sal had ever met.

"I'll give you something to do it," Esau said.

Harrison stayed with Sal as they watched him rifle through his belongings. "I didn't expect your brother to be so . . ." Harrison started, but he didn't finish.

"Rude? So much of an asshole?" Or maybe pretty. Sal knew he was good-looking, but so was Esau. Not that he thought that would mean anything to Harrison, but for the first time in a while, he couldn't help but feel fragile, insecure. He didn't like it, even though he knew it was only because he cared so much for Harrison, and that was a good thing.

Sal leaned against the cool stone of the wall while Harrison took care of his thigh. He could have done it himself or have Esau or one of the others do it, but he knew Harrison would be offended by that, and he didn't want that to happen. He had no way to be sure he'd make it out of his next meeting with Shaila in one piece or even alive, and he wanted to savor what was possibly his last moments with Harrison, the feeling of Harrison's hands on his skin, the way Harrison's care for him made him feel.

Loved. Cherished. All things he'd tried to leave behind in the past, and all things that Harrison had thrust at him again when he'd barreled into his life and had refused to back out of it.

"It would be easier if you took your jeans off, or at least if you lowered them," Harrison murmured.

"Yes, Sal. Take your pants off," Esau crowed from the other side of the cave. "It's been a while since I last saw your scrawny ass."

"Should I be worried that you want to see my ass?" Sal snapped back.

Esau made retching sounds. Sal reached down and cut the hole in his jeans larger. They were good for the trash once they got back anyway. "Just do what you can," he told Harrison. He wasn't going to let this or anything else stop him.

"She's not far," Laz said from his spot on the other side of the cave, close to the entrance.

Sal had to stay where he was until Harrison was done, but as soon as the bandage was around his thigh, he went to crouch next to Laz. His thigh only gave him a twinge of discomfort, so he knew he'd be able to walk in the desert fast enough to get to Shaila, as long as the wound Thailor had given her was incapacitating.

He could see the dark burned spot on the map Laz had been using ever since they'd met at the portal, ignoring the other ones, the ones they'd already used. "You're going to need a new map," he murmured.

"I'll make sure to add it to your account."

"I'm sure what I'm paying you is enough already."

Laz shook his head, but he was smiling. "She's not far. It shouldn't take us more than ten or fifteen minutes to catch up to her, although I can't tell if she's still moving, not unless I cast the spell again. Still, she hasn't gone far since she left here, so even if she is, we should make it easily enough. Of course, the sooner we leave here, the sooner we'll catch up. I don't know about you, but I could use another bath like last night's."

Sal nodded and rose. He turned toward his brother.

"You're coming?"

"Of course I am. I wouldn't miss this for anything in the world."

"That's what I thought." Sal took a breath. "Harrison?"

Harrison crossed his arms over his chest and arched a brow. "You think I'm going to stay here, knowing every-thing?"

"Of course you're not. But there will be rules."

"Why am I not surprised?"

Chapter Twenty-two

"You'll stay back."

Harrison managed not to roll his eyes at Sal's order and nodded instead. "I'll stay back."

Sal narrowed his eyes.

Harrison was pretty sure he was wondering if Harrison was making fun of him, and he kind of was, even though this was the worst time to do something like that.

"You *have* to stay away from Shaila, whatever happens. She's always dangerous, but especially so when she's hurt."

"I'll stay away from her," Harrison said. He didn't promise he would, though, because that would depend on what happened. There was no way he was staying out of it while his friends, or worse, Sal were getting hurt, and Harrison didn't care who was doing the hurting.

Sal nodded curtly. "And if something goes wrong—"

Harrison stumbled at that and almost fell face first in the black sand. "Nothing's going to go wrong."

"You can't know that."

He couldn't, but he could pray nothing did, even though he didn't believe in God. "You're right, I can't, and I'm aware of the fact that I'm only human and would break like a stick if Shaila decided to hurt me, but that doesn't mean I'm entirely useless and weak."

Sal huffed.

He'd redone his ponytail before they'd left the cave, but strands were already sliding out and sticking to his sweaty face. His cheeks were red, and Harrison wasn't sure if it was because of the heat or because Sal was so close yet so far from getting what he wanted.

"I never said you were weak. I *know* you're not. But Shaila is a bitch, and she's angry with me. She's not just going to roll to her back and give me what I want. She's doing this because I hurt her, and she doesn't care why I did what I did. She's not going to let a human get in her way for revenge."

"Revenge for what? For leaving to save your own life? I'm sorry, but from where I stand, that means she was never your friend. If you had to leave me here to save your life, I'd be the first one to push you out the door."

Sal shook his head. "You haven't spent enough time here, and you were with us the entire time. You don't know how things can be."

"Maybe not. That doesn't change that fact that she seems to think you should have let your father drag you who knows where just because then she would have known you didn't leave her voluntarily." And that made her a bitch in Harrison's eyes. He understood she'd been hurt, but she'd never even allowed Sal to explain why he'd just disappeared one night. She was clinging to her righteous anger and using it to justify herself when there was no justification for what she was doing.

"That gun won't help you," Sal said softly.

Harrison hadn't needed to use it in Hell, which was surprising to him. He'd expected to have to shoot to keep demons away, but it looked like the company he traveled with was enough. "I guess we'll see. I'm not putting it away, though." He might not be able to kill Shaila because he knew that would hurt Sal, and he didn't want her death on his conscience unless there was no other way, but he *could* wound her even more than she already was. *That*, he wouldn't have a problem doing, he thought as he looked at the already blood-dirty bandage on Sal's thigh. Sal might not feel the pain, but that didn't mean he wasn't hurt, and Harrison wanted to kick Shaila's ass for it, even though she hadn't been the one who'd thrown that blade.

"Found her," Cumar said. He kept his voice soft, but they all heard it, and a current of tension ran through their group.

Harrison licked his lips and grimaced at the taste of dust. He'd be happy once he was home and he never had to see this place ever again.

"Where?" Sal asked.

Cumar pointed at a darker stain on the sand. Harrison hadn't even thought it was possible for the black sand to look darker, but it did. "Blood. It's already drying, but with this heat, she can't be far."

Sal nodded and rushed ahead. Harrison swore and followed the others after him. Shaila was alone, or she was supposed to be, but they weren't going to let Sal face her without back-up. Whatever happened, Sal wasn't alone, and he never would be if Harrison had a say in it.

"How are you going to do this?" Thailor asked. He hadn't bothered to clean his blade yet, and the sight of the dried blood on it was gruesome.

"Confront her. There's no sneaking around in this situation." Sal straightened his back and called out, "Shaila! You know you can't go on. You're going to die soon if you do. Let us take you back to the caves so your family can take care of your wound."

There was a pause during which they all waited. The silence was oppressive, with not even a gust of wind. The heat pressed down on them, but it was also achingly beautiful. The vast emptiness of the black desert was terrifying, but that didn't take away from its beauty.

"I'd die before giving you your powers back," Shaila answered from somewhere to their left. She sounded much closer than Harrison had expected, and he tensed, ready to do just about anything to keep Sal alive.

He knew Sal cared mostly about his powers, but Harrison didn't. He wanted Sal to get them back because he didn't like the thought of Sal hurting, but if he had to choose between Sal's and Shaila's life, he wouldn't hesitate.

Sal pressed forward. Rocks and boulders dotted the sand, as black as it was, and they found Shaila behind one of them. She was sitting against it, but she got up when she heard them coming.

She looked terrible, even though she hadn't been there long. Her lips were cracked, her hair looked like she'd gotten into a fight and she'd lost, and her tunic was torn.

Then there was the wound on her calf.

Harrison could only see the front of it, but he knew there had to be a similar hole on the other side, since Thailor had said his sword went straight through. Dark blood mixed with black sand was caked onto the gaping wound, and Harrison had to breathe in and out of his nose so he wouldn't throw up at the sight. He'd seen his fair share of wounds, but never something like this on someone still alive and in obvious pain.

Sal sighed. "You know I didn't want to go," he said.

Shaila glared at him. "Yet, you did."

"He would have killed me if I'd stayed, and if he didn't, the place where he wanted to take me would have."

"Like this place almost killed me? Do you know what it was like to be suddenly alone here? To lose the only support I've ever had?"

From what Harrison had seen, Shaila had had enough support from her family an hour ago, but he kept his mouth shut.

"I am so, so sorry I did that, but I can't change the past, Shaila. I can't change what happened. We *can* be friends again, though, if you let go."

She laughed painfully. "And if I give you your powers back."

"You know what you did was cruel."

"Why do you think I did it? I never want you to be happy again. I want you to feel the way I did when I lost the most important part of my life. I want you to know you won't ever get it back, because you won't. Whatever you do to me, I won't give in." She grinned. "Whatever you come up with won't be worse than what you've already put me through anyway. I don't care if you drag me back to your friend in the human realm. I don't care if he decides to lock me up or to kill me. *Nothing* will make me give your powers back. You don't deserve them. You don't deserve to be happy, and this way, I know you'll think of me until you die." Her smile widened, and it was manic and worrying. "And it will be a short life, won't it? Because now, you'll start aging, and *that's* the best punishment for you."

She'd gone crazy. Harrison hadn't known her before, but between the way she was behaving now and what she'd done to Ilyhas and Esi, it was obvious she was missing something.

That made her even more dangerous than he'd thought she was.

This wasn't going well. Not that Sal had expected it to, but he'd hoped Shaila would realize how bad her position was. And maybe she did, but if that was the case, she didn't seem to care. Sal wanted to help her, but he wanted his powers back more.

He raised his hands to show Shaila he wasn't armed. "Please. Try to put yourself in my place, okay? What would you have done if my father had wanted to drag you along with him? You know what he was involved in." What he might still be involved in if he was still alive, although Sal doubted he was. His father was violent, cruel, and he enjoyed torturing other demons and robbing them before leaving them for dead. That hadn't changed in the years of Sal's child-hood and teenage years, and he doubted it ever would if the demon was still alive. He didn't want to know, though. The less he thought about his father, the better he felt.

Shaila licked her lips. "Of course I know. All our fathers were into that kind of stuff. That doesn't excuse what you did."

Harrison moved behind Sal, and Sal moved with him, placing himself in front of him. Shaila's gaze went to Harrison, but she looked back at Sal right away. Sal couldn't afford for her to realize what Harrison meant to him. *He* wasn't even sure what Harrison meant to him. He hadn't let himself think about it, because he had to focus on Shaila and everything else.

"I want to fix things, Shaila. Please. I've been trying to do that for decades, and you never let me come close enough to explain what happened then. I know you're still angry, and I get it, I really do. But now you know why I did it. Now you know that while, yes, I did things the wrong way, I didn't mean to hurt you. I never did."

He took a step toward Shaila, then another. Holding his breath, he reached for her, but he didn't touch her, not yet. "Come on, Shay. I was young. I panicked. I know I should have come to you and told you what was happening. I wanted to. But I needed to get out of here as fast as I could. I didn't even tell Esau about it, which was another shitty thing to do." Because their father might have taken Esau instead. He al-most had, apparently, and the only reason he hadn't was that Esau had hidden in the desert.

They were desert children, the three of them—and Laz, of course. Sal's father had never stuck around, so the fact that he hadn't found Esau wasn't surprising.

"I was wrong, Shay. I knew that back then, and I still do. I want to do whatever it takes to make you forgive me. I always did. That's why I tried reaching out to you so many times over the decades."

Shaila stared, and Sal risked it. He put a hand on her arm.

Her skin was too hot, and the fine dust of the desert dotted every inch of it. It was gritty under Sal's fingertips.

Shaila's gaze suddenly moved away from Sal and behind him. He tensed, praying Harrison had gotten the hint earlier and that he'd moved back, but he knew better. Of course Harrison wasn't going to move. He was focused on protecting Sal, be it against real or imagined dangers, so he wasn't going anywhere.

And of course, Shaila had noticed that. How could she not? She'd always been one who noticed details no one else did, and Harrison wasn't subtle.

"How much do you care for him?" she asked without looking away from what Sal was now sure was Harrison behind him.

"Shaila—"

"How much do you care for him, Sal? Why else would you have brought a human along? You know better. You *know* better."

She finally looked back at Sal, and he relaxed, only for a moment.

Then she lunged.

It was a decision Sal had only a second to make. Shaila suddenly had a knife in her hand, and she was moving toward Harrison. Harrison's eyes were wide, and even though he was holding his gun, Sal didn't think he was going to have time to use it. Shaila was too fast, no doubt thanks to some of the spells inked on her skin.

Thailor and Cumar were there, and they moved, but Sal knew it wouldn't be fast enough because he'd asked them to stay back. No, the only one who could do something—who could stop Shaila from planting the knife she was holding in

Harrison's neck—was him.

He reached for her. He wrapped his hands around her waist, and he felt his claws dig in with the force he needed to use to keep her still. She dragged him a few inches, and Harrison had the splendid idea of jumping back, but that didn't stop her. She screamed and slashed at Sal's hand with the knife. It hurt, and Sal's hands slipped.

"Do something!" Laz yelled.

Sal understood why Thailor and Cumar weren't moving, though. They'd have to kill Shaila, and they knew what that would mean for Sal. They wouldn't be the ones taking that step.

It would be Sal. He didn't even have to think about it. He wanted his powers back, more than anything in the world, or more than *almost* anything. But he wasn't going to exchange Harrison's life for his powers. Harrison was much more precious.

He dug his claws deeper into Shaila's stomach. She cried out, and the knife fell from her hand. Sal still didn't let her go. He couldn't risk her wiggling away. He couldn't risk her hurting Harrison.

Shaila stopped moving. A tear rolled down Sal's cheek.

He knelt in the sand and turned Shaila on her back. She wasn't dead yet, but between the wound in her calf and the blood seeping through her tunic where Sal had dug into her stomach with his claws, it wouldn't take long.

Harrison had closed his eyes when Shaila had cried out, convinced she was about to stick that knife of hers into him. Even if she didn't get his neck or his chest, it would hurt.

It never did, because she didn't stab him.

There was the sound of something heavy falling on the sand, and he opened his eyes.

Sal was kneeling on the sand. Shaila was stretched out next to him, her head in his lap as he leaned over her. Harrison couldn't see his face, but that wasn't necessary for him to know what was happening and how Sal felt about it.

"Please, Shaila, please. Don't die," Sal said, his voice breaking at the end.

Harrison didn't know much about Shaila's anatomy as a demon, but if her body worked like a human's, or even only somewhat similarly, then she didn't have much time left. He wasn't sure what had happened, although he could take a guess, since Sal's hands and claws were covered in blood. Shaila was losing more blood with every beat of her heart, and since Harrison doubted there were any hospitals around, there wasn't much to do. Sal was trying, though. He was pressing his hands against the wound to try to stop the blood loss, and Laz rushed next to him, kneeling on Shaila's other side and rustling in his bag.

Sal looked at him. There was a streak of blood on his cheek, and white hair clung to it. "Can you do anything?" he asked Laz.

Harrison expected Laz to say he'd at least try, but instead, he shook his head. "No. I can give her something for the pain, but that's it."

"No," Shaila said. "I'll be dead before it does anything."

There were no more chances for Shaila, but she could still give Sal his powers back. Harrison understood the kind of decision he'd made, though. He could have let Shaila go, and while she would have stabbed Harrison, possibly killing him, she wouldn't have been hurt more than she'd already been. Sal would have had a chance to talk to her and make her change her mind, and even if she hadn't right away, he could have taken her back and kept her with him until she did.

But now she was going to die, and Sal might lose the only way for him to get his powers back. He'd had to decide between Harrison's life and his powers, and he'd chosen Harrison. He'd chosen to make sure Harrison would be okay, and Harrison didn't know what to make of that. He knew Sal cared for him, no matter what had happened between them and the decisions Sal had made, but was he more important than getting Sal's powers back?

"Shaila, please, I beg you. Unlock my powers. I'll never have that possibility after you die. If you care for me even one bit still, please."

Shaila smiled. Her teeth were red with blood, and the sight was freaky, especially when she said, "Oh, I do care for you. But I'm not going to do it."

Sal whimpered. Harrison moved toward him, but Thailor grabbed his arm and shook his head. He was right, of course. No matter how much Harrison wanted to support and comfort him, it was partly his fault if Sal wouldn't get his powers back, and Sal wasn't going to forget that easily or to forgive it. Harrison had wished he wouldn't get them back because he'd wanted Sal to be with him. Now he realized that even if Sal stayed mortal, even if he was never able to cast a spell again, Harrison had lost him, because it would always be his fault if Sal was less than he'd been before.

"Shaila. Why are you doing this to me?" Sal wasn't crying, but it sounded like he wasn't far from it—because of Shaila's death or because of his powers, Harrison couldn't tell.

Shaila's smile widened. "It's for the best. You need to live, and that won't happen if you can never die."

Harrison was pretty sure that was bullshit, at least on her side. She was holding onto the grudge even through death, and at this point, Harrison was pretty sure she'd never intended to give Sal his powers back. She'd taken them knowing that, or she'd made that decision soon after. The *when* didn't matter. The result did, and that result was that Sal wouldn't be able to cast spells again, not spells as powerful as he had before. Sal would die of old age.

And he'd probably go back to his lake house as soon as they set foot in the human realm again.

CHAPTER TWENTY-THREE

Hands pulled Sal away from Shaila. He tried to resist, but she was dead. He didn't have a reason to stay there, to look at her, to beg her to make him whole again.

He'd never be whole again.

"Come on," Laz said. He helped Sal to his feet, and Sal came with him after laying Shaila's head on the sand. No matter what she'd done — or hadn't done — she didn't deserve to be mistreated, even now that she was dead.

Sal tried to speak, but only a croak came out. He swallowed and licked his lips, tasting sand and blood and bitterness, and tried again. "We need to bury her."

Laz squeezed Sal's arm. "I'll take care of it."

"I want to help."

"I don't think you should." He hesitated. "I know now isn't the right moment to say this and that you probably won't want to listen, but your life isn't over because you don't have your powers."

Sal chuckled darkly. "Not yet, but give it sixty years." Sal frowned. "You will die, too, eventually. I can try to cast the spell I used before, but —"

"But I don't need you to. I don't mind growing old. I should have done that all along. The only reason I didn't was you. I never wanted to leave you alone, and now I know I won't." He tightened his hold on Sal. "You're not alone anymore, Sal. Don't push your friends and Harrison away. I know it's what you're going to do now because it's what you always do when you're hurt, but they care for you. They love you, and you're going to need their support now more than ever."

Everything Laz was saying made sense, but Sal didn't know if he could do this.

He wasn't whole, and he never would be. He couldn't stop thinking about that. He couldn't stop feeling like his life was over.

"Do you regret it?" Laz asked, his voice stronger.

Sal blinked at him. "What?"

"Do you regret choosing Harrison's life over your powers? Because that's what you did, isn't it? You could have let Shaila go. She'd have gotten to Harrison, and she'd probably have killed him. You could have let it happen, caught her, and found a way to convince her, even if it had taken you years. But you didn't. You chose Harrison's life over any chance of getting your powers back. Do you regret doing that?"

Sal shook his head. "How could I?"

Laz smiled. "Then you'll be okay. It's going to take a while to get used to this. You've been so focused on coming after Shaila that you didn't give yourself time to think about not having your powers anymore can bring you."

"Apart from death?"

"Death is such a small part of life, Sal. You've never had to think about it for yourself because you knew you couldn't die. But now you can, and you're going to have to learn what it means and to live your life like it has an end, because it does. Take your time, Sal, but don't lose sight of that."

There was no way Sal could think about the future right now. The only thing he felt was despair, and he had no idea how to deal with that, what to do with himself—what to do, period.

Laz gently pushed him toward the small group formed by Thailor, Cumar, Harrison, and a bit further away, Esau. Sal was surprised he wasn't laughing his ass off. He had to find this situation hilarious.

Sal put one foot in front of the other, slowly walking until he reached Thailor and Cumar. Harrison looked like a sad puppy now, his eyes wide and worried. He reached for Sal as soon as Sal was close enough, but Sal couldn't bear to be touched, not by him.

He didn't regret choosing Harrison, but that didn't mean his decision didn't hurt. It didn't mean that he could forget about what he'd lost forever and that in small part, Harrison was responsible for it.

Sal jerked away, and Harrison dropped his hand. He looked like Sal had kicked him while he was down, all pout and hurt expression. Sal couldn't worry about that, though. Not right now. Not yet.

He turned and headed toward Esau. He had no idea what his brother would say, if he was going to make fun of him, if he was going to try to hurt him more than he already was, or if he was going to try to kill him. Sal had managed to save himself the last two times, but he didn't have his powers anymore. He didn't feel like fighting and defending himself. It would be easy for Esau to do whatever he wanted.

But Esau didn't attack. He didn't laugh. He didn't say anything. He stayed where he was, and when Sal was close enough, he patted his shoulder. "What now?" he asked.

"I don't know."

"Why don't we go home for a bit?"

Sal didn't know if he had a home or if that home was the cave where he'd grown up or the lake house. Right now, he felt like he didn't have anything. He wasn't who he'd been before. He didn't think he ever would again.

He was going to have to find out, but not now. Now, he mourned, both for his lost self, his lost powers, and his lost childhood friend.

Harrison moved to join Sal and Esau, but Thailor caught his arm and shook his head." Leave him be."

"He's hurting." And Harrison wanted to comfort him, to make sure he knew that even though he didn't have his powers anymore, he still had friends.

"I know he is. But right now, he's emotional, and considering how this happened, he's probably going to snap at you. He'll regret it later if he says something he doesn't mean, but the words will be out between you two. Give him a little time. He just lost his powers and one of the few people he's known all his life."

Harrison wanted to be the one comforting Sal, but he could understand that Sal didn't want the same thing, so he stayed back. He was in part the reason all of this had happened after all. He wasn't sure why Sal had chosen him over his powers, but he was grateful.

He still wished things were different.

What was Sal going to do? He'd been so convinced that he'd get his powers back that he'd never mentioned what he might do if they didn't. He'd refused to think about it, but now it had happened, and that left a lot of questions, both for him and between them. Would Sal even want to try to live now?

That was what Harrison feared the most. Sal wasn't suicidal, but he'd also never had to contemplate a life like the one waiting for him once they got back to the human realm. He'd been immortal. He'd had so much power that he'd been one of the most powerful demons in the human realm, one of the only ones who could manage Caelan's exorcism. His powers were what had given him his reputation, his home. He was going to have to reinvent himself, and that would only happen if he faced the truth.

Harrison suspected he wouldn't, not if he could get away

with it. Knowing Sal the way he did, Sal would rush back to the lake house and lock himself inside until he died of old age. Of course, that was without considering the bracelets they were going to have to wear for the rest of their lives now.

Harrison raised his wrist and peered at it. It was still as shiny as it had been when he'd put it on, even though he'd been sweating for the past week. It was the sign that he and Sal were one, and Harrison didn't regret getting it done and putting its twin on Sal. He might not have done a lot to help during this trip, but he'd been there, and he thought he *had* helped Sal in a way.

Would Sal see the things the way Harrison did, though? Or would he think that Harrison had ruined his life by putting the bracelet on him and forcing him into a bond they couldn't break now? The spell was the only reason Harrison had been there for Shaila to try to kill. If he'd let Sal come here without him, things would have been different. There was no way to know how, but Sal wouldn't have had to choose between his powers and Harrison.

Harrison still couldn't believe he'd chosen him. He knew Sal cared for him in his own way and that he'd do just about anything to keep him safe, but his powers were his life. He felt like he didn't *have* a life without them, yet he'd thrown the possibility of getting them back away when he'd chosen Harrison's life.

"Can I get some help?" Laz asked from behind them.

Harrison turned and blinked at him. He looked sad, standing next to Shaila's body, and in a way, Harrison shared that sadness. He hadn't known Shaila before, but it had been evident that the main reason she'd done what she'd done was that she was hurt, wounded by the decision Sal had made back when they were little more than teenagers. That didn't excuse her behavior or what she'd done to Esi and Ilyhas, but it gave Harrison a new point of view of the situation.

All of it was a mess. He'd been selfish. Shaila had been selfish. And now Sal was the one who was paying for that.

"What do you need from us?" Cumar asked.

"We should carry her back to the village. There's a patch of desert close by where we bury our dead."

Cumar nodded. "Thailor and I will take care of it."

"I can help."

"Sal is going to need you once we catch up to him. You're his oldest friend here, and I'm not sure how useful his brother will be."

"He won't hurt Sal."

"Not intentionally, maybe. But from what I saw, their relationship isn't exactly traditional, and I wouldn't put it past him."

"They'll be fine. They sound like they'd rather kill each other than talk, but they're brothers, and they were close when they were kids. When Sal left, it hurt a lot of his relationships, but Esau was never one to hold a grudge."

Harrison was grateful he wouldn't have to carry Shaila's body. It was partly his fault she was dead, although he suspected she'd known exactly what she was doing when she'd lunged for him.

"He's going to be fine," Laz said,

Harrison shrugged. "If you say so." He couldn't look away from Sal, even though by now, he was little more than a silhouette in the distance.

"I do. He's strong, far stronger than he thinks. He needs time. He's never had to think about death, or what living a life that would end in it was like. He's going to have to now, and he'll manage. He'll have to change a lot of things, though, more importantly, himself and the way he views the world. That's not going to happen in one night, and I have no doubt he'll try to push us all away. I think we should allow that for a bit, give him the time he needs to wrap his mind around everything and get used to it."

"He's going to isolate himself forever if we give him the chance."

Laz smiled. "That's why I said we should give him *some* time. I agree with you. He's going to try to push all of us away. He thinks his life is over. He hasn't realized it's just started, but he will."

Harrison hoped Laz was right. Objectively, he knew that what had happened wasn't his fault. It was Shaila's. She'd hurt Esi and Ilyhas, had taken away Sal's power and run. And when they'd found her, she'd refused to unlock Sal's powers even though Sal promised that was all he wanted. She could have still been alive and well, and they could have been on their way back, with Sal whole. Instead, she was dead because the grudge she'd been holding had been more important than her life.

But even knowing that, Harrison felt guilty, and he had no way to be sure if *Sal* thought it was his fault or not. There was no way Sal was thinking clearly right now, and Harrison wouldn't be surprised if he lashed out against him.

"He's going to need you," Laz said.

"Why? I doubt he'll want to see me again once we're back in the human realm."

"Ah, but he won't have a choice, will he?" Laz tapped the bracelets on Harrison's wrist. "You two are stuck together. He'll grow weak if he goes too far away from you, and I know you won't allow that."

Harrison groaned. "It's going to be a disaster."

"Maybe, and might I point out that you really should have thought better before you did this."

"I know." But he'd only been thinking about keeping Sal safe—and about the fact that he couldn't know if he'd ever see him again if he didn't do it.

"Things might also go well, though. You're human. You

know how to live like one. You can show him that."

"If he ever speaks to me again."

"He will. And if he doesn't, *you* are going to have to talk to him."

Harrison wouldn't have minded in any other situation, but right now, he couldn't help but wonder if Sal was going to try to kill him if he came within grabbing distance of him.

CHAPTER TWENTY-FOUR

Sal kicked a pebble on the road and watched it bounce ahead of him. He could hear Cumar and Thailor talking behind him, but he was far enough away that he couldn't hear what they were saying. Probably pitying him or something.

They all were, even Esau, who was walking with them to the city. Sal didn't want to talk to him either, and he wished Esau has stayed home. He wanted to talk to his brother a while longer, to catch up with him and reconnect, but not now, not when he still didn't understand what all of this meant to him. Maybe he could come back later, once he did — if that ever happened.

"You're acting like a bitch," Esau pointed out. He'd caught up to Sal, even though Sal was doing his best to isolate himself.

The asshole.

"How would you act if something like this had happened to you?"

"I can't tell you that, now, can I? I've never been nearly as powerful as you."

"Then what the fuck do you want?"

"Nothing for myself. I'm used to you acting like a bitch. But your boyfriend looks like his pet just died a violent death, and it's making even me uncomfortable."

"I don't have a boyfriend." Even though now Sal's main reason not to be with Harrison was gone, he didn't know what he wanted, or rather, what he could stand. He still liked Harrison. He was still half in love with him. But he didn't know himself anymore, so how could he be with Harrison? He couldn't just ignore what had happened and throw himself into a relationship with him, even though it was what he wanted to do because it would be the easier way out.

"A puppy, then. He looks like it anyway, and he looks like you kicked him while he was down."

"I can't do anything for him right now."

"At least smile at him. You know he thinks it's his fault."

"It's not." Sal had been angry with Harrison right after everything happened, but now that he'd had a few hours to think, he wasn't anymore.

It was Shaila's fault. It had started with Sal, but that had been decades ago. He didn't know why Shaila had held onto that grudge for that long. He understood how hurt she'd been — he would have been, too, if she'd been the one who'd left without saying anything back then — but it had been close to two hundred years. No one held a grudge that long, except apparently Shaila. Sal wouldn't have the chance to ask her why she was still so hurt, what she'd done since the last time they'd seen each other, how her life had been. He wanted to believe she'd been happy, at least some of the time.

"Why do you think she did it?" he asked even though he hadn't meant to bring his brother into this.

Esau didn't miss a beat. "She saw a chance to get back to you."

"By *dying*?"

"You know, I think you and I, and most of the demons who live as long as we do, don't understand death and what it means."

"It means that you're done, Esau."

Esau bumped their shoulders together. "I'm aware of that. What I was trying to say is that we don't fully live our lives because we know it doesn't have an end. What have you been doing since you left here? Honestly."

"I worked. I bought a house."

"What about a family? Not that I know how families work, but you were always softer than me when it comes to feelings, and I doubt that changed once you moved to the human realm. Humans are nice and soft, if your man is an indication of it."

"Some of them are." Harrison *definitely* was.

"So, no family? That's why you're ignoring my question, right?"

"I've had a few people I loved."

"When? How long ago? Because I have to say, I was surprised not to see you all over Harrison when you got here, but especially after what happened with Shaila. You saved his life, but you haven't looked at him twice since then, and he seems uncomfortable and almost afraid."

"Are you trying to tell me that losing the powers I've had since I was born and my immortality don't matter? That's easy for you, since *you* still have it."

"And what am I doing with it? I haven't left this place, ever. My days are all the same, and let me tell you, it gets boring after a few years, let alone a couple of hundred years."

"*Why* are you still here, then?"

Esau shrugged. "Where else would I go? This is what I know. And *that's* what I was trying to tell you. If I'd only had seventy or so years, would I have stayed? Part of why I'm still here is that I have time. I have all the time in the world to explore, so there's no urgency to do it, to go out there and explore and *live*. You've been doing pretty much the same thing, except in the human realm. That's going to have to change, and while it *is* sad that you lost a lot today, it doesn't have to bring only bad things. You can have a life with Harrison, or whoever else you love. A *fulfilling* life, a life that isn't spent waiting and wasting time. Life is supposed to be lived, Sal, and that's what you should do from now on."

Suddenly, Sal didn't want to let go of Esau. He didn't want to never see his brother again. "You'll visit me in the human realm?" he asked.

Esau gave him a half-smile. "Why should I?"

"Because maybe it's time for you to start living, too. You might have dozens of years left, but it doesn't mean you have to spend them here."

Esau's smile widened. "Maybe not. I'll think about it."

They didn't have to hate each other just because they were demons, or because of what their relationship had been in the past. Sal had never realized how significant his brother's absence had been, what it had meant for him and his life, but Esau was right, just like Laz had been.

Sal needed to start living now that he had so few years left. He wasn't sure how he was going to do that, but he was going to try — as soon as he was done feeling sorry for himself and mourning his losses.

CHAPTER TWENTY-FIVE

Sal had been keeping to himself ever since they'd left his village, and Harrison hated it. They were back at the smaller tavern tonight, which meant that tomorrow, they'd be home, and Sal would go back to his lake house. Time was slipping away, and Harrison wasn't sure what to do.

He didn't want to push. That never ended well, not when the other person didn't want to talk — and Sal *obviously* didn't want to talk. He'd never been the quiet type, not since Harrison had met him. Even right after Shaila had locked his powers, Sal had still been upbeat, albeit less than usual. He wasn't anymore. Harrison didn't think he'd said a word since they'd left Esau behind, and even before that, Esau had been the only one Sal had talked to. Harrison was dying to know what they'd talked about, but he knew Sal wouldn't tell him even if he asked, and Esau had just laughed in his face when he'd tried with him.

"I can't *wait* to eat dinner," Cumar said, his tail swishing behind him in a gesture that reminded Harrison of a puppy wagging his tail.

"It's only going to be bread and meat," Thailor pointed out. "I don't know about you, but I miss ice cream."

"Don't remind me about it. It feels like we've been gone forever."

Harrison let them walk into the tavern first. Laz and Sal were behind him, and he wasn't surprised when as soon as Sal stepped into the tavern, he said, "I'll be in my room."

Harrison sighed and turned to face him. "You're not eating

with us?"

"I'm not hungry."

"You have to eat."

"I will. Just not tonight."

Harrison gritted his teeth. Maybe the time of pushing had come. "We'll share the room." Sal and Esau had shared last night, while Harrison had been with Laz. Esau had stayed behind, though, and there was no way Harrison was letting Sal stay on his own, not now that he needed love the most.

Laz linked his arm with Harrison's. "Come on, let's go eat. You can go yell at him later."

Harrison let himself be pulled along. It was late enough that they didn't have time to wash up before eating, not if they wanted to find food. Harrison didn't like the dust coating his skin, but he didn't have a choice, and he was getting used to it anyway. He'd still be glad to be home, though, where the only dust around was the stuff on his furniture, and where he had access to a shower any time he wanted.

Harrison wasn't sure if the demons in the tavern's main room were the same who had been there last time, and he didn't particularly want to find out. He kept his head down and followed the other three to an empty table.

"It's weird not to have you ask a dozen questions for every breath you take," Laz said when they were sitting down.

Harrison shrugged. "I haven't been in the mood lately."

Laz patted Harrison's hand. "He'll get out of his funk. It's only been a day and a half, you know."

"I know." Was Harrison in too much of a rush? He wanted Sal to be okay, and he knew Sal would need time. He also knew that Sal wouldn't heal if he hid in his lake house, away from everyone. He could live a good life alone, but his life would be better if the people who loved him were there with him. Harrison wasn't even thinking about himself, although he did hope that he'd be part of Sal's life from now on. It would do Sal no good to be alone and to push his friends away.

Harrison picked at his plate—the same meat he'd eaten on the way to Sal's village. He was hungry, but he was too worried to eat much. His thoughts kept returning to Sal and how alone he was upstairs. He knew he'd be worried as long as he didn't at least try to talk to Sal. He'd left him alone until now, but that was over. Two days to think and reflect were enough to start coming to terms with what the rest of his life would be. Harrison didn't expect Sal to be over everything—it was way too soon for that—but being on his own wouldn't help him, either.

He pushed his plate away. "I think I'm going to go to bed."

No one at the table believed that. Laz wrapped several pieces of bread into a napkin and thrust it into Harrison's hand. "Be careful, and make sure he eats at least part of this."

Cumar rose from his chair, maybe to walk Harrison upstairs, but Harrison shook his head. "I'll be fine. I'm armed, remember?"

"No demon would be happy if you tried to shoot them. That would probably make things worse."

"I'll go straight to our room, don't worry. Eat, rest. You deserve it."

Harrison left before Cumar and Thailor could insist. He *really* did think he was going to be okay.

He was wrong.

Harrison should have expected it, but he was so focused on Sal and how he was doing that the demon caught him by surprise. A hand wrapped around Harrison's throat when his foot touched the top step of the stairs and pulled him forward. He spluttered and dropped the bread as his back was slammed against the closest wall.

The demon—he couldn't tell if it was the one who'd tried to buy Harrison from Sal the last time they'd been here—

leaned closer. His breath was warm and smelled of meat and beer and smoke, and Harrison choked. Or maybe that was because of the giant hand around his throat.

The demon grinned. "Looks like I'm going to have you after all."

Harrison could take out his gun. He could shoot this demon and hope he'd kill him with the first shot, because he'd be the one dying otherwise.

He kicked his feet against the wall, trying to make some noise. He wasn't sure it would be enough, but a door creaked open somewhere along the hallway. Moments later, the demon was pried off Harrison and thrown on the other side of the hallway.

Harrison slid down to sit on the floor as he tried to breathe.

"Are you okay?" Sal asked. He looked formidable, with his wings extended and his fangs exposed, his hair floating around his face like a halo.

Harrison nodded. "Thank you."

Sal nodded back and turned toward the demon, who was getting back to his feet. "What did I tell you about not touching my human?"

The demon charged, but Sal was waiting for it. He extended his arm and grabbed the demon around the throat, just like the demon had done to Harrison. Harrison saw his claws dig into the skin and spill blood. Then Sal slammed the demon against the wall again and raised his other hand, claws extended. He'd stopped filing them when they'd gotten to Hell, and they were even longer than they'd been when he'd killed Shaila with them. He'd slice right through the demon's throat if Harrison let him.

"Sal. Stop," Harrison croaked.

Sal froze. "What?"

"Don't kill him."

"Why not? He hurt you. He would have hurt you even

worse if I hadn't stepped in."

"You're better than him, that's why. You don't hurt people intentionally, even if they deserve it. Come on. Drop him."

Sal did. Harrison was surprised but relieved, and he didn't waste time. He grabbed Sal's hand and dragged him toward the bedroom they'd share tonight, needing to get him away from the demon and what had almost happened.

It was good to see Sal had left his self-imposed isolation and misery, but this wasn't what Harrison had had in mind when he'd thought it was needed.

Sal let Harrison drag him away even though he wanted nothing more than to tear that demon's throat out. But he needed to make sure that Harrison was okay. He knew he'd gotten there just in time, but still, the demon could have slammed him against the wall too hard, or he could have done something to him before Sal got there. He'd come running as soon as he'd heard the sound of Harrison being slammed against the wall and that horrible demon telling him he'd have him this time, but maybe he hadn't been fast enough. He needed to be sure.

Harrison closed the door once they were inside the bedroom and leaned toward Sal. "Are you okay?"

"I should be the one asking you that. It was you that demon was molesting."

Harrison smiled. "And you saved me. I'm fine."

Good. That was good.

Sal grabbed Harrison's hand and pulled him close, wrapping his arms and his wings around him. Their lips met, and Sal sagged in relief. Harrison was okay. He wasn't hurt, and he was still there, pressed against Sal as if he'd never left.

Sal had missed him more than he'd cared to admit to himself. He'd been the one to push Harrison away, but how he'd missed him.

Harrison put his palms on Sal's chest and pushed him away. "What are you doing?"

"I'm kissing you." Sal needed more skin, though. He hadn't been able to stop thinking about the night they'd spent here on their way to the village. He hadn't felt so close to someone in decades, and he wanted that feeling back.

"*Why* are you kissing me?"

Sal huffed. "Because I want it. I want *you*." Sal tried to bring Harrison closer again, but Harrison didn't let himself move.

"Why do you want me? Or wait. You mean you want sex, right?"

Sal frowned. "Well, I thought that was obvious."

"It is. I'm trying to understand *why* you want to have sex with me. Is it revenge for what happened?"

Sal let go of Harrison. "What do you mean? Revenge?" What was Harrison talking about?

Harrison cleared his throat. "If I hadn't put that bracelet on you, if I hadn't followed you here, Shaila would still be alive, and you'd still have a chance to get your powers back. You know how much I care for you and that I'd do just about anything to be with you and have a future with you. So is that why you want to have sex? So you can discard me once we're done and hurt me?"

Sal jerked back. "What the fuck?" Was that what Harrison thought of him? That he could do something like that? "I'd never do something so cruel."

Harrison's shoulders slumped. "I know. But I needed to be sure. You haven't been yourself lately, and I get why, but I don't know how much what happened changed you."

Sal raked a hand through his hair. It was still damp from the bath he'd taken earlier. "I'll admit I'm shaken by everything. That doesn't mean I'm going to turn into a monster."

He was surprised when Harrison gently took his hand

since Harrison thought he could have sex with him and throw him away. "I'm sorry. I know you wouldn't do that. I'm just confused and worried, and I thought the worst of you because what I told you is the worst I can imagine happening to me right now." He smiled. "Well, apart from what you saved my ass from out there. I think we need to talk, though. I want to make love to you as much as you seem to want to, but I want to know where we stand before I let myself be vulnerable like that. I won't be a distraction from your pain, not if this is the only way you can think of to deal with it."

Sal should have known Harrison would make him talk about it. Wasn't that what humans usually did? Of course that was better than the demon way, where everyone tried to kill everyone and never thought about it again.

Harrison took off his shoes and dropped onto the edge of the mattress. He briefly closed his eyes, and Sal could see all the exhaustion he felt on his face for a moment, just before he schooled his expression and opened his eyes again. "I want to help you, Sal. I can't even imagine what you're going through, and I feel so fucking guilty for what I did."

It would be easy for Sal to blame Harrison for everything that had happened, but he couldn't. He had, for those first few hours right after Shaila had died. He'd had more than enough hours to think about it, though, while they walked back. Harrison had just given Shaila more ammunition to hurt Sal. She'd known Sal would do whatever he had to do to save Harrison, and she'd acted accordingly. If Harrison hadn't been there, she'd have tried to hurt Esau or Laz, because she knew Sal cared for them.

He swallowed. "It wasn't your fault."

"If I hadn't—"

Sal caught on of Harrison's hands. "I know. If you hadn't put the bracelet on me, you wouldn't be here, and Shaila wouldn't have tried to hurt you. But she would have found another way to goad me into hurting her, and if I hadn't, well, I doubt she would have given me my powers back anyway. I don't think anything I could have said or done would have convinced her to do that. She was ready to die over this."

Harrison nodded. "I'm glad you realized that. It helps a bit. And I know how hard everything is for you right now. I can't be the comfort you need, though, not if that comfort is only going to last a few days, just the time you get your feet under you and decide what your next step is going to be. I want to help you get used to this new life of yours, but not if I'm going to have to pay for it with my heart. Our friendship means a lot to me, but I'm in love with you, Sal. I can't be used and thrown away, even if it would help you feel better."

Fuck. Was Sal so bad that this was what he'd been asking of Harrison? "I don't want to hurt you."

Harrison smiled, but it was sad and small. "I know. But I also know that you have no idea what's coming next. You have to deal with the fact that instead of hundreds of years, you might only have forty of them waiting for you. You have to make decisions you've never even had to think about before. I can't be there to hold your hand through it, not unless you want me to hold your hand for the rest of your life. Because that's what I want from you, Sal. I want you and me to be together for as long as we can. So think about that. Think about everything. I'm not going to rush you. No one is. And when you know, come find me. I'll be there for you."

Watching Harrison get up and leave was one of the hardest things Sal had ever done. He hadn't realized it until now, and he was terrified that once he knew what he wanted to do with his short life, it would be too late to get Harrison back.

CHAPTER TWENTY-SIX

Harrison had to blink a few times to get used to the darkness—and the smell of the sewer. After spending more than a week in the desert of the demon realm, with its heat and doomed light, it felt weird to see something familiar, as familiar as the sewers could be.

"All right?" Thailor asked, gently patting Harrison's shoulder.

Harrison nodded. "Although I'll feel better once I take a shower and eat something."

Cumar groaned. "Pizza. No, wait. A big, juicy burger, and some ice cream to top it off. Fries. Maybe even cake."

Thailor chuckled. "You'd think spending some time with your mate was more important than eating all the food you can get your hands on."

"I can do both." Cumar wiggled his eyebrows. "Especially if I put the ice cream *on* Yo'ash. Mmm, I wonder if he's working tonight. I'm going to need some time with him and the ice cream."

Harrison forced himself to smile, but he was pretty sure it came out more like a grimace. He'd tried to put up a brave front since last night when he and Sal had talked, but Laz, Thailor, and Cumar knew something was happening. Harrison had shared Laz's bedroom again, and he'd stayed quiet ever since. Sal was even quieter than him, which wasn't something they were used to.

Harrison didn't want to talk or to think about what was happening, but he also wasn't sure he wanted to be alone.

"Laz, what will you do?" he asked, not looking in Sal's direction.

"I'm going back. I shouldn't have crossed the portal at all, to be honest. I want to make sure Shaila's family isn't going to try to kill Esau or something."

Harrison frowned. "Is that something they might do?"

"Possibly. I can't say any of them particularly cared about Shaila, but they might find it fun to torture Esau and use that as a reason. Not that they need a reason to do that, of course, but everyone always tries to keep the peace in the village, so violence tends to be frowned upon."

"Should we have tried to convince him to come with us?"

Sal snorted, but he didn't say anything. He was already inching his way along the sewer, no doubt eager to go home. Harrison wasn't sure where that home was for right now. Sal's stuff was still at his apartment, so he'd have to come back sooner or later, especially if he was planning on running back to his lake. Harrison didn't know how he'd take it if he had to share the apartment with Sal, but not sharing it with him came with its own set of problems. Harrison wanted to keep an eye on Sal to make sure he was okay and that he wouldn't do anything stupid, and he couldn't do that efficiently if they weren't living together.

Laz smiled. "We could have tried, but Esau only does what *he* wants, so I doubt we'd have managed. He can defend himself. I just want to make sure he's okay."

There was a round of handshakes, and for Sal, of crushing hugs, and Laz disappeared back into the portal. Harrison stared at it for a few seconds, wondering if he'd ever see the demon again. He hadn't liked him in the beginning, but he couldn't deny that he was going to miss his quiet presence and his knowledge of Sal. Getting him to tell childhood stories about Sal had been fun, and it had distracted them on the long walks to and from the village.

Cumar swung an arm around Harrison's shoulder. "Want to go to Underworld for a drink?"

Harrison narrowed his eyes. "Why are you asking?"

Cumar shrugged. "Why not? We're friends, aren't we?"

"Since when?" Harrison was aware of the fact that demons mostly tolerated him. They certainly didn't like him, especially not the badass League warriors who could skewer him with a thought.

Cumar looked offended. "We were always friends. And trekking through the desert to find a rancorous ex tightened the bond between us."

Harrison had to smile. "Okay, we're friends. I'd still rather go home, though. Like I said, I need food and a shower, and to sleep for the next twenty hours." And to mope around for a bit. It wasn't the first time Harrison had been dumped, and it wouldn't be the last.

He'd survive. He might hate it, might wish Sal could see how good they could be together, but this was out of his hands now. Sal was going to have to take the next step, because Harrison couldn't put his bruised heart even more at risk than he already had. He loved Sal, but he loved himself more. Things hurt now, but they would hurt worse if he let Sal use him to feel better and then discard him.

"How are you getting home?" Cumar asked.

Harrison was grateful Cumar wasn't pushing. "I don't know. I'll probably cab it or something."

"I already texted Jordan for you."

Harrison blinked. "What?"

"I thought you could use the ride and the friend. Thailor and I will take Sal back to HQ. Jadon will probably want our healers to examine him again, considering everything that happened and that didn't happen. That'll get him out of your apartment for a few days. Thailor and I might come over to grab some of his things so he doesn't come himself."

"What about the bond between us? Won't the distance make him feel weak?"

Cumar grimaced. "Well, I hope he'll get his head out of his ass soon. He knows he can't just go back to his old life, and he needs some time to think things through and make decisions. I think things will be okay if he only stays away a few days, but I'll make sure to ask our healers, just in case. You two are going to have to work things out, though."

"We will. I just need a few days, just like he does."

Harrison wasn't sure what to say. He hadn't expected this, not from people he hadn't been close to. He, Thailor, and Cumar were friendly enough, mostly because of the people they were connected through, but that was where it ended, or at least where it had ended before. It looked like the trip to Hell and back had changed things, though, and through the heartbreak, Harrison was glad for that. He might have lost a piece of his heart, but he'd found friends, and that was better than anything he'd expected.

Jordan was waiting for him by the time they trudged out of the sewers. They probably stank as badly, if not more, but Jordan didn't say anything as he gently pushed Harrison into his passenger seat. Harrison watched Sal, Thailor, and Cumar disappear and sighed heavily. "What did he tell you?" he asked Jordan. He knew Cumar had at least hinted that something had happened.

"Just that you got your heart broken. I have no idea how or by whom, although I can take a wild guess. You don't have to talk about it, though. We can hang around, get some pizza and beer, and celebrate the fact that you made it to Hell and back alive and in one piece."

Harrison could have cried in relief. Jordan wasn't going to interrogate him about what had happened. They could chill out for one evening as Harrison got used to being in the human realm again. He could face the heartbreak and everything else tomorrow, and it would be soon enough. For now, he'd rest and wrap his mind around everything. No matter what had happened and how *hellish* it had been, the trip had been interesting enough that Harrison was glad he'd gone.

Chapter Twenty-seven

Sal stared at the white ceiling and tried to stop thinking.
It didn't work. His mind was full of questions, and he
didn't have answers to most of them, not any more than he
had when he'd come back from Hell three days ago.

He'd spent most of that time in the League's infirmary getting poked and prodded so Jadon could be sure he was okay.
He'd started feeling nauseous and weak a few hours ago, but
he hadn't told anyone that. He knew why he felt that way,
and no one except him could do anything about it.

Yet there he still was, stretched out on his bed staring at the
ceiling. At least he had a private room in the infirmary. He
could still hear the people outside of it, moving around and
healing and sometimes, screaming, and he hated it. He
wanted to go back to Harrison's quiet apartment, but Harrison had been clear. As long as Sal wasn't sure he wanted him
in his life, he wasn't welcome there.

And Sal still didn't know what he wanted.

It should have been easy to make that decision. The one
reason Sal had not to let himself fall in love with Harrison was
gone. He wasn't immortal anymore. He would age and die,
just like Harrison would. He wouldn't have to watch Harrison do that on his own. He'd be right there with him.

That wasn't a problem anymore, but something else was.
Sal had never thought about what he'd do if he wasn't immortal anymore. Why should he have? He'd never even
dreamed about something like that happening. He hadn't
thought it was a possibility until recently.

And now it was his reality. What the fuck was he supposed to do with that? Especially with the bond between him and Harrison. He hated that they were bonded, not because he didn't want Harrison, but because he wasn't sure what he could offer him.

He couldn't cast spells anymore. He'd tried, and but all his magic was gone. Even the simplest locating spell was out of his reach. That meant he'd have to go out of business, and how was he going to earn his living now?

He didn't know who he was anymore. He was still Sal, but a big part of him had been made up by his powers and his ability to use them, and now that was gone, and a big, black hole had taken its place.

The door slammed open. Sal jerked, but he didn't get up. It was probably a healer wanting to check on him or something. They were all fascinated by Sal's sudden loss of powers, and while a few had been able to feel them behind the lock Shaila had put on them, none could help. The only one who could unlock them was the person who had the key—who'd cast the spell—and that person was dead.

Sal wasn't sure if that was even worse. If his powers had been gone, it would have been as horrible as things were now, but at least he could have made his peace with it. But as things were, his powers were still there. They always would be. It wasn't something anyone could take away from him. They could lock it away, though, like Shaila had, and that was almost worse than having them ripped out of you.

"You're still feeling sorry for yourself, I see," Jadon said.

"What do you want?"

"For you to stop. You're making my warriors sad, and I can't have that, not when they have to go out every night to kill demons."

Sal sat up, crossed his legs, and glared. "Easy for you to say that, isn't it? You didn't lose the only thing you were good at in life."

"Oh, shut up."

Sal blinked. The only person who'd ever talked to him that way was Esau, and his brother was still in Hell. It looked like Jadon might be channeling him, though. Maybe Esau had decided to possess him? It wasn't possible for demons to possess other demons, but it sure looked like it right now. "What?"

Jadon sat on the chair next to Sal's bed. "Are you done crying over something you can't change?"

"It's not as easy as you seem to think it is, Jadon."

"I know that, and trust me, I hurt for you. No one should have to go through what you have. It's not fair. But life seldom is fair, and you're not dead. You still have most of your life in front of you, and you're wasting it by moping around in my infirmary."

"I can't get over losing my powers in a few days."

"No, but you can let people in to help you go through it. You have friends here, including me." He raised his feet and put them up on the edge of the mattress.

Sal wrinkled his nose, but he didn't protest. This *was* Jadon's turf after all. "I know that."

"Then maybe it's time to stop thinking about everything you've lost and start building up your future. Like I said, you have friends, and if my intel is correct, a boyfriend, at least once you get your head out of your ass and go talk to him. You also have a job if you want."

Sal tensed. "I don't have a job anymore."

"That's why I'm offering you one, idiot. I know you don't have experience as a healer, not without your magic, but you know herbs, right?"

"Of course I do. You have to know herbs and ingredients to cast spells."

"Then you can take the job of making the pastes and potions the healers use."

"Don't you use modern human medicine?"

Jadon snorted. "Who's going to hand me over a box of painkillers? Besides, human pills don't work as well on demons. Our anatomies are too different in most cases. So? Are you going to stop digressing and give me your answer?"

What could Sal say? He didn't have anything to go back to at the lake except his house. He *couldn't* go back to it, not without hurting himself through the bond that now tied him and Harrison.

And Jadon wasn't wrong. However Sal still felt after everything, however hurt he was, he still had friends. He could build a home here and a good life.

He could have a boyfriend, share his life with him, grow old with him.

He licked his lips. "I—"

Jadon swung his feet to the floor and got up. "Think about it, all right? Like I said, I want you to take care of the potions side of the infirmary so that the healers can focus on the wounded. If possible, I'd also like you to help with the longer recoveries. Some of the warriors can't go back to their job once they're done, and it's always hard for them to get used to a new life." Jadon smiled. "You'll know all about that soon enough. And for anything you need, I'm here. I hope you know that. But you really should go apologize to that man of yours."

"Apologize for what?" Sal knew he wasn't behaving the right way when it came to Harrison, but Harrison understood why he was doing what he was doing. He understood Sal needed time, and he'd given it to him. He'd given him a choice, and while they would have to sort things out between them, he'd always be in Sal's life.

Jadon chuckled. "Trust me, you always have to apologize for something, or at least that's what Esi and Ilyhas seem to think."

"I don't know how you deal with two of them." Sal didn't even know how to deal with only Harrison. The thought of having to face two sets of needs and feelings was terrifying.

"I love them, that's how. Everything is easier when you have someone to love and who loves you, even the complications that brings. Make your decision, Sal, and go talk to Harrison. He doesn't deserve to be kept waiting like he is."

Sal was off the bed as soon as Jadon left the room. He had no idea what he was going to tell Harrison or if Harrison would forgive him and take him back, but he had to try. And if Harrison didn't want him, well, they were going to have to find a way to live together. They were bonded. That wasn't going to change. They could be friends, housemates.

But Sal hoped they'd be lovers.

Harrison trudged to the elevator and pressed the button. It wasn't that late, but he felt like he'd run a marathon, and he couldn't wait to pass out on the couch with the TV on and pizza in his stomach. He should probably try to cook instead of eating takeout again, but he didn't think he had enough energy to do that, not today, and probably not tomorrow, either.

Pizza it was, then. Maybe he'd get Chinese tomorrow, just to have a variety.

"You look like something the cat dragged in," Icha said from behind Harrison.

Harrison whimpered. "Please, not tonight."

Icha stepped closer. "Not tonight, what?"

"No flirting. No trying to get in my pants. I might have taken you up on it any other time, but not tonight."

Icha's eyes narrowed. "You might have taken me up on it? Now I *know* something is wrong with you. What happened? Who broke your heart?"

The elevator doors slid open, and Harrison sighed in relief. He shuffled inside, but of course, Icha was right behind him.

"Come on, Harrison. Who broke your heart?" he insisted.

"I don't want to talk about it."

That managed to do what Harrison had never obtained. Icha snapped his mouth shut and stopped talking. He leaned against the wall, and Harrison could still feel his gaze on him, but at least he didn't have to answer questions. He hoped Icha would leave him alone, but when they left the elevator, he leaned closer and put a hand on Harrison's arm. "If you need anything, you know where to find me. I hate to think about you all alone in your apartment."

"He won't be alone."

Harrison blinked at the voice. He hadn't noticed Sal sitting in front of his door, his legs stretched out, his feet almost touching the wall in front of him. He was wearing black jeans that were ripped at the knees and a bright orange t-shirt with a kitten on it. His hair was loose, and his wings were trapped between his back and the wall in a position that couldn't be comfortable. Yet there he was, and Harrison had no idea why. The sight of him was enough to make Harrison's heart race, though.

Harrison licked his lips. "What are you doing here?" he asked.

Icha leaned closer as Sal hauled himself to his feet. "So he's the guy who broke your heart? He looks like he could have broken mine, too, to be honest." He patted Harrison's arm. "Don't let him walk all over you, no matter how gorgeous he is. You're a good guy, and you deserve someone who will make you happy." He disappeared into his apartment while Harrison unlocked his door.

He was keenly aware of Sal's presence next to him, of his wings slightly fluttering and the way he was shuffling. That wasn't like him, or rather, it hadn't been. Sal had always been confident, for as long as Harrison had known him. He'd lost some of that after Shaila had locked away his powers, but especially after she'd died. Harrison wasn't surprised. He might have asked Sal to be sure of what he wanted before coming back, but he did understand how hard everything must have been for him.

His life was completely different now, and it would always be. He had to deal with the fact that he couldn't live forever now, that he'd grow old. He had to deal with the fact that he didn't have his powers anymore and that his life would never be the same.

No wonder he was insecure. Harrison wanted to see him like he'd been before, though, and he wanted to help him get back to that.

"What are you doing here?" he asked as he stepped inside. He knew Sal would follow him, and he couldn't help the hope bubbling in his chest. Sal wouldn't break Harrison's heart on purpose, and since Harrison had told him to come back only when he knew what he wanted, that meant he knew, and that Harrison was about to find out.

"Jadon offered me a job."

That wasn't what Harrison had expected to hear. "Yeah? That's good."

"It is. He wants me to take care of the medicinal side of the infirmary. You know, mix the potions and everything else. That'll free up more time for the healers to deal with the warriors."

"I know it's not what you wanted from life."

"No, but it's better than I would have otherwise. Along with a job offer, Jadon gave me a piece of his mind. He told me what he thought of me and my behavior."

Harrison toed off his shoes and flopped on the couch after taking his jacket off. "I'm almost afraid to ask what was said."

Sal chuckled. "He wasn't nasty or anything. He just made

sure I knew the truth even though I was trying to ignore it."

Harrison swallowed. "So you're here because you want to move in again? I know you don't like living at HQ." And he'd told him he'd be there for him, whatever he needed to make his new life work.

And he would. If Sal had decided he didn't want Harrison as a lover, then Harrison would accept it—eventually. But he'd promised, and he did want to be there for Sal if Sal needed him. They could be friends. Harrison would get over what he felt for Sal. He'd have to.

"That's not why I'm here, although yes, I'd like to move back here with you. The healers seem to finally be done with all the things they wanted to do to me, and I'm allowed to leave the infirmary. I'm not looking forward to going back to the room I had before and having to listen to my neighbor and his girlfriend having sex."

"You can come back any time."

Sal gestured at the couch. "Can I sit?"

"I can grab your stool if you want."

"No, thank you. I want to be next to you."

That sounded good. Didn't it? "Of course. I just want you to be comfortable, and I know that the couch isn't easy on your wings."

Sal's answering smile was soft and gentle, and when he sat next to Harrison, he tentatively reached for his hand.

Harrison let him take it. He still didn't know what to think, but he was about to find out, and his heart was racing.

"I'm a mess right now," Sal said. "I'm pretty sure I'll be a mess for a long time. Dealing with the loss of my powers and my immortality isn't easy, not even when I try to focus on the things I still have. I'm going to be angry sometimes, then sad. I'm screwed up. There's no denying that. But I want to try to be the man you deserve. I want to love you and spend the rest of my life with you, if you'll still have me."

Harrison was still breathing, but barely. He couldn't believe what he was hearing, yet Sal was right there, still holding his hand, playing with his fingers and avoiding looking at him.

He'd come even though he wasn't sure Harrison still wanted him. He was insecure in a way he'd never been, and while Harrison didn't like it, he knew he could change it, with time and love.

A love Sal wanted.

"Yes," he croaked.

Sal looked up. "Yes? You want to try, too?"

"Of course I do. I already told you I love you. That hasn't changed. I don't think it ever will."

Sal's smile widened. "Good. Because I love you too."

Harrison hesitated. "Is it because of the bond? I'm not sure how that works, exactly."

"I think we're both aware of that. But no. I don't love you because of the bond. It doesn't create feelings. We're bonded, but that's all there is to this."

"I'm sorry we can't break the bond."

Sal shrugged. "I'm not. Not that our lives wouldn't have been easier without it, if anything because we *have* to stay close by, but we'll deal with it, just like we dealt with everything else. And why should we take things slow when we both know we're in love?"

Harrison's heart clenched and released. "Why, indeed."

When Sal leaned closer to kiss Harrison, Harrison let him. He'd wanted this since that day in Hell when he'd pushed Sal away. He'd yearned for it, and for Sal, and now he had him. He didn't know what he'd done to earn himself this, but he wasn't going to protest.

He wrapped his arms around Sal's shoulders and pulled him along when he stretched out on the couch. This was the easiest position for Sal, and his wings cradled both of them in a half-darkness that made this encounter even more intimate.

They hadn't known each other long, not this way. They'd spent a glorious night together, learning each other's bodies, but this felt different. They'd both been enthusiastic the last time, and they still were, but there was a reverence in the way Sal stripped Harrison of his clothes, in the way he touched his bare skin and stroked his body, that hadn't been there before. Harrison didn't know if it was because Sal had kept it hidden or because he hadn't yet been in love, and he didn't care. What mattered was the present and the future, not the past.

It was slow and soft and gentle. Sal kissed every inch of Harrison's body, and when Harrison tried to sit up to do the same with him, he pushed him back down.

Harrison let go. He understood why Sal was doing this, why he was taking care of him. He wanted to show him he could do this, that they could be together, and that he wasn't going to run again. He needed to prove himself, even though Harrison didn't need him to.

Sal wrapped his lips around the head of Harrison's cock. He did something with his tongue, and it was enough to have Harrison beg to be fucked. "I don't want to hurt you," Sal murmured against the skin of Harrison's inner thigh.

"You won't."

"I haven't done this in a long time."

Harrison couldn't help but smile. "Does that mean you're out of practice?"

"Very much so."

"You don't want to do it?"

Sal moved up Harrison's body until they were face to face. "I want to do everything with you and to you. But I won't deny I'm wary of this."

Harrison cupped his cheek and wrapped his legs around Sal's. "Nothing you can do will push me away, especially not when we're naked. We don't have to do anything that makes you uncomfortable, but God, Sal, I want you inside me, branding me and showing me how much I am yours."

Sal licked his lips. "You'll tell me if I hurt you?"

"Of course I will. But you won't."

Sal raised a hand. "I doubt you're used to these."

His claws were short again, but there was no denying they weren't human fingernails. Harrison grabbed Sal's hand and kissed one of the claws, then darted his tongue out to lick it. It was hard and smooth but filed, and it *wouldn't* hurt him, not even when it was inside him. "I'll get used to them soon enough."

Sal's pupils were huge, and he was staring at Harrison's mouth. Harrison smiled and gestured toward the coffee table. "See that drawer?"

"Of course I see it."

"Open it."

Sal arched a brow, but he hung the top half of his body off the couch and obeyed. His eyebrows shot even higher when he took out a small pot. "Where did you get this?"

"I might have done some research."

Sal sat up on Harrison's groin. "When?"

"Before we left. Ah, right after I first met you, I guess." Harrison knew he was blushing, but he supposed he should get past that since he and Sal were together now. "I've always hoped you'd see more in me than an annoying human."

Sal's smile was soft. "You are so much more than that."

"I notice you didn't deny that I'm annoying."

"You can be. I don't mind."

Harrison relaxed as Sal opened the pot and sniffed the paste inside. "This is good quality."

"That's what I was looking for." And Harrison was thankful for that, because he'd paid a lot for that little pot of what was essentially lube.

Sal wiggled down Harrison's body. Their skin dragged

together, and Harrison's cock was painfully hard. He opened his legs, hoping it was enough for Sal to get the idea and get to the point. Sal's grin was wicked, but he slicked his fingers with the fragrant paste in the pot and put it onto the coffee table. He spread the lube over his fingers. "We don't need much, not when it's this good."

"We do need it to be in the right place, though."

"I should have known you wouldn't be quiet during sex. You never are, so why would this be different?"

Harrison opened his mouth to answer, but just then, Sal decided to get to it finally. He reached between Harrison's legs and pushed a finger inside him. That shut Harrison right up, and he had to close his eyes because of the onslaught of feelings. Making love with the man he loved, knowing Sal wasn't going anywhere when they were done, was all Harrison had wanted during their trip to Hell, and now he had it.

Sal's cock was as well-built as the rest of his body. Harrison knew it well enough by now, but it still felt so much bigger than he knew it to be when it pushed inside him. He bit his lower lip against the pain, and when Sal noticed and moved back, he kept him still, wrapping himself around him. It still hurt, and the fullness of it was uncomfortable, but he knew it got better.

It did. Sal gave him all the time he needed to relax, and when he finally started moving, Harrison was in heaven. It wasn't the sex, but the emotions that came along with it, the feeling of being cherished and revered. It exuded every movement Sal made, from the kisses he peppered all over Harrison's face, neck, and shoulders, to the expert way in which he wrapped his fingers around Harrison's cock to make sure he came before him. Harrison clung to him as he rode the pleasure, grateful for the wings that made this moment intimate even though they were alone.

They opened when Sal came inside him, tensing along with

Sal's body as he moved faster and harder. He came with Harrison wrapped around him, his wings wide opened, his face buried against Harrison's neck. Harrison wanted him to stay right there forever, or since that wasn't possible, to stay in his life forever.

And it looked like that was precisely what he'd get.

EPILOGUE

"**B**e careful with that, asshole!" Sal yelled at Cumar, who was juggling with two pots that contained rare herbs Sal had paid a fortune for.

Cumar yelped and almost dropped one of them. "I had them before you started yelling in my ear," he complained.

"Put them in the box and stop playing around with my belongings. I'll need that for my new job."

"You'll need all of the stuff you're packing? Because I'm pretty sure no one needs all of that, Sal."

It was true that Sal was packing a lot of stuff, but who wouldn't in his place? He was moving for the first time in a hundred or so years, and even though he wasn't selling his lake house, he was terrified of leaving something he'd need behind. He could come back—he *would* come back when he and Harrison needed a vacation—but the lake was too far away from the city to make it convenient.

Cumar put down the containers and grabbed a pile of books. Sal winced at his rough treatment. He needed Cumar and everyone else's help to pack everything up, but he couldn't watch as they did so, not when they threatened to break something with every move they made.

He left Cumar in the study and headed to the porch. The air was cool, and the humidity rising from the lake prickled his cheeks. He wrapped his wings around himself and looked out at the lake, and the place he'd called home for so long.

Leaving hurt. He'd known it would, but he'd thought of this house as only a few walls and a roof. He'd thought it would be easy enough, that he was starting a new life and that leaving everything of the old one behind was the right thing to do. He still thought that was the case, but he hadn't expected to feel so much. Being here reminded of him of what he used to have, and the memories, the feeling of something missing inside of him, had resurfaced, and he didn't know how to push them back down. Usually, he lost himself in Harrison's presence, but Harrison was busy somewhere in the house, and Sal realized that he was relying too heavily on his lover. He needed to learn to deal with the memories on his own, and what better occasion than this one?

"What did Cumar do?" Harrison asked.

Sal jerked in surprise because he hadn't heard him, or the door. "Nothing."

"That's what he told me, but I call bullshit. I know you were with him in the study."

"I should have asked Thailor and Chase to take care of the study. They'd be more respectful of the things there."

"Probably." Harrison pressed his front against Sal's back, trapping Sal's wings between them. It wasn't uncomfortable because he didn't put any weight on them, and Sal rather liked being wrapped in Harrison's arms. It made him feel safe, something he'd never thought he'd need. Before, he'd had the means to protect himself. Now he didn't, but he'd gained *someone* to do it.

"Are you okay?" Harrison asked softly.

"I will be. It's just hard. There are so many things I won't need anymore because I can't use them, yet I don't want to throw them away."

"Then don't. We're not going to use the house, so you could leave them here and deal with them when you feel ready to. It's only been a few weeks, Sal. I know you want to start this new life of yours in earnest because it makes it easier to try to forget the old one, but that old life made you who you are today. There's no need to cancel it, although I do understand why you want to ignore it. We'll be back, Sal. Focus on what you're comfortable doing, and we'll deal with the rest later."

Sal turned into Harrison's arms. He wrapped his wings around both of them, isolating them in a cocoon of black leather and warmth. They could still hear the bustle of the people moving inside the house, and Sal winced when he heard something break and Cumar swear, but he stayed where he was instead of charging inside and trying to rip his head off with his bare hands.

Harrison smiled and ran his hands up Sal's back, stroking to spot where his wings were anchored. "I thought you were going to rush inside."

"I want to. But I want to stay here with you more."

"That's good. I always want to stay with you."

"Me too." It had taken Sal's life being turned upside down for him to realize that he didn't have to be alone. He wasn't sure if he'd be there if he'd managed to convince Shaila to unlock his powers, but he doubted it, and at night, when he was in bed with Harrison and Harrison was sleeping wrapped around him, he wondered if losing his powers hadn't actually been a good thing.

He wanted to think he'd have eventually given in and that he'd have stayed with Harrison even if he'd been able to leave, but he couldn't be sure of that. It didn't matter anyway. He didn't have his powers anymore, but he had something else, something better, in a way. He was loved, and he loved in return.

It had been his choice when he'd killed Shaila to save Harrison, and he'd never regretted it. He didn't think he ever would.

YOU MAY ALSO ENJOY THE FOLLOWING FROM EXTASY BOOKS INC:

Elemental Union
Catherine Lievens

Excerpt

Quillan wasn't sure what to make of Rhea—or of the fact that they were soulmates. He couldn't deny they were, and he didn't want to, but he couldn't deny he was shocked and that he didn't know how to deal with everything. It was easier to focus on Rhea and on getting him first to a phone, then to safety.

Not that there was anything more secure than this building. He had to scan both his fingerprint and his iris before the doors finally opened for him. At least Rhea looked impressed.

"You weren't kidding when you said this was a secure building," he mused as he followed Quillan inside.

"I didn't want to take you somewhere that wasn't safe."

"Why not? You didn't know I was your soulmate when you pushed me into the trunk."

Quillan scowled. "I didn't push you into the trunk."

Someone laughed. Quillan closed his eyes. He'd known this was going to happen.

"Still as romantic as ever, I see," Dakota said.

Quillan turned his scowl toward his ex-boss—and possible ex-friend, if he didn't stop messing with him. "Shut up. You wouldn't recognize romance if it hit you in the face."

Dakota laughed again. It made him look less intimidating, and Quillan didn't miss the way Rhea relaxed. He knew what Rhea saw—Dakota was close to six feet five, and his shoulders were so broad he looked like a brick wall. The big man could probably grab Rhea and throw him against the wall without breaking a sweat, but he was one of the gentlest men Quillan had ever met. That was one of the reasons he'd gone into security—so he could protect people.

Dakota Pulled Quillan into a bear hug. Quillan wasn't small by any means, but he always felt tiny next to his friend. "It's good to see you. We miss you around here."

Quillan found himself smiling back. "And I miss you guys."

"You know your spot will always be there for you. Just say the word, and you're back."

Quillan patted Dakota's back and moved away. "I know. And I might take you up on that, but not for a while." He'd left this job because he wanted to do something different, something that would finally allow him to have a private life. It wasn't easy when you had to follow clients around the world to protect them.

Dakota's smile widened. "Great. So, what can I help you with? I doubt you're here to say hello."

Quillan rolled his eyes. "You saw me letting Rhea out of the trunk. Rhea, this is Dakota. Dakota, Rhea."

"Of course I did. You know there are cameras everywhere."

"He needs a secure phone to call his father, if that's okay. I'll tell you everything while he's on the phone."

Dakota arched a brow in surprise, but he didn't protest. "Of course. Right this way."

Rhea stuck close to Quillan as they followed Dakota deeper into the building. Everything looked professional, but it became homier and more comfortable once they crossed into the side of the building reserved for the employees. There was everything there, from a large living room that housed every game station one could think of to guest bedrooms in case one of the employees needed a quick nap, to an infirmary that was so well-stocked that the docs could probably perform surgery there. Rhea and Quillan would be safe there until Rhea could go home.

Dakota led them into his office. He gestured at his desk. "You can use my phone, and feel free to sit down. Quillan and I will be right there on the couch." The office was big enough that part of it had been furnished with a couch, a few armchairs, and a coffee table. Quillan flopped into one of the armchairs, but he didn't look away from Rhea, following him with his gaze as Rhea carefully sat on the edge of Dakota's chair and took the phone.

"What's going on?" Dakota asked, going straight to the point.

"I have no idea."

Dakota sat on the couch. "You're going to have to give me a better explanation than that."

Quillan raked a hand through his hair. "I really don't know, though. I went out to throw away the trash this morning and stumbled on two guys pushing Rhea into the trunk of his car."

"So of course, you jumped in to help him."

"Well, yeah."

Dakota smiled and shook his head. "I still wonder why you left this job sometimes. Protecting people is in your blood."

And he didn't know the half of it when it came to Rhea. "We can talk about that later." The reason Quillan had quit still stood, especially now.

Dakota took his phone out and texted someone. Quillan cocked his head at him when he looked up again. "I asked someone to park the car in the garage. I'm still not sure how Rhea ended up in the trunk, but I know it's not yours."

"It's not. Like I said, those two guys were trying to get Rhea into the trunk. They managed, and I took them out, but before I could help him, another two guys arrived, so I slammed the trunk shut and got the fuck out of there." He leaned forward. "They were fire wielders."

"Uh. What about Rhea?"

"He's one, too. And he's my soulmate."

Dakota blinked. "You're a water wielder."

"So? You're an earth wielder. We're friends anyway, aren't we?"

"True. How did you and Rhea find out, though?"

"You didn't look at the entire footage? He attacked me when I finally let him out of the car here in the parking lot."

"Pity I didn't stick around. I'll have to check the recordings."

"You do that."

"What's going on, then? Why were those men after Rhea?"

"He says he doesn't know, but I think he has a good idea. He wanted to talk to his father first, though, and I didn't think it was a problem."

They both looked at Rhea, who was still on the phone. Quillan didn't want to listen in on him, but he couldn't avoid it.

"I'm fine, Dad," Rhea said. He sounded exasperated. "I promise I'm safe."

Quillan looked at Dakota. "I hate to ask you this."

"And you don't have to." Dakota patted Quillan's knee. "You two can stay here for as long as you want. Take whatever guest room or rooms you want. Just let me know so I put them down as unavailable. Rhea will be safe here."

"I know." Quillan was relieved. He could keep Rhea safe on his own, but this was better. There was no way anyone would get to Rhea as long as he stayed in the building, even if Quillan wasn't with him. Not that Quillan was planning on going anywhere. He might have to go home for a bit to grab clothes and his computer, but he wasn't leaving Rhea. He realized he felt that way because Rhea was his soulmate, although Dakota wasn't wrong when he said that Quillan protected people. But the reason why didn't matter, as long as Rhea was safe.

"We need to talk to him," Dakota murmured. He was watching Rhea, who looked more relaxed now that he'd talked to his dad.

"We will. I have no doubt he'll tell us everything we want to know. Whoever the guys were who tried to grab him, he's afraid of them."

"As he should be. Four men tried to grab him. That's not a mugging gone wrong. They wanted him for a specific reason." Dakota hummed. "Money? Do you know who his father is?"

"No, but Rhea says it's not that."

"I suppose we'll find out soon enough." They needed to know if they had to protect Rhea to the best of their ability.

ABOUT THE AUTHOR

Catherine lives in Italy, country of good food and hot men. She used to write fantasy as a child, but it was reading her first gay erotic romance novel that made her realize that that was what she really wanted to write.

After graduating from college in English language and translation, she divides her day between writing, reading, taking care of her son and reading some more.

You can find her on Facebook and Twitter or on her website: authorcatherinelievens.wordpress.com

Email: lievens.catherine@gmail.com

Newsletter: http://eepurl.com/c-uvKn